BIRTHRIGHT

Julia Quinn

INTIMATE MOMENTS®

Published by Silhouette Books

America's Publisher of Contemporary Romance

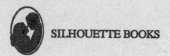

SILHOUETTE BOOKS

ISBN 0-373-07540-5

BIRTHRIGHT

Books by Julia Quinn

Silhouette Intimate Moments

Wade Conner's Revenge #460
Birthright #540

JULIA QUINN

decided to become a writer before she was out of high school, and she's never regretted her decision. First as a newspaper reporter and now as a romance novelist, she has found that writing gives her a voice for her creativity and an outlet for her imagination. She and her husband honeymooned in Paris and live on the Florida coast with two small children. She fulfills a continuing interest in sports by working part-time for a newspaper sports department. She makes time to write while her children sleep.

To my lovable daughter Paige, who contributed to
this book in ways she doesn't yet understand

Chapter 1

Her heart was pounding so intensely that Tessa Daniel frantically tried to think of a way to remain calm. Dr. Morgan was due to come through the office door at any moment, and it wouldn't do any good if she was too nervous to listen to what she had to say.

A dim memory of the breathing exercises she had used while in labor with Abby surfaced, and Tessa exhaled two short breaths and then inhaled three times. Was she remembering the sequence correctly? Was she out of her mind? It was ludicrous to believe breaths of air could stem the growing horror she felt when she thought about the debilitating blood disease she might have passed on to her child.

She shifted in her seat, oblivious to the luxurious feel of the leather chair and the rich look of the doctor's private office. Instead she saw Abby's dear face and the way her long brown hair swayed when she walked. *Please, God,* she prayed, *please don't let my daughter have the disease.*

Tessa had been almost frantic with worry since Dr. Morgan called and requested that she come to her office. When the phone rang, Tessa had been sure that the doctor's office was calling to tell her their blood tests had come back negative. She'd never thought for a minute that Abby had Cooley's anemia, even after Tessa's cousin discovered while undergoing testing that she was a carrier of the disease.

There was no indication that Abby's bone marrow wasn't producing enough red blood cells. She was a normal three-year-old, so full of energy that she couldn't sit still for more than a minute. A child with Cooley's anemia was breathless, inactive, always tired. Of course, the pamphlet she'd read before she and Abby had provided their blood samples stated the disease could lie dormant for several years. It was still possible that Abby was tragically anemic and had endless blood transfusions and a shortened life span ahead of her.

Tessa took some more short breaths, but her heart seemed to be pounding faster and more loudly than it had before she started the breathing exercises. She was astute enough to know that a doctor could reveal a routine result over the telephone. The doctors she'd encountered never wanted to speak to her in person unless something was wrong.

She had learned that lesson through grim experience when Chris had died almost three years ago. The voice on the phone would say only that her husband had been in an automobile accident and that she should come to the emergency room as quickly as possible. Tessa had known then that Chris was gone. The emergency-room doctor had only confirmed the awful truth.

Tessa jumped in her seat at the sound of the door opening, and one hand flew to her throat. Dr. Samantha Morgan had been her family physician for nearly ten years, but now Tessa felt nothing but dread when she looked at her. The doctor, dressed in a crisp white coat and wearing her customary glasses, had barely settled in her seat when Tessa blurted out her fear.

"Please tell me that Abby doesn't have Cooley's anemia," Tessa said, and her voice cracked on the name of the disease. Dimly, she noted that her palms were sweating.

Dr. Morgan looked at her, surprise and concern clouding her even features. She removed her glasses and delivered the measured, reassuring gaze that had calmed Tessa so many times in the past.

"Abby's just fine," Dr. Morgan said, but she still seemed concerned. "She tested negative for the disease."

"Thank God." Tessa exhaled, relief making her so weak she clutched the sides of the chair for support. "Then I don't have the gene that causes Cooley's anemia."

"On the contrary, you do."

The relief that her daughter had been spared a life of sickness was so great that Tessa couldn't be sure she had heard Dr. Morgan correctly. "What did you just say?"

"I just said that you carry the gene that causes Cooley's anemia," Dr. Morgan said slowly.

"Then, Abby could still develop the disease." Fear, even stronger than before, once again gripped Tessa and she leaned forward in the leather chair.

"No. As I said, Abby's blood tested negative. The gene that causes Cooley's anemia is a recessive gene, which means you're a carrier of the disease without actually being afflicted with it. If Abby's father also carried the recessive gene that causes the disease, Abby would have a one-in-four chance of inheriting both defective genes and thus coming down with a full-blown case of Cooley's anemia."

Abby allowed herself to relax against the back of the chair, grateful that the crisis was over. Her heart was no longer beating a tattoo inside her chest, and she was filled with sweet, blessed relief.

It was impossible to know if Chris had carried the defective gene, because his blood hadn't been tested before he died. Sadly, it didn't matter anymore. Abby was fine, and Chris would never father another child. Tessa blinked determinedly, fighting the familiar rush of tears that threatened to fall whenever she so much as thought his name. Abby was fine, and that was reason to rejoice.

"So that's what you wanted to tell me," Tessa said, and she no longer sounded as though she were on the edge of hysteria. "You wanted me to know that if I ever have another child there's a possibility that I could pass on the disease. I can tell you right now, there's nothing to worry about. Abby is all I want, all I need."

Dr. Morgan picked up her glasses and replaced them on the bridge of her nose. She looked down at the papers strewn across her desk, and Tessa got the impression she was trying to figure out how to delicately phrase something. Finally, she looked up at Tessa.

"Do you know anything about blood types, Tessa?"

"Blood types?" Tessa was confused. She thought back to the college biology classes that had convinced her she'd be a better teacher than physician. "I know about the ABO system, that everyone has either A, B, AB or O blood."

"That's right," Dr. Morgan said, nodding. "Did you also know that a child inherits two blood-type genes from her parents? And that she can't possibly belong to any blood group unless one of her parents carries a gene for that type?"

"That makes sense," Tessa said slowly, wondering why Dr. Morgan was giving her a crash course in blood chemistry. She waited for the doctor to continue.

"The blood test that you and Abby took to screen for Cooley's anemia also revealed your blood types," she said, staring at Tessa intently. "You're type O-negative, and Abby is type AB-positive."

"So?" Tessa asked, not understanding.

"Tessa, do you remember what blood type Chris was?"

Tessa smiled, because she remembered very well. Chris's younger sister had needed a complete blood transfusion at birth to save her life, and Chris regularly donated blood as a form of payback. Since his blood type made him a universal donor, Dr. Morgan had been in the habit of phoning him whenever one of her patients needed a transfusion and the hospital's blood supply was low. "Of course I remember. Like me, he was O-negative, the universal donor."

Tessa didn't add that, unlike her, Chris wasn't squeamish around needles. The one time Tessa had accompanied him to the blood bank, she had blacked out halfway through the procedure and awakened to smelling salts and the concerned face of a nurse who filled her with juice and cookies. Still, because they had matching blood, Chris had proclaimed Tessa and himself a match made in Red Cross heaven.

Dr. Morgan nodded, her eyes pinned on Tessa. She seemed to be waiting for Tessa to unscramble a puzzle, but Tessa continued to look at her blankly.

"You still don't understand, do you?" she asked, and Tessa shook her head. Dr. Morgan swallowed. "Tessa, you're type O and Chris was type O. Two parents with type O blood can only produce a child with type O blood. There's no possibility that a child born of that union could have type AB blood."

"What are you saying, Doctor?"

Dr. Morgan paused, and Tessa had a sense of foreboding so strong she almost asked the doctor not to continue.

"I'm saying that Chris couldn't possibly have been Abby's father."

Tessa stared at the doctor, making little sense of what she had just heard. Chris not Abby's father? Since Tessa had been a virgin before marriage and faithful during it, there was no way Chris could not be Abby's father. Tessa started to explain, but something stopped her.

"Of course Chris was Abby's father," she said instead, thinking that it was uncharacteristic for Dr. Morgan to make such a colossal blunder. "The blood tests must be wrong."

Dr. Morgan bit her lip, and her gaze was filled with sympathy. Tessa realized the doctor thought Abby was the result of an extramarital affair.

"There was no mistake, Tessa. I drew blood from both you and Abby twice. I checked the results myself. Twice. Chris was not Abby's father."

Dr. Morgan's tone softened, possibly because she read the shock in Tessa's face. "Believe me, Tessa, I wish I didn't have to tell you this. I even thought about not telling you, because Chris is dead. But of course you should have the knowledge to do with whatever you see fit. And I assure you that I will keep this information completely confidential."

Tessa would have laughed if she had not held Dr. Morgan in such high esteem. The doctor was subtly suggesting she might want to tell a man who didn't exist that he was the father of her child. It was lunacy, beyond belief. But she trusted Dr. Morgan, and the doctor insisted she had accurately identified their blood types. If Dr. Morgan said she was certain the blood tests were accurate, then they were. Her mind worked furiously.

"There must be some other explanation," Tessa said finally, and her voice sounded as though it belonged to a stranger. "Isn't there any other reason Abby's blood could be incompatible with Chris's?"

The answer, when it came, was so preposterous that the doctor obviously dismissed it as pure fancy. It was also the only explanation that made sense. Tessa had once had the wind knocked out of her as a child, but this was much worse. That had been a temporary blow to her body; this was a permanent assault on her mind.

"Only if Abby and another baby were switched at the hospital, and you brought home the wrong one."

Chapter 2

"Mommy, are we there yet?"

How many times had Tessa answered that question in the past eight hours? Too many to count. She flipped the rearview mirror down to an angle affording her a clear view of the three-year-old in the backseat of the car. In the reflection was an uncommonly pretty little girl with deep blue eyes and ruler-straight brown hair, a girl who Tessa now saw didn't bear any resemblance to herself or her late husband.

At first, of course, Abby had looked like any other baby. She was nearly bald except for some sparse dark fuzz atop her head. It was only later, when the new hair had fallen out and been replaced by strands of golden brown, that friends and relatives puzzled over who she looked like. Time and again, they'd asked how two black-haired, brown-eyed parents had produced Abby, but Tessa had always laughed it off. "We're not clones of our parents," she'd said, "and recessive genes do exist."

Tessa's hair was thick and black, and it fell just past her shoulders. Her eyes were so dark it was hard to pick out the pupils, and her skin looked very pale in comparison. The combination of light and dark was striking. Tessa's mother had always said she was like pepper and salt, obsidian hair and an alabaster complexion.

"Soon, Abby, we'll be there soon," Tessa said. Abby was squirming in her car seat, trying to escape the inescapable constraints. "If you just sit still a little longer, before you know it we'll be there."

Tessa sounded unconcerned with the passage of time, but in reality she was almost frantic to get to the rural Pennsylvania town where Abby had been born. Tessa was an elementary-school teacher, and if someone had told her a week ago that she'd be spending her summer recess in Oak Haven she would have laughed aloud. But a week ago, she hadn't known that Abby wasn't the baby she should have brought home from the hospital.

She expelled a shaky breath, finding it difficult to believe even now that Abby wasn't her biological child. But she didn't have a choice. A telephone call to Abby's pediatrician had confirmed the child's blood type, and a check of some records she kept in her file cabinet had reaffirmed Tessa's. There was only one possible conclusion. Dr. Morgan hadn't made a mistake—Oak Haven Hospital had.

Tessa fingered her shoulder-length black hair, aware of how different it was from her daughter's. Hospitals today operated like modern machines and took precautions against monumental mix-ups such as children being switched at birth, but it had happened a little more than three years ago.

A lump formed in Tessa's throat. She tried to swallow, but the lump wouldn't go away. When she'd accepted that Abby wasn't her biological child, she had been certain that someone would appear on her doorstep demanding she return Abby to her rightful keeper.

A blur of hours later, however, Tessa concluded that her fear was unjustified. Dr. Morgan had promised to keep the knowledge about Abby's unmatched blood type to herself, and there was no reason for anyone else to be suspicious. Even if someone stumbled upon the truth, Tessa was armed with a birth certificate and a powerful lie. She could concoct an extramarital affair and claim that another man had fathered Abby. She would say anything if it meant she could keep her daughter.

Tessa had never intended to return to Oak Haven. She wanted nothing more than to sweep the knowledge about Abby into her subconscious and get on with her life. But she couldn't. Abby might not have Cooley's anemia, but Tessa's birth child could be afflicted with the disease. If she was, there was a very good chance her doctors hadn't figured out precisely what was wrong. Unless requested by name, the blood test for Cooley's anemia wasn't routinely done.

In the middle of a sleepless night, with only her conscience guiding her, Tessa had reached the inescapable conclusion that was leading her to Oak Haven. She needed to find her birth child and make sure she wasn't afflicted with the disease. Only then could she and Abby sneak back to their old lives.

"Want to be there now," Abby whined. *So do I,* Tessa silently mouthed. *So do I.*

And then, unexpectedly, they were. Tessa had branched off the main highway almost an hour before and thought they had another thirty minutes of driving. But the thick growth of pine trees lining the highway suddenly thinned, and she saw a smattering of development—a service station, a convenience store, a roadside vendor selling fruit— that signaled a town was ahead.

Tessa slowed the car, unsuccessfully looking for a familiar landmark. She didn't expect to see anything she recognized, even though she had lived in Oak Haven just over three years ago. The entire experience was a blur. She hadn't wanted Chris to start a new venture that would wrench her away from her job and family when she was six months pregnant, but he'd insisted it was for the best.

He was wrong. Tessa had developed complications and spent the final three months of her pregnancy in bed on doctor's orders, preventing her from making a single friend and filling her with an aching loneliness. Chris hadn't fared much better at his latest stab at entrepreneurship. He and a childhood friend soon discovered there wasn't much demand for a video delivery service in a quiet Pennsylvania town. When Abby was two weeks old, they moved back to Virginia. Tessa never dreamed they had left with the wrong baby.

She took another glance at Abby, who was staring out the window while the rays from the setting sun bathed her in light, and a fierce protectiveness stole over her. Abby must never know about the hospital's mistake; no one could ever know.

They hadn't been in Oak Haven more than a few minutes, and already Tessa was itching to leave. It was a stroke of luck that school had just recessed for the summer, affording Tessa more than two months to conduct the search, but they couldn't dare linger in Oak Haven. Life wasn't fair. If the wrong person discovered Abby wasn't her biological child, Tessa risked losing her. She couldn't trust anyone. But she couldn't let an innocent child suffer, either.

"Are we there yet?" Abby asked again, and this time Tessa smiled.

"Yes, we are, pumpkin," she said, enjoying the grin that spread across Abby's face. "This is Oak Haven."

Oak Haven wasn't a metropolis, but it was more than farmland with a road running through it. Tessa guessed that the population was about twenty thousand. The town had a post office, grocery stores, a couple of banks and the rest of the conveniences of modern life.

She stopped at a red light and noticed leaves rustling on the trees overhanging the road. Tessa switched off the air conditioner and opened the window to let in the breeze. The wind carried with it the joyful shouts of children playing, and Tessa impulsively turned the car off the main thoroughfare to follow the sounds.

A half block down the road was a fenced yard with a swing set positioned under a huge shade tree. About a dozen children, most of whom looked to be under five, played happily. Tessa parked across the street from the children, tilting her head to get a better look at them.

She didn't really expect to stumble upon the girl she was looking for minutes after driving into Oak Haven. Even if one of the girls on the playground were the right one, chances were slim that Tessa would be able to recognize her. She knew that the girl had been born around the ninth day of October more than three years ago. Aside from that, she didn't have a clue as to whether one of the half dozen little girls frolicking on the playground could have spent nine months growing inside her.

Tessa willed herself to remember the timeworn photographs that had been taken of herself as a child, but the fuzzy images didn't help. She had white blond hair as a toddler, but it had gradually darkened to its present shade. None of the little girls had pale blond hair, and she was parked too far away to tell if any had inherited an alabaster complexion or a chin and nose that were slightly angular. But maybe the little girl had taken after Chris.

"Mommy." Abby no longer sounded tired, just determined. "Want out of the car."

Tessa bit her lip as she turned and quickly assessed the three-year-old child. Dark smudges under Abby's eyes made it look as though the tree branches were casting shadows on her face, but Tessa knew that wasn't the case. Abby was tired as well as hungry, and Tessa should have known better than to take a detour after an eight-hour trip that would try the patience of even the calmest child.

She should have found a hotel and a restaurant, in that order, and left her quest for the morning when they were both fresh. But Tessa had been so eager to get started, to do something to assuage the keen sense of helplessness that had gripped her ever since her doctor had told her she carried the gene that causes a devastating disease.

"I'm sorry, sweetheart," Tessa said, reaching across the seat to take Abby's hand. "We'll get something to eat as soon as we find a hotel."

Instead of switching on the ignition, however, Tessa shifted her attention back to the scene across the street. A child she hadn't noticed before, a raven-haired girl dressed in red, was playing off to one side of the group. Tessa squinted. She looked to be about the right age....

"Looking for something?" A deep, gruff voice snapped Tessa's train of thought, and she turned guiltily in her seat until her dark eyes collided with an uncompromising pair of blue ones. A man's face, strong and unfriendly, filled her car window so that all the sunlight was blotted out. His eyes were narrowed, his mouth set in a slit and his jaw thrust forward. He appeared to be the kind of man it would be good to have on your side in battle, but he was looking at her like an adversary instead of an ally.

Tessa swallowed and fought the flash of guilt his question had solicited. This bear of a man couldn't know that she was on a quest to find the little girl to whom she had given birth three years ago. She hadn't told anyone, not even her sister. Susan thought she was going to spend the summer in Pennsylvania to escape from the memories that filled her apartment in Virginia. Tessa didn't have to tell this man, this stranger, anything.

"I can't imagine why that's any of your business," Tessa said in her best haughty voice, while she bravely met his eyes. She had used the tone on men often in the past few years to deflect unwanted attention, but her cavalier delivery had the opposite effect on this man. He stared back, all of his attention focused on her. Despite her brave front, Tessa felt trapped, like a criminal who had been cornered by the law.

"I consider anything that goes on in this town my business," he said, and his eyes narrowed even further. Tessa marveled at his arrogance. He acted as though Oak Haven were a police state and he had been deemed its protector. She fought back her nervousness, more annoyed now than afraid. This was a free country, and this man had no right to quiz her.

"Then you're going to have to change your way of thinking, because what I do is none of your concern," Tessa said, unconsciously raising her chin a notch. She had rolled down her window to get an unobstructed view of the playground, and he was leaning on the car with his hands on both sides of the door. Her only view now was of his unsmiling face.

"Oh, no," the man said, and his dark eyebrows rose to convey doubt. "You talk like you have something to hide."

"What is this, an inquisition?" Tessa asked angrily, annoyed that he had already guessed that her reasons for coming to Oak Haven weren't entirely aboveboard. What would he say if she admitted she'd been scanning the playground for a child who might resemble herself?

"Actually, it was an offer to help," he said, but Tessa didn't trust him. She thought he was the kind of man who could twist any situation to fit his needs. And right now he wanted to know more about the reason she was parked across the street from an Oak Haven playground. "Didn't it occur to you that I noticed your out-of-state plates and wondered if you needed help finding anything?"

"No," Tessa said firmly. He had approached her car solely because he sensed something suspicious, but the fact that she was indeed hiding something didn't appease her.

"Mommy, what does that man want?" Abby's voice penetrated the silence, and she sounded curious rather than afraid. Surprise registered on the man's hard features, and Tessa was sure he hadn't noticed the child until that moment. She shifted in her seat to address Abby, grateful for a reason to turn away from him.

"Nothing we can help him with, honey," Tessa said, aware that Abby was looking at the stranger rather than at her. "There's nothing to worry about," she added needlessly, since Abby didn't look in the least bit worried.

Tessa quickly turned back to the steering wheel and switched on the ignition. If she had read Abby's expression correctly, the little girl wanted to make friends. In a moment, Abby was bound to launch into her version of the reason they were in Oak Haven. She might even ask the man to have dinner with them, and that would be intolerable. Tessa couldn't risk getting close to anyone in Oak Haven, least of all a rude, unsmiling man prying into their business.

"If you're through with your inquisition, we'll be getting on our way," Tessa said tartly when the car roared noisily to life. It needed a new muffler, but she hadn't been able to scrape up enough cash to buy one. Now, with the man passing judgment on her every action, she wished she had.

He was still leaning on the car door, and Tessa couldn't stop herself from drawing back when she turned toward him. He looked forbidding and not at all amused by her choice of words. His blue eyes were fringed by a long sweep of lashes, but they were set beneath thick brows that counteracted any hint of softness. His mouth was wide and generous, but it was drawn tight.

Tessa prided herself on her even composure, but this man made her nervous. He was so close that she could hear his deep, even breaths. When he exhaled, she imagined she could feel the warm air rustling her hair.

"I wouldn't dream of stopping you," he drawled insolently and straightened. Tessa immediately felt a sense of freedom and something else she couldn't quite identify. She put her foot to the gas pedal and pulled away from the curb, leaving the man standing in the street staring after them. As his image in the rearview mirror grew smaller, Tessa realized what the strange feeling was. Even though Abby was in the backseat, suddenly she felt very much alone.

Corey McCash watched the battered blue sedan drive off with a mixture of regret and suspicion. Maybe he shouldn't have been so confrontational, but when he'd spotted the Virginia license plate he'd immediately thought that Alise had come to claim their daughter. He should have known instantly that he was mistaken.

Corey had heard his ex-wife was living in Virginia, but that didn't explain the flight of fancy his mind had taken. Corey had sole custody of Maggie, and since their divorce two years ago Alise hadn't shown any indication that she even remembered the child's existence. But Corey didn't understand how a mother could neglect her daughter, and he sometimes wondered if Alise would reappear in their lives full of regret for giving up Maggie.

That unjustified fear didn't excuse the way he had handled the situation, but he couldn't allow a woman in an out-of-state car to stake out the preschool his daughter attended. Maybe the words "stake out" were too strong, but he was a successful private investigator partly because he was a good judge of human nature. He knew instinctively that the woman had something to hide.

For all he knew, she could be a mother without custody plotting to kidnap her own child. Even worse, she could be a woman so desperate for a family that she planned to abduct someone else's child. That would explain why she was lurking outside a preschool, but it didn't explain why the little girl in the backseat had called her Mommy. She obviously wasn't childless.

Corey didn't usually pay much attention to any child other than Maggie, but the little girl had been enchanting.

Wide-set blue eyes, a soft petal of a mouth that had smiled at him and a button nose were set in a face framed by long, straight brown hair. She was sweetness personified.

Her mother was a different matter. Corey scowled, angry that he had felt a stirring of desire when he'd noticed that her pale skin looked almost like porcelain next to her dark hair. He couldn't remember the last time a woman had riled him as much as that one. Although she didn't resemble his ex-wife, she had the same imperious lift to her chin. She'd acted as though he had no right to know why she was staring so intently at the playground where his daughter played. He refused to consider that he hadn't even told her he had a daughter.

Corey glanced across the street. Underneath an enormous shade tree, children in colored clothing played on a swing set that was a bright shade of yellow. He supposed the happy scene could have seduced the woman into stopping, but Corey was through giving females the benefit of the doubt. She was probably just like Alise, certain that her beauty and big, dark eyes would get her out of any scrape she muddled into.

Corey wasn't having any of it. Oak Haven wasn't a tourist destination. Strangers didn't end up here unless they had a specific purpose in mind. If that woman intended to stay in Oak Haven, he intended to find out what she was up to.

Feeling slightly better now that he had settled upon a course of action, Corey strode across the street to the preschool. Halfway there, he spotted Maggie playing in a sandbox and his scowl turned to a smile. He was all she had, and he wasn't about to let her down.

Darkness had fallen by the time Tessa pulled up to the two-story white house with the rooms for rent. The owner of the house was expecting them, but Tessa would have preferred to inspect the rooms in daylight. Tessa cursed herself under her breath for letting it come to this.

She hadn't thought things through when she'd made up her mind to come to Oak Haven. She was so desperate to find her birth child that she hadn't even bothered to check if Oak Haven had a hotel. Instead she'd barely waited until school had let out for the summer before she'd packed up her suitcases and dragged a three-year-old across two state lines, blissfully unconcerned with where they were going to spend the next few weeks.

She'd even taken the time to park across the street from that preschool and speculate about whether any of the children resembled her. A flood of irritation washed over Tessa when she remembered the blue-eyed stranger. What right did he have to look at her suspiciously and hurl questions at her? She was in Oak Haven to find a child who might be afflicted with a terrible disease, and no one was going to stop her.

Tessa willed herself to forget the infernal man. It was nightfall in an unfamiliar town, and she couldn't get sidetracked from finding herself and Abby a place to spend the night. After eating a dinner of fast food, they'd discovered that the only hotel in Oak Haven had no vacancy. The owner, who'd apologized profusely and seemed as surprised at his full house as she was, had steered them here.

"Here we are," Tessa said brightly, unfastening her seat belt and turning around to unbuckle the straps on Abby's car seat.

The little girl looked at her suspiciously. "This not a hotel, Mommy."

"I know it doesn't look like a hotel, sweetheart, but the lady who lives here rents rooms," Tessa said, trying to sound reassuring.

"But you said we stay in a hotel," Abby persisted. She usually scampered out of her car seat the moment the belt was unbuckled, but she was rooted to the spot. Tessa fought back impatience. It had been a long day, and it was perfectly reasonable for Abby to be wary of this unexpected turn of events.

"Just give it a chance, Abby. Maybe the rooms here are nicer than the rooms in a hotel," Tessa said, although she didn't believe that for a second.

Abby thought for a minute with her lips pursed and then silently got out of the car. A moment later, Abby's hand firmly entwined with hers, Tessa rang the doorbell on the front porch. The door swung open almost immediately to reveal a short, plump woman with salt-and-pepper hair. She smiled first at Abby and then at Tessa, and there was such warmth in her face that Tessa liked her instantly.

"Are you the two ladies who need a place to stay?" she asked brightly, and Abby answered before Tessa could.

"Mommy said we stay at a hotel, but she can't find one."

"Is that so? Well let me tell you something, young lady. Staying at Mary Moriarty's house is a wee sight better than staying at some hotel. What's your name, anyway?"

"Abby Teresa Daniel is the name," Abby said, and Tessa marveled at her daughter's pluck. Where did she pick up that stuff? She might not be old enough for kindergarten, but Abby had already mastered social skills.

"And I'm Tessa Daniel, her mother," Tessa said proudly, and she knew that everything would be all right. Abby was like a tonic, and had been since Chris's death. Whenever Tessa's spirits sagged, Abby would do or say something to lift them. Even if the rooms weren't suitable, they could weather a night's stay here as long as they were together.

An hour later, Tessa lay in one of the twin beds in the strange room and willed herself to fall asleep. Even though she had been traveling all day and her eyelids were so heavy she couldn't have kept her eyes open had she tried, she couldn't relax her mind.

The rooms turned out to be better than Tessa had dared hope. They were decorated simply, but they were clean. The large bedroom was adjacent to a compact kitchen, small bathroom and modest sitting room complete with a black-and-white television set. There was even a back entrance that gave them complete privacy.

Best of all, the cost wouldn't break Tessa's budget. Chris hadn't taken out any insurance before his death, and Tessa needed every penny of her salary to make ends meet. She usually taught summer school to provide a financial cushion, but this trip had made that an impossibility. Tessa had been tucking away some money every month in an emergency fund, and she figured she could finance their stay in Oak Haven on that if they were frugal.

"Mommy," a small voice called out in the darkness. "Can I sleep in your bed?"

"All right, pumpkin, but just for tonight," Tessa answered and listened to the sounds of Abby getting out of bed. She usually insisted that Abby sleep in her own bed, but she could make an exception just for tonight. The truth was that she needed Abby even more than her daughter needed her.

Abby climbed into her bed, and Tessa breathed in the clean scent of baby shampoo as the little girl snuggled against her. Within minutes, the even rise and fall of Abby's chest revealed that she had fallen asleep. Tessa ran a hand over the little girl's hair while love welled within her.

Since Chris had died, Abby was all she had. Tessa didn't think she could have survived the terrible months after the accident if it hadn't been for Abby. She had been barely nine months old when it happened, too small to grasp the horrible truth that she would have to grow up without a father.

Tessa opened her eyes, hoisted herself on one elbow and tried to make out the little girl's features in the darkness. She should have seen it in the beginning, she supposed. Abby didn't have any of the physical traits that ran in either her family or Chris's. But outward appearances weren't important. She and Abby had a bond that was stronger than biology, a bond forged in soft kisses, warm hugs and unconditional love.

Tessa planted one of those soft kisses on Abby's cheek, more determined than ever to accomplish her mission in Oak Haven and return home with her treasured daughter. Tessa had already lost one of the two people who were most important to her in the world. She wouldn't lose the other.

Chapter 3

"Mommy, I'm hungry." A wide-awake Abby bounced on the bed next to Tessa, creating ripples in the bed sheets and making absolutely sure her mother wouldn't get another moment of sleep.

"What?" Tessa asked, trying to blink the sleep from her eyes as she came awake. She took in the unfamiliar surroundings—the pale pink walls, the rose bed sheets—and for a split second couldn't understand why she was in this room. Then she remembered the little girl to whom she had given birth and wondered how she could have forgotten, even for an instant.

"Hungry," repeated Abby, louder this time. She stood up and lifted her legs from under her so that her little rear end landed on the bed with a soft thud. Everything shook, including Tessa.

Now I remember why I insist she sleep in her own bed, Tessa thought wryly, fully awake now. She raised herself on one elbow and peered at her daughter. "Am I dreaming, or are you jumping on the bed?'' she asked in a tone of mock reproach.

Abby became very quiet and peered at her mother, but Tessa's eyes weren't as cold as her voice and the little girl saw that she wasn't really angry. ''Yeah,'' Abby said, collapsing on the bed in a gale of giggles. ''Bouncy, bouncy, bouncy.''

Soon Tessa was laughing too; she even sat up and gave the bed a bounce for good measure. The bright mood persisted while they went through their morning rituals, but Tessa had to make a conscientious effort to keep her spirits up. In the back of her mind lurked an uneasy truth: she was ill equipped to launch a search for a girl she had never known, especially with a three-year-old tagging along.

Tessa had some half formed ideas about how to proceed, but she wasn't at all sure they were the methods a trained professional would use. *Think positively, Tess,* she told herself sternly. *A little girl's health is involved. You can't afford to fail.*

''Mommy.'' Abby's high-pitched voice brought her back to the present. ''I'm still hungry.''

''Me, too, sweetheart,'' Tessa said, realizing it was true. ''But we don't have any groceries. How does a Happy Meal sound?''

''Hurray,'' Abby squealed, jumping up and down and then heading for the door. ''Those are the bestest breakfasts of all.''

Tessa grabbed her purse from the bed and followed the scampering child, grinning at how easy she was to please. Despite the daunting task ahead of her, Tessa's spirits rose. That's how it had been these past few years since Chris's death. Her emotions were on a perpetual seesaw; whenever she started to sink into depression, Abby was there to pull her from the dark abyss that yawned so invitingly in her mind. Sometimes she did it with a silly remark or a sunny smile. And sometimes all it took was her mere presence.

Tessa opened the door and then locked it behind them. She beamed down at her daughter. "Last one to the car's a rotten egg," she said, and the two of them made a mad dash for the sidewalk.

An hour later, Tessa scrolled through the back issues of the *Oak Haven Gazette* on the library's microfiche, squinting to make out the dates that appeared in the right-hand corner of the newspaper pages. She stopped, adjusted the enlargement dial on the machine and started to scroll again. August... September... October...

"Bingo," Tessa whispered aloud when she came to October's editions.

Maybe she wasn't such a bad detective after all. When she'd seen the Oak Haven library fifteen minutes ago, she'd had a moment of panic. Tessa was used to spacious, gleaming structures bought with taxpayer dollars, and she'd never seen a library quite like this one. Oak Haven's version of a library resided in a quaint brick house.

Tessa had walked slowly up the steps leading to the door of the two-story structure and paused, wondering if she should ring the doorbell. Before she could decide, Abby had stepped in front of her and managed to pull open the heavy door.

"C'mon, Mommy," she'd said with a touch of impatience, holding out her hand to Tessa.

One glance around the interior of the building had Tessa doubting that the library would contain anything as sophisticated as microfiche. Books were crowded into every conceivable space and the aisles between them weren't wide enough to accommodate more than one person at a time. She'd grabbed Abby's hand, hoping the little girl wouldn't decide she wanted to rearrange the books on the shelves. Tessa had approached the front desk warily, prepared to ask the clerk if there was a larger library in the next town.

Despite the inauspicious beginning, it had been ridiculously easy to find what she needed. The librarian, a pretty blonde who belied all stereotypes about her occupation, took only a few minutes to find the newspaper back issues. She'd even reacquainted Tessa with the fine points of using the microfiche and given Abby a stack of children's books, which so far had kept the child relatively absorbed.

"Mommy, what are you looking for?" Abby asked so loudly that she probably could be heard in the next county. Tessa put a finger to her lips, because it was exactly the kind of question she didn't want to answer. Not even for Abby.

"I'm just looking through some old newspapers," she whispered evasively. "Nothing exciting."

The answer seemed to satisfy Abby for the moment and she went back to her book, humming to herself as she rapidly thumbed through the pages. Tessa absently ran her hands through her hair. Her dark hair was loose, mostly because she'd been so anxious to visit the library that she hadn't taken the time to pull it back. In a few moments, the wait would be over and she'd have the information she needed to find her birth child.

Small-town newspapers were noted for the space they devoted to birth and death notices. She had worked for a small newspaper in Virginia one summer, taking information over the telephone for classified advertisements. Tessa had been low on the totem pole in the newspaper hierarchy, but even she had known that a newspaper wanted to be involved whenever somebody entered the world or left it. Whatever's important to you, the newspaper's slogan went, is important to us. Death and birth were important to just about everybody.

Tessa remembered the form she had filled out at the hospital authorizing the release of information to the newspaper. The woman who had taken home her child must have filled one out, too; there was no reason not to want others to share in the joy of a new life.

Tessa's fingers trembled as she reached for the knob that advanced the microfilm. In a few moments, she would know everything she needed to find the little girl she should have brought home from the hospital. When Tessa came to Abby's birth announcement, she knew she was on the right track.

It read: Abby Teresa, weighing seven pounds, thirteen ounces and born to Teresa Anne and Christopher George Daniel in Oak Haven Hospital on October ninth.

Tessa's eyes misted at the sight of Chris's name and the memories it recalled. He had been so proud, puffing out his chest and handing out cigars to the strangers at the hospital even though most of them politely informed him that they didn't smoke. That had been almost enough to forgive him for ducking out of the labor room when her pain escalated and she needed him most. Later, he had claimed he couldn't stand the sight of her in agony.

Tessa shook off the memory and perused the other notices grouped with Abby's, but they all announced the birth of baby boys. A half hour later, Tessa looked down at her notebook beside the microfiche and wrinkled her nose. She had gone through two months of birth notices, taking into account that a few might have been placed late, and she had found only three baby girls born within a week of Abby.

"Mommy, can we leave?" Abby asked for what seemed like the hundredth time. She was sitting on the floor beside Tessa with her books scattered haphazardly around her. Sighing, Tessa bent down and starting gathering the books into a neat pile.

"Just a few minutes more, Abby."

"I wanna leave now," Abby said, her voice raised.

"I'll tell you what," Tessa said with more patience than she felt. "If you'll be quiet just a few minutes more, I'll buy

you some of those cookies you like when we go to the grocery store. Is it a deal?''

"Okay," Abby said, but she didn't look entirely molli-
fied.

Tessa's eyes swept the interior of the library and stopped
on a copy of an Oak Haven telephone book. She retrieved
it and quickly thumbed through the pages, her dismay
growing as the seconds passed. One of the surnames wasn't
listed; the other two were so common Tessa counted thirty-
five listings, none of which carried the first name of the baby's mother or father. Her eyes misted in frustration.

"Can I help you with anything?"

The voice startled Tessa so much that her hand jerked,
knocking the notebook to the floor. The librarian who had
helped her earlier stooped to retrieve it, but Tessa was
quicker. She bent and scooped up the notebook a fraction
of a second before the librarian could get to it, and then
quickly closed it so the used pages weren't exposed.

The librarian slowly got to her feet, regarding Tessa
quizzically. *Now I've done it,* Tessa thought, *I've aroused
suspicion in someone who had no intention of being suspicious.*

"No, thank you," Tessa said, trying to repair the damage. "I don't need any help. I found everything I was looking for."

"We're gonna leave right now," Abby added in a hopeful voice.

The librarian smiled at Abby and then turned back to
Tessa, doubt clouding her eyes. "Are you sure you don't
need help? I would have checked on you sooner, but I got
tied up on the telephone."

"I'm sure," Tessa said and pressed the machine's rewind
button. The whir of the microfilm rewinding pierced the silence of the library. "As soon as I gather everything up,
we're going to leave."

"Don't let me chase you away. You can stay as long as you like."

"No," Abby interjected. "Wanna leave now."

"Thank you, but we're through. Really we are," Tessa said, giving Abby a reproachful look. The other woman nodded and walked away, the staccato click of her heels sounding loudly on the wooden floor. Tessa was at a loss to explain why she hadn't heard the woman approach.

I have to be more careful, Tessa thought on a sob of panic, *or before I'm through I'll alert everyone in this town that Abby isn't really my daughter.*

"Let's get out of here, Abby," she said, standing and placing a guiding hand on Abby's back. The little girl quickly headed for the door, but Tessa was in the bigger hurry. She wanted to get away from the questions in the librarian's eyes.

"What do you mean you can't release the information to me?" Tessa's exasperation seeped into her voice, and she completely forgot that it was easier to get what you wanted with soft words than harsh ones. Abby stood quietly at her mother's side, her rigid posture betraying the fact that she knew something was wrong.

"Ma'am, you don't need to raise your voice." The hospital records clerk, a heavyset woman in her forties, glared at Tessa. They were in the records office of Oak Haven Hospital, and Tessa was becoming more agitated by the moment. This was the hospital that had managed to mix up two newborns, and Tessa was being treated as though she were in the wrong.

"I wouldn't have to raise my voice if someone around here knew what she was doing." It had been a very long day, and Tessa was beyond minding her manners. After coming up empty at the library, she had sandwiched a telephone call to the hospital between grocery shopping and a trip to the mall—Abby claimed she needed cartoon-character bed sheets if she was expected to sleep alone. Patience had never been one of Tessa's virtues, and she had run out of today's quota long ago. "All I want is a list of the babies born in the hospital during a week in October three years ago."

"I know what you want." The clerk wanted Tessa to tone down, but her voice was the louder. "You're just not going to get it."

Tessa took a steadying breath and made an effort to be reasonable. "The other clerk I spoke to on the telephone told me I had to come to the hospital in person before you could release any information. She said it would be no trouble to get what I needed."

"She must have assumed the information you wanted was about your own child. It's against hospital policy to release information about anyone else."

"I'm just wasting my time with you," Tessa muttered under her breath, aware that she had lost hold of her temper but not caring. She had to find a way to get that information, especially since she hadn't determined anything from the newspaper birth announcements. She did her best to deliver an intimidating stare. "Let me speak to your supervisor."

"I am the supervisor," the clerk said smugly, and Tessa knew she had lost. Not only would the stubborn clerk refuse to give her the records, she'd make doubly sure no one else in her office did so. But Tessa wasn't about to walk out of the hospital empty-handed. She scribbled her name on one of the release forms on the counter.

"Then I want my daughter's records. Her name is Abby Daniel, and she was born here on October ninth almost four years ago."

The clerk didn't move for nearly a minute, and Tessa felt sure she was trying to dream up a reason to refuse her even that. Then she turned abruptly, disappeared into an adjacent room and returned a few minutes later with a manila folder stuffed with sheets of paper. Tessa took it word-lessly.

"C'mon, Abby," she said, grabbing her daughter's hand and walking away with as much pride as she could muster. She was already ashamed of herself for losing control, but it was so terribly important that she track down her birth child. Even now, the little girl could be plagued with the overwhelming fatigue that preceded Cooley's anemia. Maybe she had already come down with it, and her doctors were unsure of how to treat her.

Tessa walked quickly down the long, empty corridor that led from the records office through the guts of the building and out to the parking lot. Beside her, Abby struggled to keep up on legs much shorter than her mother's. Ahead of them, a nurse pushed a stretcher carrying a sedated man into an elevator. It brought to mind how helpless hospital patients were and how much trust they surrendered to their caretakers, trust that wasn't always rewarded.

Tessa was trying to rectify a mistake, and the very hospital that had made it was thwarting her efforts. She hadn't even come close to getting any child's records except Abby's.

Tessa's eyes went to the folder in her hand, which seemed to be stuffed with original copies of forms. Her heartbeat quickened. Had that incompetent clerk allowed her to walk off with the hospital's only record of Abby's birth? If she had, it was a major victory. If the other parents discovered that the hospital had switched their baby with someone else's, there would be no way for them to track down Abby.

"Mommy, too fast!" Abby's complaint sounded like a wail.

"I'm sorry, honey," Tessa said, slowing her steps but not her mind. Even if she did have the sole records of Abby's birth, which was highly doubtful in today's age of computers, she still had what seemed to be an insurmountable problem. She'd come to a dead end in her search and didn't have the slightest idea what to do next.

The yellow pages had only two listings under "investigators," and one of them specialized in divorce cases. Tessa envisioned a sneaky man with a camera lurking outside a motel window and decided to phone the other. She had agonized over the decision to seek out a private investigator half the night and most of today, but she couldn't put off making the phone call any longer. Her hands shook so much when she dialed the number that it took her three attempts to get it right.

A man's voice, deep and clear, came across the line, and it was a few seconds before it dawned on Tessa that she was listening to a recording. She hung up before he could tell her to leave a message at the sound of the beep. Even though she fully intended to lie about her motive, she couldn't afford to leave a record of her calls. She had far too much at stake to make that kind of blunder.

Tessa jotted down the investigator's name and address on a piece of paper and shoved it into the pocket of her light-weight gray slacks. She walked to the bathroom mirror and picked up a brush, dimly noticing that her pale yellow shirt accentuated her black hair but made her skin looked washed out; a rich yellow would have been a better shade.

She hadn't taken the time to put on makeup, and she didn't look her best. Her dark eyes appeared almost haunted, the tip of her nose was shiny, and she weighed five pounds more than she would have liked. Tessa rubbed at the spot on her nose and shrugged.

It didn't matter how she looked. She was going to meet with a private investigator, not someone in the health-and-beauty industry. Mrs. Moriarty, her landlady, had invited Abby to help her make brownies, and time was at a premium. Tessa hurried out the door before she could think of another reason to delay the inevitable.

* * *

Corey McCash didn't even bother to turn on the air conditioner when he hustled into his one-room office, which was located in a strip shopping mall across from the police station. As usual, he didn't intend to spend more than ten minutes in the office, just enough time to check the messages on his answering machine.

Corey was a big man, but he moved with an easy grace that spoke of his athletic past. Although coaches had pestered him throughout his youth to join their football teams, Corey had resisted and placed his energy into track-and-field. He wanted to carry memories of foot races and pole vaults into adulthood instead of joint pain and knee operations. He didn't have time to exercise as much as he would like, but he still lifted weights a few times a week to keep in reasonably good shape. And, of course, he got a workout trying to keep up with Maggie.

At the thought of his daughter, a hint of a smile crossed Corey's face. He glanced at his watch and saw that he was due to pick her up at the preschool in a little more than an hour. He thought of the way she had interrupted her breakfast that morning to climb into his lap and whisper in his ear, "You're the best daddy ever." *Alise,* he thought, *you don't know what you're missing.*

Pad and pen in hand, Corey switched on the answering machine. Considering the time he spent here, he supposed he didn't really need an office. But his hours were irregular, and he would hate to conduct business from his home with Maggie in the next room. Besides, the location of his office was perfect because his friends on the police force sometimes referred him clients.

Corey was dressed for the summer heat in a white shortsleeved shirt of a tropical weight, but beads of sweat formed on his forehead. When he'd listened to all the messages, he pushed his chair back from his desk and stood. He figured he could squeeze in another hour of surveillance on the man who was suing the school district because he'd tripped on a crack in the sidewalk on school property. Neither the school district nor Corey believed the fall had put the man in a wheelchair. If Corey could get a few pictures of him using his "injured" legs, he could save the county taxpayers some money.

The door opened before Corey reached it, and his pulse rate increased markedly as the secretive woman from Virginia walked into his office. Her hair was loose about her shoulders instead of pulled back and she wasn't as tall as he'd thought, but there was no mistaking the beautiful pale skin and the obsidian eyes that had flashed at him so angrily a few days ago.

He hadn't been able to get her out of his mind since her car had sped away, and for a moment he wondered if he was hallucinating. But he blinked, and she still stood there. So he'd been right when he guessed she had something to hide. Now he was going to find out what it was.

He held out a hand. "I guess it's about time I introduced myself. I'm Corey McCash."

Tessa could hardly believe her bad luck. She stared down at the hand he offered, and then slowly raised her gaze up the length of his well-developed upper body to the blue eyes that were studying her so intently. Corey. She finally had a name to attach to the man who had intruded into her thoughts a dozen times in the past few days.

If she hadn't encountered him before, she probably would have thought him attractive. He was almost a foot taller than she was, even though she was five feet five. He was probably in his early thirties, but his golden-brown hair showed no signs of thinning; it was thick, even luxurious, the kind of hair a woman likes to run her fingers through.

With a square chin and broad cheekbones, he was arresting rather than classically handsome. His face, however, didn't contain an ounce of warmth and she was filled with the same blend of trepidation and anger that had assailed her the first time they'd met. She ignored his hand.

"Tessa Daniel," she said. Tessa didn't want to tell him even that much, but it would have been childish to withhold her name.

Corey fought a flash of annoyance and let his hand drop to his side. He indicated the chair facing his desk with a nod. "Have a seat and tell me how I can help you," he said brusquely, starting to return to his chair. Her words stopped him.

"I'm not staying."

"What?"

"I've changed my mind. I don't think I need a private investigator after all."

"Why don't you tell me why you came here and let me decide that?" Corey said, puzzled at her attitude. He would have wagered a month's commissions that she needed help, but she was prepared to walk away before she even asked for it.

"That won't be necessary," Tessa said, bristling. "I'm perfectly capable of deciding things for myself."

"I'm sure you are," Corey replied, trying to keep his tone diplomatic. It shouldn't matter that she was shrugging off help that she obviously needed. He had other cases that merited his attention, and he could live without a mysterious woman who showed up at his door without an appointment. Especially one who wouldn't tell him why she'd come to a private investigator in the first place. Why, then, couldn't he let her go? "But I'm a trained professional, and you can talk to me for free. I only charge the people who actually hire me."

He was still standing, towering over Tessa and making his small office appear even smaller. It would be heavenly to let someone in on her secret, but she couldn't unburden herself to Corey McCash. Tessa had only to look at his uncompromising expression to know that he would have no trouble distinguishing right from wrong. So what would she do if he thought it was wrong to raise a little girl who was yours only through a hospital's mistake?

"No, thank you," she said, turning to leave.

Corey frowned. He'd recognized the emotion that flitted across her delicate features as fear. But fear of what? Of discovery? What could she have to hide that would be so monumental that she couldn't tell a private investigator?

Something clicked in Corey's brain, and he tried to ignore the disappointment that coursed through him. He glanced down at her ring finger, saw the band of gold and thought he'd hit the mark. He'd been approached before by women who suspected their husbands of having affairs, and some of them had a hard time admitting it.

"I assure you, I'm very discreet. Nothing you say in this office goes any further. But you should know up front that I'm not the kind of investigator who will spy on your husband," he said. Tessa stopped in her retreat and went rigid, but Corey kept talking. "If you suspect him of having an affair, there's someone else I can recommend."

Tessa whirled, her fear of discovery forgotten. "How dare you," she seethed, her dark eyes boring into his, her nostrils flaring. "My husband couldn't possibly be having an affair. I'm a widow."

Corey merely gazed back at her, and despite her anger Tessa was relieved that he didn't murmur any meaningless words of sympathy. How could she possibly believe that one man was sorry a stranger he'd suspected of cheating on his wife was dead?

"Listen, Mrs. Daniel," Corey said, controlled anger running through his voice. "I have no way of knowing who or what you are, because you won't tell me. But I can tell you this. I haven't been back in Oak Haven long, but I was on the police force for eight years before I went into business for myself, and I'm damned good at what I do. You came into my office looking for help, and believe me, I can help you. But first you're going to have to tell me your problem."

She wondered what had happened to him to put the flint in his eyes and the mistrust in his voice. His very tone sent chills down the length of Tessa's body, but she refused to back away from him. She didn't doubt he was good at his job and she didn't deny that she needed help, but she didn't want anything from him.

"Why can't you just accept that I don't want your help?" she said icily. As always when she was in a jam, her chin raised a fraction in defiance. Tessa was twenty-seven, and she had an air of maturity that widowhood had thrust upon her. She had been making her own decisions since Chris had gone around that deadly curve too fast, and no one could intimidate her into doing something she didn't want to do. And she didn't want to hire him.

Why couldn't he accept it? Corey asked himself acidly. Because she was determined not to trust him, which amounted to an unfair attack on his integrity? Because she intrigued him as no other woman ever had, and he wanted to know her secret? Because he sensed her distress and knew he could alleviate it? Or because he'd rubbed her the wrong way when he'd approached her car the other day?

"If you're looking for an apology for the things I said the other day, I can't give you one," Corey said, and his voice changed so that now it sounded harsh instead of angry. "I'd do the same thing tomorrow. You have to admit you looked pretty suspicious sitting in that car across from the playground."

"I don't have to admit anything." Tessa was incredulous. "What I do is my business. I'm not about to make it yours."

Corey swallowed. "I'm a professional..." he began again.

Tessa's anger overflowed, and the truth came pouring from her. "Look, I don't care about your credentials. Yes, I have a problem. And no, I don't trust you. If there had been a picture in the yellow pages next to your name, I would never have come here.''

She whirled again, this time determined that nothing he could say would prevent her from walking out the door. But he didn't say anything, and the sunshine almost blinded her as she let the door slam behind her. Belatedly she realized that her blouse was damp with perspiration, and it occurred to her that there hadn't been a noticeable change in temperature between the inside of Corey McCash's office and the outdoors. She wondered if his air conditioner was on the blink or if it was white-hot rage that had heated her body. Corey McCash was, without a doubt, the most insufferable man she had ever met.

Chapter 4

Tessa had tucked Abby into bed and switched on the night-light barely ten minutes ago, but the even rise and fall of her daughter's chest revealed that she was asleep. Tessa bent at the waist and gently smoothed Abby's bangs from her forehead, placing a kiss on her exposed brow.

"I love you, little one," she whispered, even though nothing short of a shout would have roused Abby from sleep. Less than an hour ago, Abby had chattered so excitedly about "Aunt Mary" and the "bestest brownies in the whole world" that Tessa had feared she'd be up half the night on a sugar rush, but it hadn't taken long for exhaustion to set in.

Children were amazing little creatures, surprising their parents at just about every turn, but one thing wasn't a mystery. Once they had expended their day's supply of energy, they were a lot like batteries low on energy that needed to be recharged. But Tessa thought there was yet another reason they slept so heavily. Young children such as Abby hadn't yet developed the problems and worries that kept adults awake far into the night.

Tessa had become accustomed to staring into despair and the blackness of night after Chris's death. She had been as fragile as a piece of torn paper, but she hadn't allowed herself to be ripped apart by grief. Time—and Abby—had mended the tears in her psyche, and eventually she had looked forward to the night instead of dreading it. When she was asleep, she didn't have to face her demons.

But now the sleepless nights were back. Tessa had fashioned a life for herself and Abby that held the illusion of happiness, but those few haunting moments in Dr. Morgan's office had shattered that. This time, however, the nights Tessa lay awake had a different quality. When Chris had died, she was powerless to make things right. Now she used the night to plot so their lives wouldn't take another tumble. This time, she had hope.

Tessa sighed. No longer was she certain of the wisdom of coming to Oak Haven. It was imperative that the reason for their presence remain a secret, but Tessa couldn't stop Abby from making friends. She certainly couldn't tell Abby to be careful that no one guessed she belonged to some other mother.

Tessa turned away from her sleeping child, silently closed the door to the bedroom and stretched out on the sofa in the small den. She stared unseeingly at the ceiling. How had something like this happened?

Tessa had relentlessly searched her memory for a reason, but there was none. If Abby had been a sickly child, a mother desperate for a healthy infant could have made the switch. But Abby was so robust she hadn't suffered from even a common ear infection. No. It had been a mistake, pure and simple. A mistake that had somehow circumvented the hospital's system of identification bracelets and record keeping.

Tessa could be making an even bigger mistake by stirring waters that should remain muddy. If she hadn't discovered that Abby wasn't her rightful child, no one would have been hurt. If she stopped searching right now, no one would be the wiser. The child who should have been hers probably wouldn't even suffer any ill effects.

Cooley's anemia usually ran in families of Mediterranean descent, and Chris's mother had been Greek. That was the sole reason Tessa suspected it had tainted his blood. Her own mother was Italian, another group at risk, but descent alone didn't assure that anyone was a carrier. Even if Chris had been, any child of theirs would have only a one-in-four chance of developing the disease.

Then again, Tessa didn't know much about the health history of her late husband's family. Chris's parents had died in an airplane crash before he met Tessa, and it had pained him to discuss them. She'd never questioned Chris about hereditary diseases, assuming he would tell her anything relevant. But maybe he'd never told her because she hadn't asked.

Tessa's eyes fastened on the phone atop the end table, and she reached for the receiver before she could change her mind. She dialed a number that she knew by heart but never called, and waited for her sister-in-law to pick up the phone.

"Hello."

"Peggy? Hi, it's Tessa." She imagined her sister-in-law standing in her immaculate living room half a nation away wearing a look of shock. Peggy lived in Dallas, too far away for routine visits, and Tessa had spoken to her only twice since Chris's funeral.

"Why, Tessa. What a surprise," Peggy said after a moment's pause, and she sounded pleased. Then her voice changed. "Is everything all right? You're not calling with bad news, are you? Please tell me nothing has happened to Abby."

"Abby is fine," Tessa said, resolving to call more often. Peggy loved her niece and enjoyed getting updates on her progress, but Tessa's pain hadn't allowed her to stay in close touch with Peggy. In the past, talking with Peggy had brought memories of Chris to the surface in the same way that scratching a mosquito bite brought out the itch. If you let it alone, the discomfort was bearable. "How have you been, Peggy?"

"Fine, just fine," Peggy said and then fell silent so that Tessa could hear the crackling of the phone line. Her sister-in-law had always been straightforward, and she waited for Tessa to reveal the reason for her call.

"Peggy, this might seem like a strange question, but did your parents have any hereditary diseases?"

"This is about Abby. I knew it."

"No, Peggy. Really it's not. It's just that I'm thinking about enrolling Abby in a preschool, and they always make you fill out a form about your family's health history. It occurred to me that Chris and I never once discussed that."

"Are you sure that's all it is?"

"Yes," Tessa said, childishly crossing her fingers. The last time Tessa had lied, she was a senior in high school. Eager to fit in with a new crowd of friends, Tessa told her parents she was spending the night at a friend's. Then she used a fake driver's license to get into a nightclub. The ruse would have been worth the risk if the club hadn't confiscated Tessa's bogus license and informed the authorities. Her parents had grounded Tessa for two months. She'd never told another lie. Until now.

"Well, Aunt Hazel has a touch of arthritis, but she says it only affects her when the weather is bad," Peggy said thoughtfully, and Tessa breathed easier knowing that this time her lie wouldn't be discovered. "And one of our grandfathers had a bad heart, but he was in his eighties before they discovered that."

"What about your parents?" Tessa pressed, and there was a pause. Peggy was obviously searching her memory.

"You already know that they died when Dad crash-landed his Cessna. It was so sad, especially since Dad never suffered from anything more serious than a cold. Of course, Mom was a different story. She wasn't really sick, but she was always talking about some disease that was inside of her threatening to come out. I think she was a bit of a hypochondriac."

Tessa's heart stopped, or at least it seemed that way. "What disease, Peggy?"

"I can't remember. It seemed so unimportant, because she obviously didn't have the disease. I always thought she made it up. But looking back on it, I think she could have been a carrier for it."

"Think, Peggy," Tessa implored, trying not to sound too desperate. "What was the name of the disease?"

"Oh, I don't know. Something like thalamus or thallium."

"Thalassemia," Tessa said flatly.

"Yes, that's it," Peggy said. "Thalassemia. How did you know that?"

"Just a lucky guess," Tessa said evenly, but her heart beat in dull thuds. "I really have to go, Peggy."

"So soon? I'm not going to let you hang up until you promise to call again."

"I promise."

"I hope you do, Tessa. And please send some pictures of Abby. I know she must have changed a lot since you sent the last ones."

"I will," Tessa said, anxious to end the conversation. "Bye, Peggy."

"Goodbye," Peggy said an instant before Tessa hung up. For a long time after Tessa replaced the receiver on its cradle, she stared at the phone.

Thalassemia was another name for Cooley's anemia.

* * *

Such a gorgeous day was meant for the park, Tessa thought as she walked hand in hand with Abby. Summers in Oak Haven could be scorching, but the late afternoon sun had a sort of lazy glow that didn't give off too much heat. The park was a half dozen blocks from the house they were sharing with Mary Moriarty, and their path was shaded by the huge oak trees that gave the city its name.

"I'm so happy go to park," Abby said, skipping alongside her mother. Tessa had combed her hair into two pigtails and fastened them with bright pink bows, and they bobbed as she moved.

"Me, too," Tessa said, and she wasn't lying this time. If she had spent another minute sitting in their rented rooms thinking about her impossible predicament, she would have been certain to develop a pounding headache. Something dull had been thudding behind her eyes, waiting to grip her with pain, until the fresh air had blown it away.

The headache would wait until later, because their outing was only a temporary respite. That morning Tessa had visited Lester Speehar, the other private investigator in Oak Haven. She'd yearned to trust him, but Lester Speehar didn't inspire trust. His "office" was a room in his house, which looked as though it hadn't been cleaned in three or four weeks. That wasn't surprising, because Speehar didn't smell as though he bathed regularly.

Tessa would have been willing to overlook those faults if the man had impressed her in any other way. When he started discussing terms of payment without asking why she had come to see him, she considered walking out of his house. When he called her "doll" for the third time, she had. Even though Tessa intended to lie, entrusting Speehar with any information about Abby would have been tantamount to child abuse. But trusting Corey McCash was her alternative, and that was hardly an attractive option.

"Faster, Mommy. Faster." Abby tugged at her mother's hand.

"Are you calling me a slowpoke?"

"Yes, sirree."

Tessa put her hands on her hips and considered the little girl, who was fairly dancing with unspent energy. The sun sparkled, and she was with a gem of a child. She didn't intend to ruin the day by dwelling on the wisdom of trusting Corey McCash, especially since she hadn't figured out how to enlist his help after the way she'd treated him yesterday. Those thoughts could keep, especially since they promised to ruin her evening.

"Nobody accuses me of being a slowpoke." Tessa dropped Abby's hand and broke into a run that a three-year-old could match. Abby yelped in delight and readily followed.

By mutual consent, they slowed to a walk when they reached the park, and Tessa drank in the sights. Parts of the park were sun dappled, but trees afforded cover to every strategic location. The picnic tables looked so inviting that Tessa wished they had arrived earlier with lunch. Abby's eyes, however, were fixated on a child's paradise. A wooden play center in the distance included swings, a sandbox, monkey bars, a climbing rope and a clubhouse.

A tall man pushed a lone child on one of the swings, and Tessa recognized him instantly although they were fifty feet away. Corey McCash. Tessa's first thought was retreat, but she had barely stopped walking when Abby pulled her hand from Tessa's grasp and took off for Corey McCash in an unstoppable run.

"Last one to swing set's rotten egg," Abby shouted gleefully, pumping her little legs as hard as she could. Tessa stood immobile for a few seconds, considering her options. She decided she didn't have any.

If she yelled for Abby to come back, the child's momentum might carry her to the playground anyway and Corey

McCash would surely conclude that he unsettled her. He did, but she didn't want him to know that she hardly recognized the tense, distrustful woman she became in his company. Especially since she needed his help. Slowly, almost mechanically, Tessa followed the path of no return that her daughter had taken.

Corey gave Maggie another sturdy push, and the swing arced high above the ground, but not so high that his daughter was in danger of falling. Corey had propelled Maggie into the sky a few hundred times, and he remembered a time when swinging used to elicit shouts of glee. But Maggie was silent. Even though her back was to him, Corey knew she wasn't smiling.

His heart was so full of love and worry that he experienced a physical ache. He consistently put his daughter's needs above his own and did everything in his power to let her know she was loved, but Maggie wasn't a happy child. She had her moments—such as earlier today when she had laughed uproariously at his rendition of a break dance—but overall she was a solemn child who didn't make friends easily and spent too much time in the company of adults.

If she had been older when Alise had deserted them, Corey would have suspected that Maggie yearned for her mother. But how can you miss what you never had? Maggie had been only six months old when Alise declared she'd had enough of diapers, early morning feedings and Corey. It wouldn't have hurt very much at all if Alise hadn't run off with his best friend. Even now, his ex-wife's behavior filled him with disgust.

Corey had been glad to end the farce that was their marriage, but he'd never understand how Alise could have given up all rights to their child as though Maggie were nothing more than a piece of unwanted property. Alise had insisted they live in Philadelphia instead of Oak Haven, but she hadn't even cared when he and Maggie moved back home.

Alise never telephoned or sent cards, not even for birthdays or Christmases. She acted as though Maggie, the child who filled a corner of his heart with a pure joy he hadn't known was possible, didn't exist.

Of course, Maggie didn't know any of that. She never questioned him about her missing mother, and he tried to love her enough for two parents. Maybe the problem was with Mrs. Miller, the woman he employed to care for Maggie. Mrs. Miller loved his daughter, too, but she had a gruff, efficient manner that was intimidating even to some adults.

Or maybe Maggie needed more time around other children. Corey shook his head helplessly as he kept the swing moving. That's why he had entered her in preschool for a few afternoons a week, but the teacher reported that Maggie mostly kept to herself. Not only didn't he know how to solve Maggie's problem, Corey thought as he gave the swing another push, he didn't even know what it was.

Leaves rustled, and Corey looked up to see Tessa Daniel's sweet-faced daughter rushing at them as fast as her feet would carry her. She was still young enough that she had that funny little bob when she ran, and her pigtails flew behind her. Her grin was as open as the sky, the kind of grin he longed to see Maggie wearing. Following slowly, at a distance, was Tessa. He fought back a rush of irritation and focused on the little girl.

"Hi," she called cheerfully when she was almost to the swing set, and Corey wondered if she recognized him. But Abby was looking squarely at Maggie. "Wanna play with me?"

Corey stopped pushing Maggie so that the swing glided back and forth until it came to an almost complete stop. He waited expectantly for Maggie's response, but thought it would be tantamount to a miracle if she said anything at all.

Tessa's child had stopped running, and she wore the most lopsided, perfect grin he'd ever seen. "My name's Abby," she offered, and he wondered how Maggie could resist her.

And then the miracle happened. Maggie got off the swing, walked to within a few steps of Abby and actually reached for her hand. He stared in wonder as the girls' small fingers intertwined, and realized that Tessa's daughter had succeeded effortlessly where he'd failed. He'd been reaching out to Maggie all day, and she hadn't even noticed.

"I'm Maggie," she said, none of the earlier melancholy in her voice. "Wanna play in the sandbox?"

The little girls were fast friends even before Tessa drew even with the play center. They giggled and chattered excitedly while digging craters in the sand with the plastic shovels some other children had left behind. Just moments ago Corey had yearned to see a smile on his daughter's face, but now he couldn't seem to keep his attention focused on the children. Tessa was walking his way.

Somehow Corey knew he hadn't seen the last of her when she'd stalked out of his office. Oak Haven wasn't so large that you could stay clear of the people you wanted to avoid. Some sort of twisted fate guaranteed that you ran into the very people you would have run across the street to avoid. Not that Corey wanted to dodge Tessa. She was up to something, and he was going to find out what.

She was really quite lovely with her ivory complexion, ebony hair and eyes that were almost black. He supposed some of her features—such as the nose that dipped too suddenly and the narrow chin that lent her face a heart-shaped look—were flawed. But he liked her face. That didn't mean he liked her, Corey added quickly to himself. His disastrous relationship with Alise had taught him a valuable lesson: nobody is exactly what he seems. He thought that was particularly applicable to the secretive Tessa Daniel.

"We meet again," he said when Tessa stopped a half dozen paces short of him. Until then her eyes had been trained on their daughters; now she finally looked at him.

"Thankfully there aren't any doors around for you to slam in my face."

Corey, dressed in a T-shirt and shorts that showed off the bronzed length of his legs, leaned with his back against the supports of the play center. Tessa couldn't help but notice the light sprinkling of blond hair on his legs and arms and the glint in his eyes. Was it amusement or just the reflection of the sun? Tessa's stomach lurched, and the last thing she wanted was to speak to him. But she was an adult; she could be civil.

"I could always fling some sand in your eyes," Tessa deadpanned, her eyes flickering to the children in the sandbox. Abby was clearly visible, but Tessa's view of her playmate was obscured by one of the wooden supports that held the overhead clubhouse in place.

The traitorous Abby was actually laughing, and Tessa experienced a stab of nonsensical annoyance. Trust her to have a daughter who didn't have the discretion to check with her mother before hurling herself headlong into friendship with Corey McCash's child.

"I take it that's your daughter?"

On the heels of the question came another about his marital status, but Tessa bit it back. Before she could stop her eyes, however, they dropped to the ring finger of his left hand. It was tough to tell from this angle, but it didn't seem as though he was wearing a ring. In the next instant, Tessa got a clearer view. Corey held up his hand and wriggled his fingers. She willed herself not to blush.

"You take it right, but I'm divorced," he said, disappointed that she hadn't reacted to his gesture. He'd expected at least a blush, but wouldn't have been surprised had she flashed with anger. But nothing about her revealed that she had shouted at him less than twenty-four hours ago for daring to ask why she was seeking a private investigator. "I don't think they'll be too happy if you tell them this playground isn't big enough for the both of us."

Tessa's mouth twisted, but she didn't smile. She didn't intend to forgive him his transgressions just because he had a sense of humor. Then again, nothing about him indicated that he intended to apologize. ''Yeah, Abby's always been quick to open up to strangers.''

Unlike yourself, Corey thought. *You'd guard your secrets with your life.* She'd probably display that anger he recalled so vividly if she guessed that he'd already had her investigated. Part of what Corey did best was gather bits of knowledge until he had enough clues to come up with the truth. He still didn't know Tessa's secrets, but he knew more about her than he had yesterday.

Fifteen minutes after she had left his office, Corey telephoned an old friend who worked for the Virginia state police. Within another fifteen minutes, his friend had tapped into a computer that listed people with criminal backgrounds and found that Tessa's name wasn't listed.

He'd run her license plate number through another computer and discovered she was twenty-seven and lived in Richmond. A flip through the Richmond city directory had further showed that she taught at Richmond Central Elementary School.

All that brought Corey to the as yet unanswerable question: what sort of problem could an elementary-school teacher from Richmond have that was so grave she needed a private investigator in Oak Haven? And, more puzzling, why wouldn't she tell him what it was?

''Maggie's actually pretty shy. I'm surprised she's even playing with your daughter,'' Corey said instead of asking her. She stood about ten feet from him, and he had the odd sensation that she would turn and bolt like a skittish deer if he moved closer.

''Abby has that effect on a lot of people,'' Tessa said dryly, studying him but trying not to be obvious in her inspection. She'd known he was tall when she stood next to him in his office, but he looked even more imposing in his shorts and sneakers. The casual clothing exposed the sheer length of him, and she couldn't detect a single inch with a suggestion of softness. "Sometimes I wonder if she's made of magnetic particles that attract other humans."

"How old is she?" Corey studied Tessa's child, who was climbing out of the sandbox. She was bigger than Maggie and probably a number of months older, but her speech and movements weren't any more sophisticated. "Three?"

"That's right. How about Maggie?"

"She's three, too."

"Mommy, Mommy," Abby called excitedly, and Tessa started when she realized her daughter was standing next to her. She had been so focused on Corey that she hadn't heard Abby approach. "This is my new friend, Maggie."

Abby had trouble enunciating the letter *F,* so the word came out "sriend." The child made "sriends" more quickly than anyone Tessa had ever met. Their apartment complex was full of Abby's "sriends," and most of them were well past childhood. Maggie stood slightly behind Abby, but she took a sideways step and Tessa took her first good look at Corey McCash's daughter.

If she had tried to guess what Corey's daughter might look like, she never would have come up with Maggie. Tessa judged her to be at least seven or eight months younger than Abby, who was half a head taller; but Maggie would never be a large person. She had delicate bone structure that showed in her bare limbs and the arch of her cheekbones. Her hair was thick and a much darker brown than her father's, and her eyes matched her hair. Maggie McCash must look like Corey's ex-wife, Tessa thought, and immediately wondered what sort of woman had married a man like him.

"Hi, Maggie," Tessa said, with none of the restraint she showed her father, and Maggie's answering smile was a thing of beauty. Maggie might not have Abby's gift of congeniality, but she had hidden attributes that were just as engaging.

"You're beautiful," the little girl said shyly.

Tessa wasn't ashamed of her appearance, but she didn't harbor any illusions of beauty. Her features were irregular, and she could stand to lose a few pounds. Still, the words seemed to reach into her soul and touch it. She bent down on one knee and gently laid her fingers aside Maggie's face. The little girl leaned toward her, as though she was chilled and sought warmth, so that Tessa's hand was cupping her cheek.

"Thank you," Tessa said softly, "but I think you're the one who's beautiful."

Something twisted in Corey's gut as he witnessed the tender scene, and he felt like an outsider. Some indefinable quality in Tessa's touch enabled Maggie to respond as though she were somebody dear and beloved instead of a complete stranger. A stranger who couldn't be trusted.

"C'mon, Maggie." Abby's boisterous shout shattered the moment, and all three of them turned to see her sprinting away. "Let's play pirates. I'll be Peter Pan, and you be Captain Hook."

Maggie gave Tessa one more quick, tremulous smile and then sped after Abby. Tessa stood, turned to Corey and shrugged.

"Abby's hooked on *Peter Pan*," she said, unaware of her pun. "She'll watch the video as many times as I let her. I even had to buy her some Nerf bats so she could pretend they were swords."

"Children of that age are quite impressionable. You made quite an impression on Maggie."

She'd also made quite an impression on him. Corey privately admitted that Tessa looked even better than she had yesterday. She'd swept back her hair to expose her delicate neck, and her T-shirt clung to her enough to hint at the curves underneath. He even liked that her shorts were cut at mid-thigh, leaving something to the imagination. But Tessa Daniel had a lot more to hide than part of her anatomy.

"Maggie's adorable," Tessa said, her eyes following the children as they wielded sticks that she supposed were make-believe swords. "Your ex-wife must be quite charming."

Corey released a breath that wasn't quite a laugh. In a single sentence, she had managed to say more than most women could in a soliloquy. She didn't think that Maggie had inherited charm from a father she obviously believed was bereft of it, but she was wrong about Alise.

"You wouldn't say that if you knew Alise."

"I say a lot of things I shouldn't," Tessa muttered. Tessa believed that Corey richly deserved every verbal barb she'd flung at him, but she would have been wise to rein in her temper. Her predicament was already bad enough. It wasn't going to be easy to ask for help from the man after she'd already vehemently refused it.

"If that was supposed to be an apology, it fell short of the mark."

Tessa bristled, forgetting her resolve to control her temper. "I don't owe you an apology," she said stiffly.

"So you make a habit of visiting private investigators and then yelling at them when they ask why you've come?"

When he put it that way, she sounded irrational. And that wasn't fair, because it hadn't happened like that. She'd sought him out, yes, but that was before she'd realized he was the high-handed man who had practically accosted her beside the playground. Besides, her mother had always told her it was a woman's prerogative to change her mind. How was she going to tell him she had changed it back again?

"You were too pushy," she said, and his teeth clenched as though he were trying to bite back a retort. "I don't do anything on the spur of the moment. I simply wanted to explore my options before I made a decision about hiring an investigator."

"And have you?"

"Have I what?"

"Explored your options?" Corey asked, exasperated. Talking to her was like being a game-show contestant trying to fill in missing letters in a phrase—she left so much unsaid. "In other words, have you talked to Lester Speehar?"

Tessa walked over to one of the swings and sat down. She pushed off the trampled-down grass with one foot, and the swing rocked into motion. Should she tell him she'd checked out the competition and found it lacking? She'd rather not, but she supposed there wasn't anything to gain by refusing to admit that she'd met with Speehar.

"He talked. Mostly I just listened."

Corey heard the disapproval in her voice and laughed shortly. "Lester's not a bad guy, and he's pretty good at what he does. But what he does most of the time is try to catch husbands and wives cheating on each other."

"That's not such a great way to make a living."

"No, it's not." Corey sat down on the swing next to Tessa's.

She didn't look at him, instead concentrating on the way the sunlight streamed through the trees and created patterns of light interspersed with the shade. It made Tessa feel melancholy, as though her life would be in shadows until she could find a way to make the sun break through. If only she could locate her birth child and reassure herself that the girl wasn't afflicted with Cooley's anemia. Only then would the darkness give way to light.

"I was planning to telephone you on Monday," Tessa said after a few minutes of silence, and it took a supreme effort to make the admission. Tessa had never been very good at asking for help, but she couldn't think of herself. This problem involved another human being's welfare, and she couldn't live with that weight on her mind. "I want you to take my case."

She turned to him then, and Corey saw how much the statement had cost her. She looked drained, like soil that had gone too long without water. Her mouth drooped, her face sagged and her eyes seemed to have lost the spark that made them come alive. All of that combined to stem the satisfaction that had briefly leaped in Corey when she'd made the admission. Tessa Daniel must have one whopper of a problem.

"What makes you think I'll take it?"

"It's what you do," she said, deliberately misunderstanding. "You're a private investigator."

"That's not what I meant, and you know it." Corey stopped swinging, and he sat perfectly still, watching her.

"Fine," she said, and the word was clipped. "If you don't want to take my case, just say so. It's fine with me."

"I didn't say that," Corey said, watching the way the spark in her eyes lit her entire face with anger. He wondered if she would be as quick to respond to his touch as she was to his words, and quickly quashed the thought. "I never decide whether to take a case until I hear the problem first. And unless my memory fails me, you won't tell me what it is."

He was every bit as maddening as she'd thought when he hovered over her car. But there was a colossal difference between then and now. Then, he was an insufferable man who was prying into matters that didn't concern him. Now, he was an insufferable man whom she needed to pry into matters for her.

"Of course I'll tell you what it is . . ." Tessa began.

"Daddy. Mommy." Tessa and Corey looked away from each other and toward the two girls who were rushing them. Tessa's neck and shoulders relaxed, and she realized how grateful she was for the interruption. "Abby asked me to go to her house and play. Can I please? Please, Daddy?"

An hour ago, Corey would have given up a lot to hear his daughter beg to play with another child. But he never imagined it would be Tessa Daniel's child. He glanced at his watch, grateful to have a plausible reason to refuse.

"Maggie, you know I have to work tonight. Maybe you'll see Abby in the park another day. Mrs. Miller's probably already waiting for us back at the house."

"Don't want to go home," Maggie said, her fine features taking on a pinched look. "Want to go with Abby."

"Please, mister," Abby pleaded, exacerbating the situation. Tessa bit her lip to stop herself from offering to keep Maggie for a few hours. Her relationship with Corey McCash needed to be strictly business, and baby-sitting his daughter didn't fall into that category.

"Maggie," Corey said, and Tessa noticed the gentle tone he used with the child. Most parents would have met their child's defiance with angry words, but he favored logic. "I'm sure Mrs. Daniel has other things to do today. You can play with Abby another time."

"When?" the child asked petulantly, unwilling to give up the fight.

"Yeah, when?" Abby asked, directing the question at Tessa.

Corey glanced at Tessa and recognized the battle waging in her eyes: she didn't have the heart to refuse the children such a simple request any more than he did. Tessa's indecision spurred him to take a stance. Corey never did anything in half measures, a quality that had won him as many friends as it had lost him. Maggie needed to socialize with children her own age, even if the child in question belonged to Tessa. Corey couldn't blame them for wanting to spend time together, but he would blame himself for keeping them apart.

"Let's talk about your case at my house tomorrow," Corey addressed Tessa. Conducting business at home violated a long-standing policy of keeping his work separate from Maggie, but it couldn't hurt to mix his business with Maggie's pleasure. Not this once.

"I don't think that's a good idea," Tessa replied quickly, before the children could endorse it. Panic rose in her throat until it threatened to choke her. She had a difficult enough time keeping her equilibrium around Corey when they were on neutral ground. He riled her more than any man ever had, and she didn't want to surrender even the slightest advantage. Being inside his home was a definite disadvantage.

"We'll have complete privacy," Corey said, either misreading or ignoring the reason for her objection. "Maggie's room is stockpiled with toys, and the woman who cares for her when I'm not home works part of the day, Sundays. I'll ask Mrs. Miller to keep an eye on them while we talk business."

Two pairs of hopeful eyes darted from Corey to Tessa, and Tessa was defeated. She needed to meet with Corey in the next few days anyway, and saying no would not only disappoint Maggie, but Abby as well.

"What time do you want us there?" she asked, and even the sight of the two girls joining hands and jumping up and down didn't lift her spirits.

She tried to look on the bright side, reasoning that it might be easier to relax in Corey's presence in a room bigger than his office, but thought it prophetic that clouds obscured what was left of the day's sunshine.

Sometime between now and tomorrow, she had to come up with a monstrous lie that would both explain their presence in Oak Haven and give Corey enough information to find the missing child.

There was no way Tessa could ever tell him the truth.

Chapter 5

"They're here," squealed a high voice seconds after Abby rang the doorbell of the split-level home in one of the nicer sections of Oak Haven. Tessa still wasn't used to the gently rolling terrain that characterized western Pennsylvania.

Some of the neighborhoods, such as this one, were even built on the sides of hills. If you stood at the bottom and gazed up, the houses looked as though they were stacked like so many building blocks. Just before the door swung open, Tessa questioned whether her foundation was as strong as the ground on which Corey McCash had built his house. She seriously doubted it; if there were time, she'd have turned around and fled.

Maggie, dressed in denim shorts and a T-shirt, danced on the threshold beaming at them. Corey stood behind her, and he didn't appear particularly welcoming. He wore the same serious expression he'd greeted Tessa with when he approached her car that day across from the playground, and Tessa wondered if he ever smiled. Then again, she wasn't smiling either.

"Hi, Maggie. Hi, mister." Abby spoke before anyone else had a chance to say anything. With Abby around, Tessa thought wryly, at least she didn't have to worry about long stretches of uncomfortable silence. "Where's your room, Maggie?"

Maggie, who had yet to say a word, happily took Abby's hand. The two exchanged a look, giggled and dashed down a hallway.

"Girls, don't run," Corey called after them and shrugged when he turned back to Tessa. "I keep telling her that, but it sinks in only half the time."

Tessa instantly missed Abby's small presence and had the uncomfortable feeling that she had been using her daughter as a shield. With Abby gone, Tessa had no other reason to avoid looking at Corey. Slowly she dragged her eyes from the now-empty hallway to his face, noting that he was freshly shaven and his hair was wet as though he had just gotten out of the shower.

"Come on in," Corey said when she didn't speak. Something in the way she was looking at him warned him to turn her away without listening to her case. Her brown eyes reminded him of Alise and the fool he'd been to believe anything she said.

This woman was trouble, too. She wasn't planning to get pregnant and trap him into marriage, but she was plotting something. Corey would remember that the next time he looked into her eyes and saw only beauty and vulnerability. He waved a hand in the general direction of the inside of his house.

Only then did Tessa realize she was still standing on the doorstep, fulfilling her subconscious urge to keep her distance. She had even chosen her dress—a no-nonsense navy blue A-line that buttoned at the collar and fell below the knees—with the purpose of maintaining a measure of space between them.

He wore faded blue jeans and a soft short-sleeved cotton shirt in stripes of yellow and blue. She hadn't considered dressing so casually, because she wanted her attire to convey that this was strictly business. It was bad enough that she had to lie; it would be far worse if she let her guard down and gave him even the slightest reason to question her story.

Tessa stepped over the threshold and Corey leaned across her to shut the door, his arm brushing hers in the process. Tessa flinched as though an iron had seared her flesh and then prayed he hadn't noticed. The annoyance that briefly flitted across his face, however, told her that he had. He made her nervous, even though she knew that was absurd. She saw him as nothing more than a means to an end, a way to solve her troubles. Absolutely no reason existed to view him as anything other than a private investigator.

"I thought three o'clock was never going to come," Corey said casually, masking the momentary irritation that had coursed through him when she flinched from his touch. His reactions didn't make sense. One moment he was debating whether to let her into his house, and the next he was reeling because she didn't want to be close to him. "Maggie has been asking me what time it is every fifteen minutes."

"It's hard to be patient when you're that young," Tessa said. The reverse was true when you got older. She felt as though a time machine had transported her to the future. It seemed as though she had just gotten out of bed, and already she was in Corey's house. Logic told her that no such phenomenon had occurred; instead she had been dreading their meeting, and time had raced by.

"How about a cup of coffee? Mrs. Miller just brewed a pot."

"No, thank you," Tessa said, wishing he wasn't standing so near. She barely reached his chin even with her two-inch heels, and she had to tilt her head to look at him. She took a step backward. "Can we just get started?"

He shrugged. "Follow me."

The interior of Corey's house was decorated in shades of brown, tan and yellow. Tessa would never have chosen the color scheme, but she privately conceded that the effect was stunning. The splashes of yellow kept the overall look from being too dark, and the combination of the two darker colors created a rich, masculine feel.

Delicate french doors opened into a study that, with its wood-paneled walls and mahogany furniture, was especially attractive. Books covered an entire wall, and Tessa fought off a stab of envy. She had always yearned for a room like this, but her small apartment in Virginia was so crammed that she kept her treasured books neatly stacked in boxes. It figured that Corey McCash would have what she'd long wanted.

Tessa sank into one of the leather chairs facing his desk, grateful that she would have the length of the desk between them. Corey's eyes flickered to the chair behind the desk, but he chose the chair adjacent to hers. Tessa stifled an urge to scoot her chair back a few feet and sat perfectly still.

"Your house is very attractive," Tessa said, aware that she was procrastinating. "Have you been here long?"

He shook his head, drawing attention to the way the overhead light cast a sheen on his hair that made it look as though there were slivers of blond running through it. "Not long at all. I grew up in Oak Haven, but lived in Philadelphia during my marriage. I decided to move back because it's a good place to raise a child."

Tessa nodded because she'd thought the same thing, and then couldn't think of another word of small talk. Realizing there was no point in delaying the inevitable, she swiveled in Corey's direction and tried not to betray her nervousness.

She was about to lie to a man who ferreted out the truth for a living, but she didn't have any choice. She'd decided days ago that she needed professional help, but she couldn't risk the price a full confession would entail. He mustn't know that Abby wasn't hers.

Corey waited, watching the way her tongue nervously darted over her lips. He recognized the warmth that started low in his groin as desire, but it irritated rather than stirred him. He hadn't been able to exorcise Tessa Daniel from his mind since she'd railed at him in his office, but that made perfect sense.

He was a detective who loved a good mystery, and an air of secrecy clung to her like early morning dew settled on a flower. He desired the intrigue, not the woman. Once she explained her mysterious appearance in Oak Haven, he'd be able to solve the case and put her out of his mind. He certainly didn't have a place for a woman like her—or any woman, for that matter—in his life.

"About five years ago, out of the blue, my brother got married." Tessa addressed Corey, but looked straight at his mahogany desk. He wondered why. "He was living in Pittsburgh when he got around to telling us. We're from Virginia, so nobody in the family ever met his wife.

"Steve could be pretty secretive, and all we knew was that her nickname was Bunny. Steve called every once in a while, and before long he told us she was pregnant. It didn't take a genius to figure out that's why he married her."

Tessa paused, expecting Corey to question her about the story, but he was silent. She thought back to the first and last high-school play she had performed in. It had been a comedy, but the audience members had stared at her solemnly whenever she'd uttered a line. She knew before the curtain fell that she didn't have what it took to be a good actress. Tessa willed herself to remember the rest of the story. This wasn't a play: this was her life.

"We didn't hear from Steve for a couple of months, and then Bunny phoned to tell us he'd died in an accident on a construction site. We couldn't even say a proper goodbye, because she'd already had him cremated. She shipped his ashes home, and we didn't hear from her again until a couple of months later. It was October ninth going on four years ago. She said she was calling from Oak Haven Hospital, where she'd just given birth to Steve's daughter."

Tessa stopped once again, but this time she was trying to get her story straight. She'd concocted the tale while she lay in bed last night, and even practiced saying it aloud. It had sounded more believable in the middle of the night than it did in the daytime.

The sunlight seemed to expose all its holes. If the hospital had duplicate copies of Abby's birth record, and she suspected it did, Corey would soon find out that her story was a lie. But she had to take that chance, because she would never find her birth child without help. Hiding her distress, Tessa plunged ahead.

"My mother and sister thought about coming to Oak Haven to see the baby, but they were still too distraught over Steve's death. I couldn't travel, because I was pregnant with Abby and having a difficult time. The upshot is we never heard from Bunny again."

Corey kept the house comfortably air-conditioned, but perspiration had formed above Tessa's upper lip. Her story was strange, almost implausible, but he'd heard stranger. Not all families were blessed with the glue that kept them from splintering apart. He could believe that her brother had broken from the family unit and kept in poor touch. He waited for Tessa to continue, but after a few moments it became obvious that she wasn't going to.

"So you want me to find your sister-in-law?"

Her dark eyes rounded. "No. I want you to find my brother's baby."

"It's the same thing."

"No, it's not," Tessa denied hotly. She couldn't allow him to attempt to find a woman who didn't exist, especially when there was a baby who did. "I'm not interested in her. It's only the baby I want."

"Why?" The question came quick and hard. All too clearly, Corey remembered Tessa sitting in the car, studying the children at Maggie's preschool. If she knew for certain that one of those children was her niece, would she have been content to just gaze?

Tessa pursed her lips. "Steve had an inheritance, and I want to see that his baby gets her share."

"I thought you just said he was a construction worker."

Tessa was ready for the question, and she almost tripped over her words in an effort to get them out. "He was, but Steve's godfather set up a trust fund that was supposed to become available when he turned twenty-one. Steve never made it, so now I have the money. It's not a lot, but it's enough to make a difference in a child's life."

Corey turned the information over slowly in his mind, considering it from all angles. From each one, it didn't make sense. Why hadn't Tessa's family made any effort to find out about Bunny while she was married to Steve? And why would Bunny cut off contact with her husband's family if she knew they were in a financial position to help her?

"I still think that I should search for your sister-in-law. If we find Bunny, we find the child."

"For all I know, she could have given the baby up for adoption," Tessa protested. "Besides, I don't know a single thing about her. Steve left home with some bad feelings, and a year went by before he even called. I don't know where Steve met Bunny or where they got married. I don't even know her real name. But I do know when the baby was born, and I know that it was a girl."

"I don't suppose you know the baby's name either." Corey watched her closely, an innate sense telling him there was a concrete reason that she didn't want him to look for her late brother's wife.

Tessa shook her head. "No. Our family name is Hutton, but I'd bet anything Bunny didn't use it."

Corey didn't believe her. The more she talked, the less feasible the story sounded. He had to hand her one thing, though, she could lie with the best of them. Her dark eyes were clear, as though she didn't have any qualms about passing fiction off as fact. And no matter what he asked, her voice didn't waver. She didn't even have any of the nervous gestures—the tapping of a foot, the stroking of a chin—that sometimes pinpoint liars. But a gut instinct told Corey that she wasn't telling the truth.

"Why isn't Bunny trying to find you, if you have money for her baby?"

"She doesn't know about it." Tessa hadn't anticipated the question, but it was easy enough to answer.

He seemed to run out of questions, and Tessa watched him as he mulled over her story. Had she been believable? Conviction had run through her words, because lying was the only way to find her birth child without endangering her relationship with Abby.

One of Corey's hands half covered his mouth and he stroked his chin with his thumb, but she wouldn't have been able to read anything in his face even if it was fully exposed to her view. Corey wasn't a man who wore his emotions like his skin. She'd talked to him on three separate occasions, and she'd yet to see him smile.

"So, will you help me?" she asked when the silence stretched too long for her to bear.

Corey knew that he shouldn't agree to take her case. The paramount thing he demanded from clients was complete honesty, and he wasn't getting that from Tessa. But unless he accused her outright of being a liar, he didn't have a reason to refuse. Besides, he wanted to take the case if only to figure out the reason behind her wild story. It didn't have anything to do with the way her lips parted slightly in anticipation of his answer.

"I'll need a retainer," he said and named his usual figure. Tessa winced, and Corey remembered that she was a single mother getting by on a teacher's salary. He wondered if her husband had left her any insurance money. He wondered if she would dip into the inheritance she had earmarked for her brother's child. "Even Lester Speehar charges more. If it'll put your mind at ease, I can't imagine this case costing any more than the retainer. It shouldn't be too difficult to get the records from the hospital and track down the kids."

"Don't be too sure," Tessa said doubtfully, masking the relief that had shot through her when he accepted her case. "I already went down to the hospital and asked for them. They said it was against hospital regulations to release information to anyone but immediate family."

"There are ways of getting around regulations," Corey said, because he already knew how to get the records. Corey had worked as a policeman in Oak Haven for years, and more than a few people owed him favors. One of them was Joe Schwinn, a security guard at the hospital for more than twenty years.

If Corey hadn't been suspicious of a car parked near an unlocked hospital door a few years back, a couple of teenagers with habits would have made off with one hundred thousand dollars' worth of prescription drugs. Joe, who had forgotten to check the locks on the doors that night, would have taken the blame and never become the hospital's director of security.

"Good. That's settled then," Tessa said and pushed herself out of the leather chair. She smoothed her dress and tried to summon a smile, but only managed a weak facsimile. She was already worrying about the dent his retainer would put in her savings account. "I can get the money to you tomorrow. How soon can you start?"

"Tomorrow." Corey was also standing, and the sheer length of him unnerved Tessa. He looked as though he had been an athlete in his youth, and she guessed that he still worked out with weights. The material of his blue jeans hugged his thighs, and she could make out the definition of his chest through the thin fabric of his T-shirt.

"I really should get Abby and go," Tessa said, because quite suddenly she wanted to get away from him and the awareness that was welling inside her. *Remember,* she told herself sternly, *this is a man you don't particularly like, who is working for you. This is strictly business.* "I'm sure you have better things to do with your afternoon than to entertain us."

Corey didn't answer, and Tessa experienced a momentary jolt of disappointment that he hadn't bothered to contradict her statement. On its heels came shame. She'd sounded as though she wanted him to convince her to stay, and that was even less true than her story had been. "Can you please show me the way to Maggie's room?"

High-pitched laughing forestalled his answer, and the french doors swung open to reveal their two smiling daughters. Small, dark Maggie was an attractive counterpart to brown-haired, blue-eyed Abby. Tessa had combed Abby's hair into pigtails that morning and tied them with bright yellow ribbons to match her yellow-and-red playsuit, but Maggie's long hair was loose. She fingered the dark strands, smiling shyly at Tessa.

"Maggie wants pigtails, too," Abby announced, and Maggie nodded.

Corey glanced from the eager girls to the reluctance on Tessa's face, and he gathered that the last thing she wanted was to fix his daughter's hair. Now that they'd finished their business talk, he had no reason to want her to stay. He ignored the part of him that wasn't ready to let her go.

"Feel free to say no," he told Tessa and tried not to notice the disheartened glance Maggie sent his way. "It's just that I'm not very good at fixing hair, and Mrs. Miller thinks it's a waste of time."

He had given her a perfect out, and that's what she wanted, but Tessa couldn't refuse when she saw Maggie's face fall.

"Of course the answer's yes," she said with a false cheerfulness. She crossed the room and stooped down to the little girl's level. "I bet you didn't know that I thought about working in a beauty shop before I became a teacher. Fixing hair is one of the things I like best."

"Really?" Maggie asked, transfixed.

"Really. Now where are the comb and rubber bands?"

After they'd gathered their raw materials, the trio of females retreated to Maggie's room. Corey stood in the doorway watching Tessa as she worked with his daughter's hair. He approved of the way she leaned down to whisper silly comments in Maggie's ears throughout the process.

"What color ribbons do you want?" Abby sifted through a box of unused hair accessories Maggie had received as gifts.

"Green," Tessa answered.

"Blue," Maggie said at the same time.

"Okay, how 'bout green and blue?" Abby, the diplomat, asked.

"That's a wonderful compromise," Tessa said, and her daughter fished in the box for ribbons that were the correct colors.

Maggie was as squirmy as most children, but she sat perfectly still as Tessa worked on her. Corey watched the long, slim fingers combing through his daughter's hair and wondered what her fingers would feel like threading through his own hair.

As she worked, Tessa was aware of Corey standing at the periphery of the room. Maggie's room was done in shades of pink with pastel balloons floating from the wallpaper, and the combination highlighted his masculinity.

He was so different from Chris, so different from any of the men she had ever dated. Tessa had always preferred dark men not much taller than herself, and Corey was a relative giant with hair that looked blond in some light and eyes so blue they were startling.

Her gaze met those eyes now, and they held her as though endowed with a magnetic power. Raw need emanated from his eyes, and she knew it was reflected in hers.

Insisting to herself that he was just another man wasn't going to work. She hadn't felt this spark of attraction for anyone since Chris had died, because her grief had been all consuming. Irritation, raw and red, attacked her. She had picked a devil of a time to notice the obvious differences between a man and a woman. She had also chosen a devil of a man.

She tore her eyes from Corey's and reached for the ribbons Abby offered. With hands that shook slightly, Tessa tied them into brightly colored bows that decorated Maggie's hair.

"Ta-da," Tessa said gaily, covering her confusion with enthusiasm for her finished job on Maggie's hair. She squeezed Corey's daughter's shoulders. "Where's a mirror?"

"There's one," Abby said, hurrying to fetch from Maggie's dresser a hand mirror embellished with Snow White's beaming face. She handed it to her playmate, and Maggie's eyes rounded in pleasure at the sight of herself in pigtails adorned with ribbons. "You look wonderwul."

Tessa smiled at her daughter's mispronunciation. "Marvelous," she supplied.

"Stupendous," Corey added.

"Better than good," Maggie said, and everyone in the room laughed, breaking the thread of sexual tension that had connected Tessa and Corey. Maggie put down the mirror, turned and threw her arms around Tessa's neck.

"Abby's so lucky to have you for a mommy," she whispered so that only Tessa could hear, and Tessa's heart filled. She'd always thought that the brand of special tenderness that now assailed her was reserved only for a son or a daughter, but she was wrong. She hugged the little girl back, wondering not for the first time what had happened to her mother.

"I got an idea," Maggie said, disentangling herself from Tessa and sprinting to her father. He caught the child under her arms and spun her around so that her pigtails went flying. He looked like anything but a man who had smoldered with desire mere moments ago.

"What's your idea about, sport?" he asked, laughing. Later Tessa would remember that moment as though it were frozen in time. Corey's blue eyes came so alive that she could have sworn they sparkled, and his usually solemn mouth curved into a giant smile. It did something to his face that nearly stole her breath. He looked years younger and infinitely happier.

"It's about asking Abby and her mommy to have pizza with us?" Maggie said excitedly, her voice so high-pitched that the tail end of her sentence sounded like a squeal. "Can we, Daddy?"

"Sure we can," Corey said, only partly because it would have been horribly rude to say anything else. Tessa Daniel had looked at him with pure need a moment ago, and despite his misgivings about her he longed to follow up on that look. He smiled across the room at Tessa, who a half hour ago had wondered if he ever smiled at all. "Mrs. Miller refuses to cook on Sundays, so Maggie and I always go out for pizza. What do you say? Will you come?"

"Yes," yelled Abby, echoing the answer her mother quite suddenly, quite unexpectedly, wanted to give. But Tessa had never been impulsive, and she wasn't about to toss away what could be her only chance to find her birth child. The more time she spent in Corey McCash's company, the more risk there was of being discovered as a fraud.

"Maybe another time," Tessa said firmly, resolving to stick to her stance, no matter how unpopular. It wasn't as though she liked Corey McCash and felt compelled to spend time with him. The flash of desire she'd experienced a moment ago could be easily explained: she'd been celibate by choice for a long time, and her senses were slowly awakening. She couldn't expect to feel nothing for the rest of her life every time she looked at an attractive man.

It didn't matter what he did or said—she and Abby were going home. The plea to change her mind, however, came from Maggie and not her father. The small girl left Corey to stand in front of Tessa and looked up at her with great solemn eyes filled with unshed tears.

"Please."

Tessa's heart filled again, and she wondered what it was about this little girl that was so achingly touching. Was it because Maggie so obviously yearned for a mother and the one she had was nowhere in evidence? Tessa crouched down so that her eyes were almost level with Maggie's, and she gave one of her pigtails a playful tug.

"Will you let us take a rain check on that?" Tessa asked gently, smiling. She had meant to refuse outright, but she couldn't bear to make the little girl cry. The tears in Maggie's eyes stayed where they were.

"What's a rain check?" she asked curiously.

"It means that we can't go for pizza now, but we will another time. That is, if you ask us again. Will you?"

"Oh, yes," Maggie said, and turned to Corey. "Won't we, Daddy?"

"Sure, sport. They haven't seen the last of us." Corey's voice was soft, his eyes focused on Tessa.

A minute later, Tessa gratefully breathed in the scent of the outdoors. For the first time in an hour, she felt truly in control of her emotions. The meeting had gone well enough, and she felt a sense of relief that Corey McCash would be working on her case.

Tessa needed to keep her wits about her, because Corey would soon be asking questions she didn't want to answer.

She might be smart enough to handle the inquiries, but her common sense could desert her if he realized she was physically attracted to him. She was already at a distinct disadvantage, because there was something else she hadn't counted on: a three-foot-tall dark-haired waif with big, brown eyes.

"Mommy, may I please have an ice cream?" Abby, not one to be ignored for long, asked sweetly. She phrased the question exactly the way Tessa liked.

"Okay, honey. But just this one time," Tessa answered, even though it was barely an hour before dinner time. She felt bad that Abby hadn't been able to spend more time with her new friend, and partially blamed herself. Abby, of course, had picked up on the guilt and used it to her advantage. Belatedly, Tessa realized there were two children she couldn't resist.

Corey inserted his office key into the lock and stood dumbfounded when the door wouldn't open. He jiggled the key, turned it another time and came up with the same result. A full minute passed before he thought to make sure he was using the correct key. He wasn't.

My mind has been somewhere else all day, Corey mused when he finally settled himself behind his desk. An image of Tessa Daniel crystallized before his eyes, and he grudgingly conceded that it had been on her.

Corey marveled that he'd been able to concentrate long enough to wrap up the case concerning the wheelchair-bound man who did a little home repair work in his spare time. Today he had snapped photos of the man climbing a ladder to replace some roof tile. Corey had an excellent record of resolving his cases, but he wouldn't have cracked this one if an ambulance siren hadn't jarred him from his daydream as the man was positioning his ladder.

Daydreaming on the job wasn't like Corey at all. Since he had married Alise, daydreaming about a woman was even more out of character. But Corey couldn't seem to get Tessa and that look they'd exchanged out of his mind. He kept wondering if he had misread what was in her eyes, if she had actually been gazing at him with dislike instead of desire.

Nothing she had done since they'd first laid eyes on each other even hinted that she found him attractive. She'd sped away from him in a car and slammed a door in his face, which didn't signal a very promising start. Corey thought he had sensed a thawing while she lovingly tended Maggie's hair yesterday, but then she'd emphatically refused to eat pizza with Maggie and him. Correction, Corey thought, frowning. Tessa had refused to have pizza with *him;* he felt sure that she'd accompany Maggie on any outing.

Not that any of that mattered, Corey thought crossly. Tessa Daniel was a client who happened to have a look about her—a way about her—that he found attractive. If Corey had met Tessa five years ago, he wouldn't have had any qualms about taking her out on a few dates, having some fun and waving a cheery goodbye.

But five years ago, he hadn't known there were women like Alise. What he had thought was a lighthearted good time came with so many strings attached that in the end he had been tied in knots.

He hadn't intended to marry Alise, even after she told him she was pregnant. She'd cried and pleaded, even claiming she was too ashamed to give the newspaper permission to print a birth announcement because she was without a husband. None of it had an effect on Corey, until he'd held his infant daughter for the first time. He'd proposed to Alise in the hospital, because he wanted to give Maggie the best of everything—including a full-time father.

No, Corey wasn't foolish enough to let down his guard and get trapped by another woman. Especially a woman like Tessa, who was probably an even bigger liar than Alise.

Besides, he had an iron-clad rule against dating his clients. He conceded that he'd never before had a client he wanted to date, but it was still a smart rule. He was supposed to be solving Tessa Daniel's case, not wondering what it would be like to hold her against him.

Shrugging away the image, Corey opened the bulging manila folder he had carried into the office and took out the contents. He was sure that one of the computer-generated pieces of paper would lead to the little girl Tessa was hunting for.

Every pore in his being told him this was the wrong way to go about this case. He would have much preferred searching for Bunny, but Tessa claimed she didn't know her sister-in-law's real name or even the state in which she had married her brother.

Since he wouldn't find Bunny with his current leads, Corey had done the next best thing. Tessa's maiden name was Hutton, so he'd phoned a friend who happened to run a slick investigative agency in Richmond. Corey wanted any information his friend could dredge up on Steve Hutton. In the meantime, he'd do as Tessa had suggested. Looking for Bunny might have yielded a quicker result, but the solution to Tessa's case was also in these birth records.

Joe Schwinn had grumbled about how difficult it would be to get the records, muttering about an old friend taking advantage and breaches of security that could cost his job. Corey had listened attentively—not once reminding Joe that he had saved the very job he talked about putting in jeopardy—and said he'd appreciate whatever Joe could do. That had been at nine this morning. By four o'clock, the records were in Corey's hands.

Corey glanced at his watch and saw with dismay that it was almost six o'clock. After snapping the incriminating photographs of the school-district shark, he should have gone straight home to have dinner with Maggie. He supposed he could phone Mrs. Miller and ask her to delay the meal for a few minutes, but it wouldn't do any good. She'd insist that Maggie was almost doubled over from hunger, because it fit in with her firm belief that a child shouldn't have dinner any later than six.

I won't be that much later, Corey reasoned. He didn't have time to study the birth records, but he'd make time to sort them because he wanted to get started on the case early tomorrow. The records from each child were about twenty-five pages thick, and Joe had paper-clipped them together to make for easy sorting. Corey planned to sort them into stacks of males and females, because he only needed to investigate the female children.

Matthew, Jason, Kevin. The first three piles of documents belonged to males, and Corey started a stack of discards just beyond his right hand. Katherine. There was one for his stack of females, which would become his acting file on the Tessa Daniel case. Jonathan. Another discard.

His hand stalled on the documents at the unexpected ring of the telephone, and he swore under his breath. He'd promised himself that he would stay in his office only long enough to sort these records, but a phone call could take away precious minutes from the time he could spend with Maggie. Of course, chances were good that it was Mrs. Miller calling on Maggie's behalf. He picked up the phone.

"McCash here."

"Hello, Mr. McCash. This is Tessa Daniel." It didn't take Corey more than a fraction of a second to identify Tessa as the owner of that soft, slightly husky voice. It took just a millisecond longer for the fact to register that she had referred to him as Mr. McCash. The lady couldn't even call him by his first name, and he'd actually daydreamed that she might be attracted to him.

"Hello, Tessa," he said briskly, masking his disappointment. "What can I help you with?"

"I wanted to make sure you got my money order for your retainer. I left it in your mail slot this morning."

"Got it. Anything else?"

Corey could have sworn the pause was longer than it should have been.

"I was wondering if you had started on my case," she said.

He glanced down at the documents, trying to figure out if there was a catch in her voice. James, Daniel, Jeremiah. Three more for the discard pile.

"Actually, I have in front of me the hospital records for more than a dozen children born during a two-week span in October almost four years ago. I'm sorting them now. I'll start investigating one of the girls tomorrow."

"How many of them are there? Girls, I mean."

"Hold on a minute," Corey said. This time he hadn't imagined it: there was a catch in her voice. Suzanna and Lisa belonged on his acting stack; Clay, Ross and Brian on the pile of documents he was eliminating from contention. He picked up another bundle, studied it a few seconds longer than necessary, and placed it on the discard stack.

He counted ten packets in his discard pile and stuffed the records into a manila folder. Then he picked up the much thinner pile of records on his acting pile. "Three."

"Only three?" Tessa asked, surprised.

"Lisa Jones, Katherine Peterson and Suzanna Smith. One of them should be your niece, and tomorrow I'll make a start into finding out which one."

Again, there was the barest of pauses.

"That sounds great," she said, pausing again. "There was something I meant to discuss with you yesterday. It sort of slipped my mind."

"Yes?" Corey asked when she didn't continue. Talking with Tessa over the phone was even more frustrating than speaking to her in person. Yesterday he had observed that she left things unsaid; today it seemed as though she wasn't saying anything.

"I don't know how you usually work, but I'd like a full report on each child even if you don't think she's the right one." She spoke the first sentence slowly, but the rest of it came out in a rush. "Don't get me wrong, it's not that I don't trust you or think that you're not good at your job. It's just that I want to be positive about who this child is or isn't, and the only way I can ever be sure is to be briefed along the way. Every step of the way."

"I don't have any argument with that," Corey said. Lots of clients wanted a step-by-step progress report, and he was usually happy to oblige. In a case like this, which could be completed as soon as tomorrow, he didn't foresee any problems. Unless she had lied to him. Just as quickly as the thought came to him, Corey thrust it away. There would be time enough later to determine whether she had told him the truth.

"Good. I'm glad that's settled."

"Now I have something to discuss with you."

"Yes?" she asked, and he wished that were the answer to another, more intimate question. He closed his eyes to shut out a vision of Tessa with her soft hair framing her face, her eyes misty and her lips parted for his kiss. His fantasy was entirely inappropriate, especially considering what he wanted to talk about.

"I'd rather you didn't make promises to Maggie if you don't intend to keep them."

"What?"

"You told Maggie yesterday that you'd take a rain check on the pizza. If you didn't want to go, you should have just said no." Tessa's statement had been bothering him since the night before, but he hadn't meant to voice his opposition so forcefully.

"I meant what I said." Tessa sounded indignant. "I'm not the kind of woman who goes around disappointing little girls. Maybe I'm not too high on making it a foursome for pizza, but I'm not blind. I can see how attached Maggie and Abby already are. In fact, I was just going to ask you if I could take Maggie for the afternoon tomorrow."

Corey was glad Tessa couldn't see his face, because he felt like a fool. He did some quick calculations. Maggie's preschool class met in the afternoons, but tomorrow was Tuesday, one of two days each week that she was completely free. But, then, he was free tomorrow night too.

"Sure you can take her, but I thought you just said you wanted to be briefed on the case," he said, not stopping to analyze what he was doing.

"What does that have to do with anything?"

"I can give you my first progress report tomorrow. Lisa Jones lives just outside of Oak Haven, and I'll find out everything you need to know about her."

"Fine," Tessa said. "I'll meet you whenever you say."

"With Abby?" Corey sounded dubious.

"I might be able to get my landlady to baby-sit for an hour or so. Mrs. Moriarty is a dear."

"Mary Moriarty?"

"Why, yes," Tessa answered, reminding herself that Oak Haven wasn't nearly as large as Richmond. "Do you know her?"

"She baby-sat me when I was a boy, and you're right— she is wonderful. But I have a better idea," Corey said. "Why don't you pick up Maggie for the afternoon and let Mrs. Miller feed both children dinner afterward? You could meet me here at six."

Again, Tessa paused. "Okay, six o'clock at your office."

"Why don't we meet at Oak Haven Tavern instead? It's a lot more comfortable than my office."

Corey expected Tessa to protest, but she quickly agreed to the change of locations and rung off. She probably hadn't been suspicious, because she hadn't guessed at his ulterior motive. That wasn't surprising, because Corey, too, was having a tough time figuring out exactly what he wanted.

He could have delivered a progress report over the phone, but he'd manipulated Tessa into meeting him. Even though he was good at his profession, he couldn't guarantee that he'd have details about Lisa Jones by tomorrow.

The root of the issue was that he wanted to see Tessa again. He planned to crack her polished veneer to discover what was beneath the surface. Corey thrust the manila folder with the discarded birth records into the back of a desk drawer.

He couldn't file away his suspicions so neatly. He was sure that Tessa Daniel wasn't quite what she appeared to be, but that didn't stop him from wanting her.

Chapter 6

Tessa peered at herself critically in the mirror and grimaced. The bow on her frilly pink blouse made it seem as though she were dressing for a date to a high school prom. Feeling about sixteen, she walked quickly to her closet, peeling off the blouse as she went.

This time she chose a knit shirt of a vibrant red and a pair of black slacks of imitation silk. Tessa scrounged through a drawer containing her costume jewelry and other accessories until she came up with a chunky necklace and matching belt that contained both colors.

She made a triumphant return to the mirror and grinned at the picture she made. The necklace drew attention away from the too-generous curve of her hips, and Corey McCash was sure to notice how the outfit showed off her alabaster complexion and dark hair. Tessa instantly sobered. She took another look at the appealing woman in the mirror and stuck out her tongue.

"Traitor," she shot at her image. "This is a business meeting, remember? You shouldn't care if he thinks you look like a witch."

Tessa turned from the mirror before she could answer herself. She was due to meet Corey in five minutes, and it was a ten-minute drive to the place he had suggested; that left no time for self-analysis. Tessa doubted anything she came up with would make sense, even if she did have the luxury of time.

How could she explain the impulse that had led to her closet after she had left Maggie and Abby with Mrs. Miller? Tessa had intended to drive straight to her meeting with Corey. En route she had looked down at a pair of khaki slacks and casual shirt that had seemed perfectly suitable a moment before and found them lacking.

Ten minutes later, when Tessa stepped out of her car in front of Oak Haven Tavern, she was still mentally berating herself. She should have spent her spare time planning how to bluff her way through this next hour instead of deciding what to wear.

Corey hadn't mentioned finding Abby's birth record, but she couldn't believe that she had the hospital's only copy. If Corey knew that Abby's birthday was the very day on which she claimed her long-lost niece had been born, Tessa would have to come up with a second lie to explain the first one. At this moment, she didn't have one.

Corey had suggested meeting for drinks, but the instant Tessa opened the door of Oak Haven Tavern she realized it was more of a restaurant than a bar. The lights were turned low, and the wooden tables tucked into corners throughout the series of rooms that made up the restaurant had a sort of cozy warmth. Flickering candles further illuminated the tables. A smiling middle-aged woman stood at the reservations desk.

"Can I help you?"

"I'm meeting someone in your lounge," Tessa said, and the hostess indicated yet another room with a sweep of her hand. Tessa followed the path she had designated, trying to ignore the knot of uneasiness in her stomach.

When Corey had suggested meeting in a public place, she had welcomed the prospect of having other people around to buffer the effect he had on her. But this wasn't the sort of place she would have chosen to meet Corey McCash. She preferred fluorescent lights and a desk, preferably one about six feet wide, between them. Not candlelight and an air of romance.

Corey had been expecting Tessa to walk through the door leading to the lounge for the past fifteen minutes, but he still wasn't prepared for what he saw. Why hadn't he realized before that Tessa Daniel was one of the most compelling women he had ever met? It would be wrong to call her beautiful, because she was much more than that.

She looked sensational not only because of the interplay of light skin and dark hair and the way her body curved in all the right places, but because of what lay beneath. One look at this woman somehow told you there was so much more.

There had been more to Alise, too, Corey reminded himself harshly, and none of it had been good. As long as he remembered that, he could deal with Tessa Daniel. He wanted to get her in bed, yes, but he didn't want a relationship with her.

Tessa's eyes darted around the room until she spotted him, and Corey could tell that she was nervous. She tried to hide her apprehension as she walked briskly toward him, but Corey had already noticed the way her chest expanded as though she needed a deep breath to brace herself for an ordeal. Knowing that she viewed their meeting with something other than pleasure was a distasteful thought.

Corey rose and pulled out a chair before she reached him and Tessa slipped wordlessly into it, not quite meeting his eyes. A waitress instantly appeared at their table, and Tessa shook off the menu she offered.

"I'll just have a glass of your house burgundy."

Corey was glad she hadn't ordered a glass of white wine; a hearty, red wine had so much more substance, much as he suspected of the woman across from him. He didn't speak until they were both seated.

"I'll get right down to business," Corey said, reminding himself that she was a client first and foremost. "I'm sure you're anxious to know how things went today."

"I am," Tessa said, folding her hands primly on the table and trying to analyze the brusqueness in his voice. She feared that her charade was over, that in the next moment he would berate her for not telling him Abby had been born in Oak Haven Hospital.

"It didn't go real well," Corey said, shrugging. "I told you there were three children I needed to check out. I'm sure to hit on something with one of the other two, because we struck out with Lisa Jones."

"You're sure?" Tessa's voice cracked on the question. She should have been disappointed that he hadn't found her birth child, but blessed relief swept through her that he didn't have a clue about Abby.

"I'm positive."

Tessa tried valiantly to regain her composure, because this conversation didn't make sense. If Corey didn't know that Abby had been born in Oak Haven, he couldn't possibly be sure of anything regarding her case. How could he when she hadn't told him everything?

"I need to hear the whole story," she said, hoping she wasn't insulting him. "I need to know why you're sure Lisa Jones isn't my brother's child."

Corey rubbed the back of his neck as he thought. He fully intended to relay the day's events, but there was something unnatural about the anxiety in her voice.

"I decided to check out Lisa Jones first, because no father was listed on the birth record. None of the documents from the three children, by the way, have your brother listed as father." Corey watched Tessa closely for a reaction, but her expression was blank.

"I didn't think they would, but that doesn't mean a thing. I don't know anything about Bunny. She could have remarried before the child was born. Or she could have falsified the record."

"Why would she do that?"

Tessa thought quickly and came up with a plausible reason, realizing that her lie was growing bigger with each passing moment. "She doesn't want my family involved in her life, remember? Who knows what lengths she'd go to keep us out of it?"

Again Corey got the impression that Tessa was unduly nervous. She wet her lips, and her Adam's apple bobbed as though she was trying to swallow her unease. He waited for a minute, watching her, before he continued.

"Anyway, there was no father on this birth certificate. But there was an address about an hour's drive from here. It wasn't hard to find."

Corey paused. He didn't need to describe the one-story brick house or the sight of the door flying open to let out a little girl with curly black hair. She had jumped down each of the three porch steps on two feet and took off running when she hit the bottom one. She had beautiful skin about the color of coffee with an extra dab of cream. She looked to be about three years old.

"Lisa Jones, you come back here this instant." A blond woman in her early twenties had appeared on the porch, and she was angry. "Listen to your mother. This won't work, Lisa. I'll catch you sooner or later, and you will take a bath."

Corey hadn't even bothered to cover the last few steps to the sidewalk. What was the point? Lisa Jones was a beautiful child, but she obviously wasn't related to Tessa.

"I got a good look at the child, and that's all I needed to be sure she wasn't your niece."

"I don't understand."

"You would if you'd seen her, but I guess I shouldn't assume anything. Your brother wasn't by any chance of mixed race?"

"What?" Tessa didn't understand what he was driving at.

"The birth record lists her as Caucasian, but Lisa Jones is the result of mixed parentage. I saw her mother, who's a blonde with skin almost as pale as yours. Unless your brother was part black, there's no way he could be the child's father."

"You're right. She couldn't be the child I'm looking for," Tessa said, leaning back in her seat. The disappointment that streamed through her was palpable, but a tiny part of her was relieved.

If she never found her birth child, there would be no chance that she'd have to give up Abby. *But then I'd have to live with the knowledge that I might have passed on a deadly disease to an innocent child,* whispered a voice that sprang from her conscience. *We have to find that little girl.*

"Don't let it get you down," Corey said, and one of the corners of his mouth lifted in something approaching a smile. "This isn't a tough case. I have two more girls to check out. If your niece was born in Oak Haven Hospital when you say she was, she has to be one of those girls."

"I'm sure you're right," Tessa said, and she wondered why he used the conditional tense. *If.* Was he already doubting her story? Could she blame him if that were the case?

"Now that that's settled, I'm starved. Why don't we grab a bite to eat in the restaurant?"

"I really didn't expect . . ." Tessa stammered, caught off guard.

"What's wrong?" Corey interrupted, not giving her an opportunity to protest or himself a chance to analyze his ploy. He'd intended all along that she have dinner with him. "Have you already eaten?"

"It's not that," Tessa said, and her voice was firmer this time. "It's just that I didn't expect you to buy me dinner."

"I can see where that might be a problem, with me working on your case and all." Corey rubbed his chin as though he was trying to solve a troubling dilemma. Suddenly he snapped his fingers. "I've got it. We'll split the check."

Corey's years of police work had taught him that the decisive course of action worked best. If you acted as though an issue had been decided, others went along unless they had a strong objection. He stood up, placed a few bills on the table to cover the cost of their drinks and pulled out her chair.

"That wasn't quite what I meant," Tessa said under her breath while she rose, but either Corey didn't hear or he ignored the comment.

Minutes later, Tessa sat across from Corey in a remote corner of the dining room with only the flickering light of a candle between them. *And it's your own fault, Teresa Anne Daniel,* she chided herself. *The word "no" is in your vocabulary.*

"Is something wrong?"

"What?" Tessa almost jumped out of her chair at the question. "What could possibly be wrong?"

"You look like you're having second thoughts about having dinner with me."

Even as he made the observation, Corey wondered why. He had maneuvered it so she would accept his invitation, and now he was offering her a way out. Could it be because he needed her to want to be at his side? "If you've changed your mind, the door's over there."

He couldn't have read her more accurately, but Tessa didn't want to admit that aloud. The bunched muscles in the back of her neck gradually relaxed. Her mind had been working furiously to think of a way out of dining with him, but now that he'd given her one, she was no longer desperate to take it.

"To tell you the truth," she said, and she realized with shock that she was going to do exactly that, "I was wondering whether this was a good idea. I haven't had dinner alone with a man since my husband died."

"There has to be a first time," Corey said wryly, surprised at the turn the conversation had taken and relieved that she hadn't taken him up on his offer and walked out the door. "You might as well get it over with. Maybe it won't be so bad."

"I don't know about that," Tessa said, and a smile curled her lips. "You haven't brought out the best in me so far. Believe it or not, I don't usually speed away in cars and slam doors. This could be a dinner that will go down in infamy."

Corey shrugged. "I'm willing to give it a shot, if you promise not to throw any plates."

"It's a deal. But I'm not making any promises about my wineglass."

He laughed then, and Tessa was surprised at the sound. She'd expected the sort of deep rumble that fades to a stop almost before it begins, but Corey's laugh was rich and unaffected. His enjoyment was reflected in his blue eyes when he looked at her. "I'm starting to think we might even get along."

"Uh-uh." Tessa shook her head emphatically. "You're not my type."

"Don't worry. You're not my type either," Corey shot back airily.

"Oh, no?" Tessa asked, trying not to feel insulted. After all, she didn't want him to be attracted to her. Did she?

"No," he said, shaking his head. "I prefer to date women who actually want to be on a date with me."

"That doesn't apply to us anyway, because this isn't a date," Tessa said, enjoying herself and this unexpected side of Corey. Who would have thought that serious, stone-faced Corey McCash was capable of such lighthearted banter?

"Well, technically it is. I asked if you wanted to have dinner, and you accepted."

"Only because I was hungry," Tessa said as she took a menu from a waitress who suddenly appeared and just as suddenly retreated.

"That's no excuse," Corey said while looking over his menu. He put it down in less than fifteen seconds. "Since we've established that I'm not your type, are you going to tell me who is?"

Tessa studied him over her open menu, but she couldn't think of a teasing response. All that came to mind was the truth. "I don't really know. I haven't thought about it much since Chris died. I haven't thought about men very much at all."

She looked back at the menu, embarrassed that she had been so candid. If she wasn't careful, she'd tell him that he was the only man who had even remotely interested her since Chris's death. Interested her and enraged her.

Tessa spent an inordinate amount of time studying the entries, but lost the menu as a shield when the waitress took their orders. The lighthearted mood of a moment ago was also lost. Tessa ordered pasta, and Corey requested filet mignon. She thought that was appropriate. He looked like a meat-and-potatoes man—there was nothing subtle about him.

"How did your husband die?" he asked when the waitress bustled back to the kitchen.

"Recklessly." Tessa said the first thing that popped into her head. Since she couldn't take back the word, she explained. "It was dark, and it had been raining heavily. He tried to turn a curve, but his car veered off the highway and hit a tree. Afterward, someone who saw the accident estimated he had been doing eighty miles an hour.''

"And you blamed him for dying?''

Tessa's eyes flashed with remembered anger. "Abby was only six months old. Some friends told me he had been drinking before he got into the car. I blamed him for not taking his responsibilities seriously.''

Tessa looked down at her hands, noticing the gold band that still bound her to Chris. The finger wearing the ring was attached to hands that were shaking. Tessa had never told a soul that version of Chris's death; she'd barely admitted she felt that way to herself. Why had she just told Corey McCash?

"I shouldn't have said that,'' she murmured.

"Why not? It's the truth, isn't it?'' Corey's eyes were piercing, and she couldn't hide from the insight in them.

"It's the truth, all right.'' She sighed. "I just feel guilty for thinking it, because a part of me knows that Chris wouldn't have chosen to die in a car accident before he turned thirty.''

Tessa stopped, unwilling to finish her thought. She didn't need to, because Corey completed it for her.

"But another part of you is angry that he left you alone to raise your daughter, especially because his death was so preventable.''

"Exactly,'' Tessa said after a moment.

"Don't fight it.''

"What?''

"Don't fight the anger,'' he repeated. "You have a right to it.''

It hadn't started this way, but talking to Corey about Chris's death was like taking a shower and washing away all the hurt. She did have a right to be angry, but no one had ever reinforced that belief before. Everyone else in her life had also known Chris, and they had been as blind to his faults as she had been when she married him.

Chris Daniel had been dashing, charming and completely irresponsible in every facet of his life: he'd spent more money than they made, promised more than he delivered and dreamed up one unsuccessful get-rich-quick scheme after another.

He'd made great company, but a rotten husband. He'd never been there when she needed him—not at the hospital when she was struggling through a difficult labor and not now when she was struggling with the fact that the little girl they'd both adored wasn't really theirs.

"The only way you'll ever forgive him and get on with your life is to let out all the anger," Corey continued and recognized the irony in his statement. If what he said was true, a darkness would always shroud his own life. He had never forgiven Alise, and he never would.

"That sounds like something a psychologist would say." Tessa managed a smile.

"It is something a psychologist would say." Corey explained when he saw her raised eyebrows. "I worked so closely with the police psychologist back when I was on the force that I took a couple of night courses on the subject."

"Then you've been able to get rid of all those feelings of guilt that go along with being a single parent?" Tessa asked, turning the focus of their conversation from herself to him. She'd talked enough about Tessa Daniel for one night.

Corey chuckled wryly and held up his hand. "I didn't say that. It's a lot easier to give other people advice on how to solve their problems than it is to tackle your own. Has being a single parent been hard for you?"

His direct question again focused the conversation on Tessa, and she frowned. Was Corey easy to talk to or a master at keeping details about himself private?

"Let's just put it this way. The reason that it takes two people to make a child is probably because two people should raise a child. I think about that sometimes when I'm due at work and Abby is too sick to take to her baby-sitter's house."

"I think about it when Maggie's screaming her head off because I made her stand in the corner for misbehaving, I'm feeling like a mean old ogre and there's no one around to tell me I'm doing the right thing."

Tessa smiled, grateful for the way he'd commiserated without passing judgment about working mothers. She didn't disagree with the argument that it was best for a young child to be home with a parent instead of in child care, but that was a utopian situation. In her case, that setup was impossible. Chris hadn't even had the foresight to take out any life insurance.

Corey liked Tessa's smile, liked the way her eyes crinkled ever so slightly at the corners, liked the fact that she directed her smile at him.

"You look great," Corey said and was surprised when he heard his thought spoken aloud.

Tessa felt the blush start at her neck and work its way up and knew Corey couldn't help but notice. She had the sort of skin that showed color like a virgin canvas marked with a dab of paint. She wished he hadn't remarked on her appearance and then felt foolish. Why had she bothered to change clothes if she didn't want him to notice her? She still didn't know the answer.

"I felt pretty grubby after an afternoon at the park with Abby and Maggie." She shrugged off the compliment, making it seem as though she had to freshen up after getting down on her hands and knees in the dirt to play with the girls. Actually, the most strenuous thing she'd done all day was to push their swings. "I guess I was tired of looking like a mom."

A mom. The word called to mind the irrefutable fact that Tessa had once belonged to another man, a man who had fathered her child. Corey wondered whether Tessa had loved him, and the probable answer hurt. Then he told himself that it was silly to be jealous of a dead man. To care at all was ludicrous.

"Did Maggie behave herself?" he asked to get his mind off her husband.

"What a question! You of all people should know how sweet she is. She was an angel." Their daughters were a safe subject, and Tessa lost her previous inhibitions. "The three of us had the best time not doing much of anything. We played dress-up with all sorts of outlandish costumes, went out for ice cream and took Abby's dolls to the park. The girls insisted on swinging them in the swings. It was great. Maggie was great."

The prick of jealousy that stung Corey's heart was entirely unexpected. He'd never viewed himself as a possessive father, but it pained him to realize that Tessa Daniel could give his daughter something he couldn't. Her long, slim fingers could braid Maggie's hair. Her dresses and high-heeled shoes could create a world of make-believe.

"Yeah, I know how sweet Maggie is. I just wasn't sure if she was as sweet around females as she is with me," Corey said, not quite hiding his envy.

"Surely you've seen her with Mrs. Miller." Tessa's reply held a tinge of surprise.

"And you must have realized by now that Mrs. Miller isn't brimming over with affection. I've even thought about replacing her with someone who might be a little more of a mother to Maggie."

The last sentence escaped from Corey's lips before he thought it through. He hadn't voiced his fears aloud before, and he certainly hadn't meant to reveal them to Tessa. Corey started to say something to cover his error, but Tessa interrupted him.

"Please don't think it too presumptuous of me to ask, but where's her real mother?"

The question had been gnawing at Tessa since the first time she'd seen Maggie McCash, and she'd been wondering how to ask it. Corey had given her an opening, but the closed expression on his face told her he hadn't meant to. When the silence stretched, she fully expected him to tell her to mind her own business.

"Alise voluntarily gave up that title when Maggie was six months old. We haven't seen her since."

Although his mug had a few swallows of beer remaining, Corey downed the liquid with one gulp. The waitress appeared with their food, and Corey ordered another brew.

A hundred questions about how a mother could abandon her daughter swirled in Tessa's brain, but she sensed that this was not the time to ask them. Still, she didn't understand: she could no more give up Abby than she could stop her next heartbeat.

That was one of the reasons she had hired Corey McCash in the first place. Tessa realized with a start that for a few minutes she had forgotten why she was here with him. This wasn't a date. They were two people with a business relationship, who just happened to be in a restaurant at dinnertime.

She picked up her fork and twirled some pasta around it, thinking about the irony of the situation. She should be quizzing Corey about the next step in the investigation, but all she could think about was the woman he had married. He spoke as though he hated Alise. Why, then, had he married her?

"Alise must be very beautiful," she said after a few minutes of silence.

Corey chewed on a piece of succulent steak, annoyed that Tessa hadn't taken the rather broad hint that he didn't want to talk about Alise. If he were completely fair, however, he'd concede that he had cajoled her into talking about her late husband.

"It's not easy to say whether a woman is beautiful until you've known her for a while," Corey said. "If Alise walked in this room right now, every man in the place would say she was beautiful. Every man except me. I know what kind of person is underneath the exterior, and that woman is far from beautiful."

"Where is she now?"

The questions weren't going to stop, Corey realized, but she wasn't going to pry the whole sordid mess from him. In a way, though, he owed Tessa a few more nuggets of information, if only because it explained why he had acted so rudely the first time they met.

"When I left her, she was in Philadelphia. But the last I heard, she was in Virginia. That's why I came up to your car the day we met. I saw the Virginia license plate, and I had to make sure Alise wasn't in the car."

"You thought she'd come back for Maggie," Tessa guessed, because she would have assumed the same had their situations been reversed.

"Exactly. It's still hard to believe that a mother who carried a child for nine months has absolutely no interest in her. But Alise doesn't. In exchange for a lump sum in our divorce settlement, she even signed a document relinquishing all rights to Maggie."

Tessa blanched. No wonder he had made the statement about the difference between surface beauty and inner beauty. His ex-wife must have ice water running through her veins.

"Does Maggie know any of this?"

"No, of course not," Corey said.

The waitress delivered his second beer, and he immediately took a swallow. He noticed a strange look in Tessa's eyes and immediately knew the reason: her late husband had died partly because he hadn't known when to stop drinking. She was wondering if Corey had a similar problem.

"My limit is two, in case you're wondering," he said. Corey usually didn't pay attention to the impressions others had of him, but he didn't want Tessa to think he was a drunk. She inclined her head slightly as though she believed him, and Corey relaxed.

"Maggie hasn't asked any questions about her mother," Corey said. "I've thought about it a lot, but I won't know what I'm going to say until she does ask."

"No child should have to hear that her mother doesn't want her." The force behind the statement surprised even Tessa.

"I agree," Corey said, twisting his lips as he wrestled with how to finish his thought. "But not every child has a mother like you, Tessa."

Tessa picked up her wineglass and took a swallow to camouflage her feelings. Not every child had a mother who really wasn't her mother. Not every child had lost a father before she even knew the identity of her biological father. *If only you knew, Corey McCash,* she thought. *If only you knew.*

The McCash house was surprisingly dark when Tessa pulled her worn sedan into the driveway behind Corey's sleek white sports car. She could barely make out the glow from a single interior light shining somewhere in the bowels of the house. Tessa opened her car door and peered up into the night sky where cloud cover obscured even the brightest stars. No wonder it seemed so dark.

"Mrs. Miller doesn't believe in wasting electricity," Corey explained as he walked toward her, answering her question before she'd even asked it. "She's one of those annoying people who follow you around the house shutting off the lights as soon as you leave a room."

"She doesn't believe in porch lights, either?" Tessa guessed, slanting a look at the shadowed porch.

"She says they're a useless invention. She probably thinks the reason God made the stars and the moon was so you could find your way into the house at night."

Tessa laughed. "Too bad she didn't take cloud cover into account."

As they started up the sidewalk toward the darkened porch, the toe of Tessa's shoe caught on a crack between the cement slabs and she stumbled. Corey's hand was instantly under her elbow, righting her. She murmured her thanks and tried to pull away, but Corey held firm.

"Oh, no, you don't. If you fall, all I have in the house to patch you up are some Mickey Mouse bandages," he said, grateful for a reason to hold on to her.

The skin on her arm where he touched it was so warm that Tessa waged a private battle to keep from pulling away again. Not for anything would she let him know how nervous he made her.

"She probably didn't expect you home so late. After all, we were only supposed to go out for drinks."

"No. I told her we were having dinner."

Tessa's head whipped around at his pronouncement, but she couldn't read his expression in the darkness. Irritation bubbled in her at his implication: they had arranged a business meeting, and he had turned it into something personal. "Rather sure of yourself, weren't you?"

"Shouldn't I have been?"

The words came out in a whisper, and warnings sounded inside Tessa's head like sirens. They had reached the porch and were standing just outside the door with his hand still resting on her arm. She looked up at him, intending to set him straight with a tart retort, but nothing came to mind except that his lower lip was slightly fuller than his upper one. She wondered what it would be like to taste him, to feel those lips on hers.

"No. I mean yes," she said, forgetting what question he had posed. "What did you just say?"

His face was in shadows, but a brief smile showed a flash of white teeth, and then his head moved toward hers and his features became so clear she couldn't look away. She couldn't think, not about a relationship that was supposed to be strictly business, not about Chris, not about anything but this man.

Corey had been subconsciously planning this moment since yesterday when their eyes had met and held in his daughter's room, but he hadn't counted on the sweet anticipation that flowed warmly through his veins. He stopped his descent just inches from her lips, savoring the anticipation and the answering eagerness he saw on her face. Tessa didn't turn away, but closed the merest of gaps with a tip of her head.

She was faintly aware of a little gasp of pleasure that sounded deep in her throat. The moment seemed suspended in time so that she was in tune with the way all her senses responded. Everything was heightened: the smell of his shampoo coupled with an earthy scent that was uniquely his. The taste of his tongue as it made maddening circles around hers. The sight of his eyes closed, with long lashes fanning his cheeks. The sound of his answering moan. The feel of her heart pounding frantically, because it had been touched in a way it never had before.

She was sweeter than he had imagined possible. He kept one hand at her waist, but moved the other to the curve of her cheek just to touch the smooth skin there. She opened her mouth wider, and he eagerly explored the softness. He didn't want to stop kissing her; she was like a bag of candy to a chocoholic, so sweet, so irresistible....

Light, harsh and sudden, filled the porch and penetrated their darkened world of pleasure. Tessa and Corey froze, like deer caught in the headlights of an oncoming car. The sound of a doorknob turning propelled them into action, and they sprang apart until about six inches separated them.

The inner door came open, and two young faces peered through the screen door onto the porch.

"Hi, Mommy," Abby said gaily.

"Hi, Daddy." Maggie giggled.

Mrs. Miller stood behind the girls wearing no particular expression, as though she didn't have the faintest idea that she had just interrupted something momentous. "I thought I heard your cars pull up."

Corey recovered first, pulling open the screen door and scooping Maggie into his arms. After his insane reaction to Tessa, he was relieved to have something to do with hands that wanted to pull Tessa back into his embrace. What had just happened between them, and what would have happened had their welcoming trio not been home?

"Hi, sport. Did you have fun?"

Maggie nodded so vigorously she was in danger of giving herself a headache, but it was Tessa's heart that was aching. Corey sounded so cheery, so completely unaffected by their kiss, that Tessa bit back a sob. She forced herself to smile at Abby.

"How about you, Abby? Did you have a good time?"

In answer, Abby skipped out the door and threw her arms around Tessa's thighs. She looked up at her mother, grinning broadly.

"Maggie asked me to go to Story Bank Sort next day," Abby said excitedly, and Tessa's brows drew together. Next day meant tomorrow in Abbyspeak, but Tessa had never heard of Story Bank Sort.

"Story Book Forest," Corey supplied, laughing. He planned to take tomorrow off from work so that he could spend time alone with Maggie, but the prospect was no longer quite so appealing. He wanted to have Tessa—and Abby—along. "It's a theme park about an hour's drive from here, where storybook characters come alive. You know. The old woman who lives in a shoe is there, and the crooked man in his crooked house. How about it? Will you come?''

He smiled across at Tessa, and somehow this invitation was different from the one that Maggie had issued last night. Maggie might have precipitated this request, too, but Corey didn't look as if he had any qualms about asking them along. Some of the warmth he had conjured up with his kiss seeped into her smile, and she forgot to feel embarrassed about what had just happened between them.

"We'd love to," Tessa said, and she meant it, even though she knew with every cell in her brain that she was making a mistake. Something told her that Corey wouldn't tolerate fools or liars, and she was both.

Chapter 7

The ten-foot-tall storybook rose out of the earth, a monument to the little children who weren't even old enough to read the words on its open pages. Abby and Maggie stood absolutely still, gazing up at the gigantic book that served as the entrance to Story Book Forest.

"What's it say, Mister Maggie?" an awed Abby asked, directing her question at Corey.

One of Corey's eyebrows rose at the name she'd pinned on him. Dressed in dark shorts and a gold shirt that brought out the blond highlights in his brown hair and made his skin appear even more bronzed, Corey didn't look the slightest bit feminine. The knit shirt hugged his chest so that Tessa could see the way his pectorals flexed when he drew a breath, and his long legs filled shorts just tight enough to make her fantasize about what was above the hemline.

"Tell you what, Abs," Corey said, leaning to minimize the difference in their heights. Tessa waited for the inevitable protest that came whenever anyone bastardized her daughter's proper name, but Abby just smiled at Corey. "I'd like it a lot better if you just called me Corey."

"Mister Corey?" Abby asked, evidently remembering Tessa's lesson that adult names went with courtesy titles.

"No. Just Corey."

Abby looked at Tessa for permission, and she nodded. "Okay, Corey. What does that say?"

Corey straightened to his full height and read in a deep, clear voice. "Here is the Land of Once upon a Time. Step through the pages of this big storybook and visit the people and places every child knows...and loves. Here, dreams are real...."

Tessa imagined he looked directly at her and softened his voice as he read the last sentence, but the sun was bright and his aviator sunglasses prevented her from telling exactly where his eyes were focused. She smiled anyway, because being here with Corey, Maggie and Abby in this impossible setting of make-believe was something she desperately needed.

Here, she could think about little boys who fell asleep in haystacks instead of her needle-fine chances of finding a little girl who would probably rather stay lost. Here, she could pretend that she was an ordinary mother trying to introduce her child to fairy tales. It didn't matter that they had never come true for Tessa and would probably elude Abby. This day wasn't real. This was a slice of make-believe.

She reached for Abby's hand, but her daughter was still grinning up at Corey. Maggie's lips quivered until they formed a hesitant smile, and the child tentatively held out her hand. Tessa took hold before the little girl could change her mind, and an incredible peace filled her at the feel of the small hand in hers.

"Abby's mommy?" Maggie asked softly, sweetly. She twirled one of the dark ponytails that Tessa had braided before they'd embarked upon the hour-long trip to Ligonier and Story Book Forest. "Can I call you Tessa?"

"Of course you can, sweetheart," Tessa said and led Maggie through the door that was cut into the storybook. Preceding them into the park were Corey and Abby, their hands firmly gripped in each other's.

Maggie and Abby took only a few moments to look around, decide they liked what they saw and take off running down a gravel path lined with tall, shady trees. The path meandered through the woods from one slice of childhood to the next. In the distance, Tessa could see a park worker dressed as Raggedy Ann.

Tessa's hand felt strangely empty without the warmth of little fingers, and she had a crazy urge to link herself with Corey. She clenched her hands into fists, resisting the impulse while she watched the retreating backs of their daughters.

"It's wonderful that you do things like this with Maggie," Tessa said, a wistful note in her voice. She had been far too busy working to keep bills paid and grief at bay during the past few years to visit the kind of places kids viewed as paradise. If Corey hadn't insisted on paying their admission today, Abby would have missed out on this trip, too.

"I like to spoil her," Corey said, reading between her words the things that she was trying to hide. Tessa was really saying that she couldn't afford to shower treats on her daughter, but he wanted her to understand that didn't matter. "But we both know that the most important thing about raising a child isn't trips to Story Book Forest or the toy store. It's loving your child, and letting your child know you love her. Abby knows."

Tessa impulsively touched Corey on his bare arm, letting her hand linger for a moment because she didn't want to break the connection. Why had she thought him coldhearted when he could not only read what was in her heart but also put it into words?

Corey gazed down into Tessa's upturned face, admiring the way the sun brought out the black sheen of her hair and the luminance of her skin. She looked like some sort of mirage, and he was afraid she would disappear if he blinked. Tessa blinked first.

"C'mon," she said, taking her hand from his arm but tempering the withdrawal with a smile. "If we don't follow our daughters now, we'll never catch up."

By the time they crossed the wooden bridge that swayed over the tombstone of a troll and visited the Pussy in the Well, Old Mother Hubbard, the Three Men in a Tub and Little Miss Muffet, Tessa was giggling as much as the two girls.

Corey watched her, not attempting to disguise the fact, and got a glimpse of the carefree child she must have been. Not that she looked anything like a child. The red sleeveless shirt she wore with black-and-white checkered shorts drew attention to the curve of her chest and made him long to touch her. But touching her in the middle of a semicrowded theme park wasn't a good idea, especially since he wasn't sure if he would be able to stop.

They walked down the gravel path four abreast, humming "Mary had a Little Lamb," when the children noticed a costumed character handing out treats aboard the Good Ship *Lollipop.* They simultaneously tore into a run, not bothering to glance behind to see if any adults followed. Corey looked around, but he didn't notice any other children dashing madly from attraction to attraction.

"Why are our children the only ones who are running?" he mused, and Tessa rolled her eyes. She wasn't wearing sunglasses, and her dark eyes were quite beautiful.

"Don't be such a dragon," she said, her voice teasing. "I, for one, heartily approve of unbridled enthusiasm."

"Oh, but if I were a dragon, I'd hold you captive in my lair just as that big guy did to sweet Guinevere." Corey nodded toward the statue of a dragon that scowled at them from the bottom of a shallow valley. "I can promise you I'd be enthusiastic about it."

"Maybe you wouldn't have to kidnap me," Tessa said, surprising herself by daring to play along with his word game. She sensed that Corey's lair would be a place of exquisite pleasure, a place she wouldn't want to leave. "But I couldn't stay, of course. See Good Sir Knight over there on his horse. It's his job to put up a fight for me."

"If I were fighting for you," Corey said, his voice so low she had to strain to hear it, "I wouldn't lose."

Heat flooded Tessa's cheeks at the thought of the sensual pleasure he would be fighting for, and she silently berated herself for imagining she could handle his sophisticated brand of sexual banter. They had barely started the word game, and already her face burned.

She trained her eyes on the gaily painted ship that was mercifully only steps away. Abby and Maggie were on board, tearing the wrappers off the lollipops the ship's captain had given them.

The captain, an elderly woman who looked as though she belonged in a shoe figuring out what to do about so many children, beamed at them. A basket full of lollipops, producing a rainbow of color, hung from her neck.

"You have a lovely family," she said in a voice loud enough to carry to Tessa and Corey. "Your daughters are cute as buttons."

Tessa and Corey exchanged a puzzled look, and the realization that the woman thought they were a married couple with two children hit them at once. Corey merely smiled at the woman and nodded, but Tessa felt an overwhelming need to correct her.

"Actually, we're not married," Tessa pronounced, and the woman's face went white. Tessa bit her lip, realizing the conclusion the woman had reached. At her side, Corey chuckled lightly.

"I mean, we're not married to each other," Tessa amended, and the woman's mouth dropped open. She obviously didn't belong to the permissive generation, but neither did Tessa. Corey laughed aloud.

"That's not what I meant either," Tessa said, trying again. "I did mean that we're not married to each other, but we're not married at all. Abby's my daughter, and Maggie's his."

The elderly lady, unsmiling now, nodded. During their exchange, Abby had cajoled Corey into hoisting her onto his shoulders so that her legs straddled his neck. Maggie had placed a sticky hand into Tessa's.

"I see the resemblance," the woman said, obviously mixing up their daughters. Tessa opened her mouth to explain further, but Corey's hand gently covered it before any words escaped from her lips.

"Thank you," he said loudly, removing his hand and giving Tessa a little push. "And I promise we'll think about making it legal before the girls are grown."

"Devil," Tessa hissed at him as they walked away from the dazed woman. With a couple of flippant words, he had redone all the damage she'd tried to repair. It hardly mattered that her initial comments had caused the confusion. The woman obviously believed they were living and reproducing together without bothering to marry.

"I thought I was a dragon," Corey laughed. Atop his head, Abby giggled madly and bobbed with every step Corey took. Her red lollipop loomed precariously near his hair. She giggled again, and her hand dropped slightly.

"You mean a red dragon," Tessa said, erupting into laughter at the stricken look on his face. "Make that a sticky red dragon."

"What a day." Tessa settled deeper into the chocolate-colored leather couch in the family room of Corey's house, letting the material swallow her. Her shoes were off, and she stretched down to her toes. Then she closed her eyes and smiled. "What a beautiful day."

"What a beautiful, long day." Corey, sitting next to her on the sofa, raised his arms above his head and yawned. "I can't believe it's only eight o'clock. And I can't believe Maggie and Abby are already asleep. Maggie usually manages to stay up until ten."

Tessa opened her eyes and gave him a sidelong glance, noticing his thick hair was mussed and his clothes were endearingly rumpled. "We shouldn't have let them talk us into taking them to the amusement park."

"Silly woman," Corey said, smiling. "Why do you think the amusement park is next door to Story Book Forest? No parent gets out of that place without visiting both, especially since you get into both places for the price of one admission."

"Then we shouldn't have let them go on every kiddie ride in the park."

Corey frowned. "That wasn't so bad. What we shouldn't have done is let them go on every ride twice."

Tessa furrowed her brow. "Do you think we were too indulgent?"

"Indulgent? Us?" Corey laughed shortly. "No way. Just because we let them ride until they didn't put up a fuss about leaving and let them stuff themselves with cotton candy and popcorn until they refused to eat dinner doesn't mean we were indulgent."

"You forgot the way we let them badger us into playing game after game until we'd won each of them a stuffed animal."

"And some people actually have the nerve to call that indulgence."

This was nice, Tessa thought as she laughed with Corey. Chris had been gone for so long that she'd forgotten how it felt to share Abby. It felt right. She could almost believe, as that old woman on the Good Ship *Lollipop* had, that they were a married couple with two adorable, adored daughters.

Abby had played into the scenario by falling asleep in Maggie's room, causing Corey to insist that the little girl stay the night. Tessa went along with the charade by giving in to her fatigue and sinking into his couch instead of driving herself home.

But Tessa couldn't afford to play make-believe with Corey for much longer. They had left Story Book Forest hours ago. If she didn't soon stop pretending that they were an established couple, the next stop in the Land of Make-Believe would be his bedroom. Tessa's cheeks flamed at the direction her thoughts had taken.

"Are you going to work on my case tomorrow?" she asked to cover her confusion. The last thing she wanted to talk about was her case, but it was becoming more and more difficult to think of Corey as anything other than a virile man. She had to forcefully remind herself that he was someone she had employed to look for a lost little girl. He was a means to an end, and the end wasn't his bedroom.

Corey sighed inwardly, wondering what had possessed Tessa to change the subject. He didn't want to discuss her case, not when she was sitting within reach on the sofa. His thoughts ran more to touching her soft skin and hearing a feline sigh of contentment. But his line of business was the only reason she was here at all.

"As a matter of fact, tomorrow I'm driving to a little town east of Pittsburgh called Fox Chapel to check out another child," Corey said. "The family moved there a few years ago."

Why hadn't she known that before now? *Because you didn't ask,* Tessa chided herself. *Because you allowed the fact that he has beautiful blue eyes and a gentle way of talking to his daughter distract you from the reason you're in Oak Haven.*

"Can I come with you?" Tessa asked, and knew she should have posed the question before. The mixed-race child Corey had already investigated wasn't hers, but the next child might be. Tessa needed to be on the scene to identify her and reassure herself that she wasn't stricken with Cooley's anemia. She couldn't trust Corey to do those things, because she hadn't trusted him with the truth.

"That's not necessary," Corey said. "I can give you a full report when I get back."

"I know that, but it's just so hard to sit here in Oak Haven waiting for information. Besides, if I came along, I could probably tell instantly if the child were related to me."

Corey's eyebrows drew together as he studied her. A hundred reasons he shouldn't take her along resounded in his brain, but he didn't listen to them. Corey usually enjoyed the solitude that came with taking a long drive, but the prospect of spending a day alone with Tessa was infinitely more appealing. Maybe she would be able to immediately identify a child whose blood was similar to her own. But if he allowed himself to capitulate to her request too easily, she would guess how much he wanted to.

"It might be a long day," he warned. "I did some groundwork and found out that the mother stays home with her children, but there's no guarantee that they'll be at home when we get there."

Tessa dismissed his warning and pressed her advantage. After all, he hadn't said no. "I don't care about that. I can be ready by nine o'clock. I just need to make sure Mrs. Moriarty can look after Abby while we're gone."

"Mrs. Miller can do that," Corey said, aware that he'd surrendered his resistance before putting up a fight.

"That would be wonderful, but are you sure she wouldn't mind?" *Careful, Tessa,* she warned herself as soon as she'd asked the question. *If you're not careful, you'll talk yourself out of a trip you desperately need to take.*

"I'm sure," Corey said. "After she watched the girls the other night, she said that she'd be happy to baby-sit Abby anytime. She said watching two was easier than watching just one."

"That's settled, then," Tessa said, anxious to nail down the details. "I'll meet you here tomorrow morning at nine, and I'll bring a change of clothes for Abby. That is, if you're sure it's okay for her to spend tonight here."

"Of course I'm sure," Corey said. He had spent much of the day alternately giving piggyback rides to Abby and Maggie, and he thought he might fall asleep if he closed his eyes. But he didn't want to close his eyes, because if he did it would shut out the vision of Tessa's shapely body and the way her sexy black hair framed her face. "I bought Maggie bunk beds so she could have friends spend the night. After they both fell asleep on the floor, it wouldn't be practical for you to take Maggie home anyway."

"I could have awakened her."

Her comment conjured up a vision of the two little girls stretched out on the floor fast asleep amid a slew of toys. They had been sleeping so heavily that taking off their shoes and socks and lifting them into the bunk beds hadn't roused them.

"Oh, sure," Corey said. "And that stuffed thing we saw sleeping in Baby Bear's Bed at Story Book Forest was really the Big Bad Wolf."

"I thought you were the Big Bad Wolf," Tessa teased, forgetting how dangerous it was to let their conversation become personal. She didn't want to analyze why it felt so natural sitting here with him while their children were safely tucked away in their beds.

"No. I'm the Red Sticky Dragon, remember?" Corey ruffled his hair, which he had washed out in a water fountain hours ago, to remind her. Then he indicated the couch. "And this is my lair."

"Oh, pooh. I'm not afraid of you," Tessa said flippantly. When Corey closed the space between them, she suspected that the lethargy that had invaded her body had overtaken her brain. She had spent one day in an enchanted fairyland and had forgotten that she lived in the real world. The world in which men such as Corey McCash viewed protestations as challenges. Ignoring the way her body wanted to lean into his as though she were chilled and he was the only one who could warm her, Tessa stood up.

She's afraid, Corey thought in wonder. She had been flirting with him a moment ago, but he hadn't even touched her and she had sprung away. Truth be told, Corey hadn't even been thinking about putting a move on her. Oh, he wanted her all right, enough so that the lower half of him ached at the thought. But he had moved closer to her simply because their intimate chat had made him feel closer to her. Corey longed to put her at ease, to go back to where they'd been a moment ago.

"I don't want you to be afraid of me." That, Corey thought, was an understatement.

"I'm not," Tessa said, but her voice cracked. Corey still sat on the coach, his long limbs at ease and his eyes half lidded. Bedroom eyes, she thought. "It's just that I'm tired, and I need to go home. It's a good thing Abby and I drove over here today, because you couldn't very well leave them here to drive me home."

She was rambling and talking so rapidly she barely took a breath between sentences, a nervous habit Corey had picked up on a few days ago. "You could have stayed here tonight," he said softly. "You still can."

Tessa didn't move, although he had given her a clear sign that she should sprint for the door. The trouble was that while she couldn't run toward him, she couldn't make herself run away. A part of her wanted to take him up on his offer and experience what it would be like to be in his arms. But that wasn't the part that housed her brain.

"I think it's better if we keep our relationship strictly business," Tessa said, hating the way her voice cracked. She already sounded like a broken record. "I can't sleep with you, Corey."

He savored the breathy way she said his name, even if the words weren't what he'd hoped to hear. Corey, however, wasn't a man to show his disappointment. Alise had taught him that it was better to be kicked in the gut than to let a woman know she had wounded him. That kind of knowledge gave a woman power, and Corey would never again let himself be beaten by it.

"I think we should keep our relationship strictly business, too. I was talking about the spare room," he said, emotion stripped from his voice. The barbed sentence hit its intended target, and Tessa's large brown eyes looked as wounded as those of a felled deer who lay dying. Then her face flamed, the telltale flush rising from her delicate neck up her porcelain skin.

"I thought... Never mind what I thought," she murmured, feeling like a fool. Was she really so out of touch with the way single men related to women that she could misread desire where there was none? Had her years of marriage to Chris and then her years of grieving rendered her unable to recognize a simple come-on? Or had she been the one who was coming on to him? "I think I should just go."

Tessa squared her shoulders in a show of bravery and turned away from him, aware that the pervasive feeling dragging her down wasn't fatigue settling in after a long day. It was disappointment, and it was all the more knifing because she shouldn't be experiencing it. The last thing she needed from Corey McCash was a complicated romantic entanglement that could rip her life apart. The last thing she needed was his hand on her arm, stopping her from taking another step.

Corey knew that letting Tessa walk out the door would be the smart move. If she walked away, she'd never know that all day long he'd had a devil of a time keeping his hands off her. But when Tessa's face crumbled in embarrassment at his implication that he didn't want her, Corey couldn't let her take another step.

He expected some resistance when his hand stayed her progress, but she stopped so completely that she didn't even seem to be breathing. Then he turned her, tipped her chin and saw that she was holding her breath. Her eyes, large and luminous, slowly rose to meet his until he felt as though he couldn't have looked away even if their daughters awakened and wedged themselves between them.

Corey lowered his head slowly, as much to give himself time to think about what he was doing as to give her a chance to withdraw. But they were past the point of thought when she released the breath she'd been holding and he caught it with his kiss.

Tessa had placed her hands on Corey's chest when he turned her, as though poised to push him away. But she'd been lying when she said she wanted to keep their relationship strictly business, and that point had been driven home when he'd so blithely agreed with her. Her relief when he detained her had been so great that she reached out to touch him rather than push him away. Her hands traveled up his body and wound around his neck, settling in the short, soft hair at his nape and pulling him closer.

His lips were soft, incredibly so, and they molded to hers as though her mouth were a special type of clay fashioned just for him. She already knew the magic of his kiss, but still couldn't stop a gasp of pleasure when his tongue slipped inside her mouth and explored the hidden recesses.

She could no more fool herself than she could hide her response to his kiss. Something about this man made her want him more than she had ever wanted any man, even more than she had wanted Chris. Her nipples hardened into points of desire even before his hand found her breast through the thin jersey knit of her blouse.

She was like honey, Corey thought as he kissed her and felt the physical evidence of her response. So sweet, so sweet. The fact that she hadn't stopped him from touching her, had in fact leaned into his hand, inflamed him so that it would have been impossible to hide the evidence of his own response.

He yearned to be closer to her, but the difference in their heights frustrated his efforts until his muddled brain somehow got across to him that they were just a few steps from the couch. He backed up, taking her with him in a glorious heap onto the sofa.

"Sorry," he murmured, concerned he might have hurt her in his clumsy eagerness.

"About what?" she rasped back, as though she'd barely noticed that they were no longer standing but sitting. Not that sitting exactly described how they were positioned. Corey was half lying across the couch, and Tessa was stretched out across his length. This way, there was no mistaking that he wanted her as much as she wanted him.

Wantonly, she pressed her lower body against his hard shaft, and one of his hands slipped inside her shirt. The feel of his bare flesh on hers elicited another gasp, and she thought she would die from waiting for him to unfasten the front clip of her bra.

Corey had never lost control of himself during an encounter with a woman, but he was fast approaching that point now. When she pressed herself against him, he thought he might climax right then, like a teenager with a delicious date who had let him go too far.

But Tessa was a woman, not a girl who was trying her wiles on a novice who could barely contain himself long enough to get inside her. That distinction didn't seem to matter at the moment, but Corey hadn't yet had enough of her. Maybe he never would.

Corey's mouth left hers, and Tessa would have protested but it soon replaced his hand on her breast. She sucked in her breath as his tongue teased and circled her nipple, and sensations long dormant flooded her. On top of them came an almost overwhelming need to make him feel what she was feeling, and Tessa boldly ran her hand down the length of his body and stroked him through his shorts.

He moaned against her breast, and slipped one of his hands inside the waistband of her shorts. He hesitated slightly when he reached the elastic of her panties, but Tessa didn't make any move to stop him, and his fingers slipped inside to find her hot, moist and waiting for him. Bells went off in Tessa's ears from the wonderful things he was doing, but the bells rang and rang until it dawned on her that it was the phone.

"Aren't you going to answer it?" she managed, reluctantly moving her hand upward until it rested on his rib cage. Sensing a subtle change in her, Corey slowly pulled his hand from her panties and slid his mouth from her breast.

"No," he said, shaking his head to emphasize his point even as the phone stopped ringing. He tried to claim her lips once more, but with a supreme effort Tessa turned her head so that he met her cheek. He drew back, puzzled and frustrated.

"What's wrong?" Corey asked, and she wanted to tell him that nothing was wrong. But it was. The nerve endings in her body were pulsating, wanting him to finish what they'd started, but the rational part of Tessa had literally been saved by the bell.

She couldn't go to bed with this man, not when her future—and Abby's future—lay in the balance. Not when she'd known him only for a few days and hadn't yet decided if she could trust him. She didn't even know yet if she could like him.

"I want you to stop," Tessa managed in a shaky voice, knowing that they were past the point when she should have made the request. Corey's blue eyes widened in shock, and it cut her to the quick.

"Stop?"

"Yes, stop."

"That's not what you wanted me to do a few minutes ago," Corey said, hating the way he didn't want to listen to what she was saying.

"It's what I want you to do now."

Her hands were still clutching his shoulders and she didn't sound as though she meant what she said, but somewhere Corey found the resolve to shakily put her from him. He sat up, willing himself to breathe normally.

He hadn't been asked to stop after going so far since he was a teenager, but he wasn't the kind of man who forced himself upon a woman. Back then, he would have angrily called the female in question a tease and demanded to know why she had changed her mind. Now he simply waited.

Beside him, Tessa fastened her bra with shaking hands and tried to smooth her clothing into some semblance of order.

"I'm sorry," she whispered miserably. "I know you have every right to be angry. I shouldn't have let it go so far."

"I'm not angry," Corey said and was surprised to find that he meant it. He was disappointed and frustrated, yes, but not angry. Tessa Daniel wasn't the kind of woman who took a romp in bed with any man who wanted her. She was a single mother with responsibilities, who still hadn't taken off the wedding ring linking her to her late husband. "I understand it's been a long time for you. It must be hard to let go of that final link with your husband."

Chris, Tessa thought dazedly, he was talking about Chris. Corey seemed to think that making love with another man would sever the bond she had with her late husband. She looked down at her left hand, resolving to take off the wedding ring as soon as she returned to Mrs. Moriarty's house.

In actuality, Tessa had let go of Chris the first time Corey had kissed her on his porch under the darkened moon. The realization was so shocking that all she could do was nod.

Corey tried to smile, but it was a failed effort. He smoothed his own shirt and ran his fingers through his hair.

He figured that if he kept his hands busy they wouldn't have a chance to stray across the space that separated them and continue their sensuous exploration.

"I'll walk you to the door," he offered, and even that took an effort. "You'd better take this chance and get out of here now, or I won't be held accountable for my actions."

"I'm going," Tessa said and sprang off the sofa, smiling despite herself. Corey McCash was full of surprises and so unpredictable she couldn't begin to guess what he'd do next. Most men would have railed at her for calling a halt to their lovemaking, but Corey not only had the decency to stop but the compassion to consider her feelings. He'd even made a joke about it, albeit a feeble one.

She covered the distance to the door quickly and stepped back to allow him to open it. She paused on the threshold, not wanting the evening to end, not knowing what she wanted.

"Can I still come with you tomorrow?" she asked, and she no longer knew whether she needed to take the trip to find her birth child or to savor the pleasure of being with him.

"Nothing's changed," Corey said, although he knew everything had.

She looked up at him then, a smile curving lips he couldn't resist. He couldn't stop himself from tasting them any more than he could stop blinking, but his lips stayed where they longed to be for only short, sweet seconds.

"Tomorrow," he whispered while she gazed at him, her mouth slightly agape at the gentle, reverent way in which he'd kissed her. This last kiss had said something more profound than what had almost happened on his sofa.

Tessa turned with an effort and hurried down the sidewalk to her car, yanking open the unlocked door and sliding inside. If she was running from him, it was only to keep from running toward him.

* * *

Corey watched Tessa pull out of the driveway and quietly retreated to the family room, forsaking the sofa where they'd almost shared paradise for a matching leather chair. He'd intended to look over a file for a case he was considering, but he wouldn't be able to concentrate on business.

His body still ached from unfulfilled desire, but Corey wasn't a teenager anymore. Tessa had made him feel things tonight that he hadn't known since the wild abandon of his youth, but he was a man who was fully in control of his emotions and his body's responses. Until Tessa Daniel had come along, Corey amended with unwelcome honesty.

All it took from Tessa to make him want her was a big-eyed stare. He could still feel the way her long, slender fingers had moved over his body, but the truth was that she didn't even have to touch him to arouse him. What's more, he was beginning to like her.

It wouldn't take too much more for Corey to believe that Tessa Daniel was exactly what she seemed, a widow who loved her daughter and was trying to locate her niece. Why had he thought that an elementary-school teacher from Virginia had come to Oak Haven with a mysterious ulterior motive? What could someone who projected such innocence possibly have to hide?

Corey had been so quick to jump to the wrong conclusions, so ready to believe that lies could drip from Tessa's shapely lips as easily as they had from Alise's. His ex-wife had soured him on women for long enough. Corey would never allow himself to fall prey to someone like Alise, but not all females had claws. Not all women lied.

He smiled to himself, looking forward to spending tomorrow with Tessa trying to crack her case. Corey could already feel the sweet anticipation of being with Tessa and knowing that sometime soon they would make love. But Tessa wasn't the kind of woman who indulged in one-night stands. While she was in Oak Haven, they would share more than just a bed.

The shrill ring of the telephone snapped Corey to attention, calling to mind the other phone call that had taken paradise away from him. Grumpily, he glanced at his watch. It wasn't yet ten o'clock, but it was late for anyone to be phoning. He answered the phone before it rang again, even though nothing short of a sonic boom would awaken Maggie and Abby.

"Hello."

"Corey, it's Mike. I hope I'm not catching you at a bad time."

Corey came instantly alert. Mike Turner was the private investigator in Richmond who was checking out Tessa's brother. He and Corey had been friends since their police-academy days. Since Corey had emphasized that his request was low priority, something that certainly could wait a few days, he wondered why Mike was phoning with news in the late evening.

"No, of course not," Corey said. Now wasn't a bad time to phone. A half hour ago had been. "Is anything wrong?"

"Yes and no," Mike said, and he sounded perplexed. "You wanted me to check out a dead guy by the name of Steve Hutton, right?"

"Right. He was the brother of a woman named Tessa Hutton Daniel."

"No, he wasn't."

"What?" The word was clipped.

"There was never a Steve Hutton, Corey. Tessa Daniel never had a brother."

Chapter 8

Tessa pulled her aging sedan into Corey's driveway at exactly nine o'clock, and this time she didn't even notice the noisy muffler. Was it possible that it had been twelve hours since she'd last been in Corey's house? When she closed her eyes, she could almost feel his mouth on her breast and his hands on her skin. Determinedly, Tessa opened her eyes and got out of the car.

She'd spent an inordinate amount of time deciding what to wear and had settled on tight-legged white pants and an oversize short-sleeved shirt in a jungle print of brown, white and black. Since Tessa didn't know how Corey planned to extract information from the parents of the girl they were going to visit, she wasn't sure if she had dressed correctly. Even if her ensemble wasn't appropriate, at least she'd be comfortable during the long car ride and secure in the knowledge that she looked good.

Before Tessa could get nervous at the prospect of seeing Corey again, the door flung open and Abby barreled down the sidewalk, almost tackling Tessa with a bear hug to the knees. On her heels was Maggie, and they were both clad in their nightclothes.

"Hi, Mommy."

"Hi, Tessa."

The little girls started to chatter simultaneously, and Tessa couldn't make out a word they said. Laughing, she stooped and hugged Abby with one arm and Maggie with the other. Four short arms returned the affection.

"Where were you when I woke up, Mommy?" Abby whispered in Tessa's ear, and Tessa was momentarily concerned that her absence had been traumatic for her daughter. Then Abby extracted herself from her mother's embrace and danced in place.

"Corey made us sugar flakes for breakfast. Yum, yum," Abby said, using her name—which came out "sugar slakes"—for the sweetened breakfast cereal that lined the shelves of the grocery store but not the shelves of their cupboards. Tessa didn't deny Abby treats, but she drew the line at breakfast. Abby's usual cereal had wheat and rice as ingredients, but an occasional lapse wouldn't hurt.

"Daddy said Abby play with me all day," Maggie added.

"Can I, Mommy? Please?"

"Sure you can, sweetheart," Tessa answered, and this time both girls did an impromptu dance.

Tessa laughed again and straightened, taking one small hand in each of hers. This time, with two chattering children at her side, it wasn't at all difficult to cover the ground to the door of Corey's home. She felt happier than she had in a very long time.

Corey watched Tessa and the girls enter the house, and he wanted to rail at the injustice of the scene they created. Tessa was the picture of glowing motherhood, and both children gazed at her as though they worshiped her. As though she weren't a lying, scheming manipulator.

Tessa smiled at him with more wattage than the bright night-light that illuminated his porch whenever Mrs. Miller bothered to turn it on. Corey wondered what kind of game she was playing.

"Good morning, Corey," she said cheerfully, not even noticing his lack of response when the girls started clamoring for her. Tessa laughed again, ruffling their hair. "Just give me a few minutes to get these girls dressed, and I'll be ready to go."

Maggie and Abby scampered off with Tessa following before Corey could tell her that he would get Maggie dressed, thank you very much. But that would have been childish and a dead giveaway that he was on to her charade. Corey's first impulse when he'd hung up the telephone last night had been to dial Tessa's number and force her hand, but he'd quashed it. At the moment, he preferred to keep her as much in the dark as she thought she was keeping him.

Corey hadn't been mistaken that first afternoon when he'd sensed that she was up to something, but Tessa wouldn't blurt out the truth if he accused her of lying. The only way to satisfy his curiosity was to play out her little drama and make damned sure she tripped up somewhere in the process. Hell, he might as well stay on the case. She was paying for his services.

"Look at me, Daddy," Maggie squealed, running full speed into Corey's arms and breaking into his thoughts.

"Me, also," Abby shouted, calling attention to the fact that both girls were wearing black shorts and Mickey Mouse T-shirts. Even the pigtails in their hair looked the same. The ensembles would have been identical if the T-shirts had been the same color. Maggie's was red and Abby's pink.

"What's this? The Mickey Mouse twins?"

Abby giggled, but she had never been a child with an identity problem. "No, we're not mouses. We're kids."

"You could have fooled me."

"Me, too," said Tessa, trailing into the room behind the children. "You certainly look like Mickeys."

This time Maggie giggled. "Mickey's on our shirts, not on our faces."

"Good point," Corey conceded, smiling indulgently at his daughter.

"I thought the girls might get a kick out of wearing similar shirts," Tessa explained. "Abby has two of them because she loved that red one so much that I bought her another in a different color when she grew out of it. Now it's a perfect fit for Maggie."

"Can I keep it?" Maggie piped up.

"If your father says it's okay."

Corey nodded, and Maggie let out a gleeful yelp. "Hurray!"

When the doorbell sounded, both girls ran to answer it and a moment later reappeared with Mrs. Miller in tow. She dismissed Tessa's attempts to thank her in advance for watching Abby, and practically pushed them out of the house.

"It's a long drive to Fox Chapel," she said gruffly. "The sooner you leave, the sooner you'll get back."

Maggie and Abby didn't play favorites when they noisily saw them off, babbling about all the fun things they were going to do together. Tessa and Corey got a hug, a kiss and orders from each child.

"Be careful," warned Abby, probably because she'd heard Tessa say it so many times since Chris's accident.

"Come back soon," Maggie said sternly.

And then there was silence, disrupted only by the hum of the engine as Corey maneuvered his car out of Oak Haven. Tessa glanced at her watch and saw that it was ten o'clock, an hour past the time they'd planned to leave.

Tessa wasn't surprised, because caring for a child had a way of eating up scads of time. She used to fret if she was a minute late for anything, but she'd given up watching the clock soon after giving birth to Abby. Tessa's mouth drooped. Only she hadn't given birth to Abby at all, a thought that always filled her with despair.

Tessa didn't want to be searching for another child when Abby was all she needed, but she wanted to spend the day with Corey. If she were honest, she'd admit that she had also wanted to spend last night with him. She glanced down at her naked ring finger and wiggled it self-consciously. Wanting Corey had given her the impetus she needed to remove her wedding ring, and he hadn't even noticed.

"I hope Abby didn't give you any trouble," Tessa said, although she knew her daughter had been on her best behavior.

"None at all," Corey answered and lapsed into silence.

Tessa turned and studied him. Even though her view was of his profile, she could pick out faint dark smudges under his eyes, as though he hadn't gotten a good night's sleep. After the way she had left him the night before, she could guess the cause.

Corey hadn't seemed upset last night, but now she wondered if he was channeling some well-justified anger her way. Now that they were alone in the car without their daughters to distract them, it dawned on Tessa that he had barely said a word to her all morning. She summoned her nerve to broach the subject.

"I wouldn't blame you if you were angry with me."

"Come again?"

"I said I'd understand if you were angry because of last night." Tessa had to force herself to make the admission. Corey, who had been so understanding the night before that he'd even sent her away with a tender kiss, certainly wasn't making things any easier on her.

"I'm not angry."

His tone was almost flat, but Tessa detected a hint of anger. She wasn't accustomed to talking to a man who hid his feelings. Chris had been loquacious when it came to making his needs known—if she had angered him, he didn't hesitate to tell her. But Corey wasn't Chris, and she didn't want him to be.

"You sound as though you are," Tessa said. Corey started to speak, but Tessa interrupted. "Wait, just give me a minute to explain. Actually, I don't know if I can explain. It's just that I don't know you very well, and things went a little further than I intended.

"Don't get me wrong. It's not as though I intended things to go anywhere at all. Oh, darn. That sounded wrong, didn't it? I'm afraid that I'm explaining things badly."

If circumstances had been different, Corey would have found her rambling to be oddly charming. Tessa was trying to explain why she'd asked him to stop making love to her when she hadn't wanted him to stop. Corey steeled his heart against her words, biting his lip to keep himself from interrupting and giving her a graceful way out of her verbal jam.

"Oh, nuts," she said finally. "I'm not very good at this sort of thing. Let's just say that I'm sorry about what happened."

Corey debated whether to add anything to what Tessa had said. He was angry, and she seemed to need a reason to justify that anger. He wasn't about to tell her what really bothered him, but he couldn't let her think he was an oversexed jerk who didn't believe in a woman's right to say no. That didn't mean she had to know he'd spent the evening yearning for her, even after he'd discovered what sort of woman she was.

"Listen, you had every right to stop me last night. It stopped both of us from making a big mistake." Corey kept his eyes trained on the curving road. "Pleasure doesn't mix with business, and we both should have remembered that. I think you're trying to say you're sorry you let anything happen. Period."

Tessa hadn't meant to say that at all, but the rigidness in Corey's voice prevented her from telling him so. This Corey was like the man who had approached her across the street

NO RISK, NO OBLIGATION TO BUY...NOW OR EVER!

GUARANTEED

PLAY "ROLL A DOUBLE" AND GET AS MANY AS FIVE FREE GIFTS!

HERE'S HOW TO PLAY:

1. Peel off label from front cover. Place it in space provided at right. With a coin, carefully scratch off the silver dice. This makes you eligible to receive two or more free books, and possibly another gift, depending on what is revealed beneath the scratch-off area.

2. Send back this card and you'll receive brand-new Silhouette Intimate Moments® novels. These books have a cover price of $3.50 each, but they are yours to keep absolutely free.

3. There's no catch. You're under no obligation to buy anything. We charge nothing – ZERO – for your first shipment. And you don't have to make any minimum number of purchases – not even one!

4. The fact is thousands of readers enjoy receiving books by mail from the Silhouette Reader Service™ months before they're available in stores. They like the convenience of home delivery and they love our discount prices!

5. We hope that after receiving your free books you'll want to remain a subscriber. But the choice is yours – to continue or cancel, anytime at all! So why not take us up on our invitation, with no risk of any kind. You'll be glad you did!

NOT ACTUAL SIZE

*You'll look like a million dollars
when you wear this lovely necklace!
Its cobra-link chain is a generous
18" long, and the multi-faceted Austrian
crystal sparkles like a diamond!*

THE SILHOUETTE READER SERVICE™: HERE'S HOW IT WORKS

Accepting free books puts you under no obligation to buy anything. You may keep the books and gift and return the shipping statement marked "cancel." If you do not cancel, about a month later we will send you 6 additional novels, and bill you just $2.71 each plus 25¢ delivery and applicable sales tax, if any.* That's the complete price, and – compared to cover prices of $3.50 each – quite a bargain! You may cancel at any time, but if you choose to continue, every month we'll send you 6 more books, which you may either purchase at the discount price...or return at our expense and cancel your subscription.

*Terms and prices subject to change without notice. Sales tax applicable in N.Y.

from that preschool, filled with accusations. The Corey to whom she'd almost made love yesterday was gone.

Tessa couldn't detect any of the affection he'd bestowed upon their daughters and certainly none of the gentleness he'd used with her. She acknowledged that she had behaved poorly last night, but she didn't deserve this treatment in return. Her feeling of injustice gave way to anger.

"Yes, that's exactly what I meant," Tessa said, even though it wasn't true. "It was a big, fat mistake."

A full minute of silence greeted her remark, during which Tessa stared blindly out the passenger window of the car. She told herself that it was best not to have a personal relationship with Corey, but she couldn't pretend that she didn't want one.

"Then we'll both have to see that it doesn't happen again," Corey said, emphasizing the word "both." He reached across her to open his glove compartment, and Tessa reflexively pulled her knees out of the way as though she couldn't bear for him to touch her. His lips pursed, but he didn't say anything.

The audio tape Corey popped into the car stereo was the first of many that played during the drive, but Tessa wouldn't be able to identify any of the recording artists later. She was trying to solve a puzzle more difficult than a Rubik's Cube.

She needed to hate Corey for holding her refusal to make love against her, but a sixth sense told her that wasn't the reason he'd turned so cool. Something had happened between last night and this morning, but she couldn't fathom what it could be. The only thing that made sense was that Corey had been gripped by second thoughts about venturing into a relationship with her. How could she blame him for that when she knew getting involved with Corey wasn't wise?

Two hours after they'd gotten into the car, Corey stopped curbside in Fox Chapel and switched off the ignition. That was the only signal Tessa received that they'd arrived at a point that might irrevocably change her life.

The house wasn't as grand as many of the others that lined the wide street, but it was still impressive. Massive maple trees shaded a yard that was lush, green and immaculately landscaped. Beyond the green paradise was a two-story brick house, complete with a wraparound white porch, that was obviously built to resemble a colonial mansion.

"Coming?" Corey asked, gripping the door handle. A panicked Tessa grabbed his arm to detain him and then yanked back her hand as though her fingers had been scorched. He'd made it abundantly clear that he didn't welcome her touch.

"Hold on a minute," Tessa said and cursed herself for waiting until now to familiarize herself with Corey's plan of action. She'd been too busy feeling dejected that her relationship with him had ended before it had even begun. "We can't just waltz right up to the front door."

"Why not? Katherine Peterson lives there," Corey said, deliberately misunderstanding. He didn't intend to make this easy for her. The trouble with a lie was that the bigger it got, the harder it was to keep it straight. He waited to hear her version of why they couldn't tell Katherine Peterson's parents their true reason for visiting.

"Exactly. I don't want Katherine's parents to know I could be her aunt. I don't want anyone to know until we're absolutely sure she's the child we're looking for."

"Isn't it a moot point?" At Tessa's raised eyebrows, Corey, spurred by smoldering anger, continued. He could barely keep the sarcasm out of his voice. "If Katherine's mother is Bunny, won't she recognize you?"

Tessa's eyes dropped. "I already told you we've never met."

"But surely she'll notice a family resemblance. Brothers and sisters usually look alike."

"Steve and I didn't resemble each other," Tessa mumbled, and Corey thought at least that much was the truth. How could she look like a man who had never existed?

Corey hesitated before he spoke again, unsure of whether he was doing the right thing. He could end Tessa's charade before she carried it into the Petersons' home, but it had become nearly an obsession to determine what she was up to.

It would be different if he were risking his professional reputation. Corey couldn't in good conscience continue the investigation if he believed he was putting the Petersons at risk, but he knew one thing instinctively about Tessa Daniel. She wasn't a danger to anybody but him.

"Listen closely, because I'm just going to say this once," Corey said, and his voice was gruff. "We're from the local health board, and we're investigating an outbreak of lice at Katherine's preschool. We need to have a look at Katherine to make sure it hasn't spread. You're going to be my silent partner. In other words, you don't say a word. Understood?"

Tessa nodded quickly, so relieved that he had a plan that she hadn't even bristled at his caustic tone. They got out of the car and walked side-by-side up the long sidewalk. Tessa resolved not to give him reason to rethink his position on letting her tag along. Still, she couldn't quite hide what bothered her.

"Isn't this a bit, well, dishonest?"

Corey laughed shortly and looked up at the clear blue sky instead of at her. Tessa questioning his integrity was a little like a sinner casting stones at an innocent man. Maybe that was a bit of an exaggeration, because Corey hadn't been innocent since his boyhood, but the analogy seemed fair enough.

"Does that mean that you never lie?"

Tessa hesitated. "I try not to."

Corey's hand shot out and clasped Tessa's elbow, causing her to stop abruptly. Her eyes went wide with shock, and Corey cursed her for being so beautiful and himself for noticing. He wanted to shake her until she told him the truth, but instead he released her.

"Look," he said roughly. "Mrs. Peterson won't let us in the door if we tell her you could be Katherine's aunt. You hired me to solve your case, and that's what I'm going to do. This is just the way you play the game."

Tessa smiled gamely, determined not to cower in the face of his mystifying anger.

"Then let's play."

The woman who answered the door was a pretty blue-eyed blonde who would have been even prettier if she lost some weight, but Corey figured Mrs. Peterson had more important things to worry about than working out at the gym. She balanced a tow-headed boy who looked to be about a year old on one hip. The baby grinned when he saw they had visitors, and he didn't have more than three or four teeth.

"Can I help you with something?" the woman said, and she seemed friendly if not welcoming.

"Grant McQueen, health department," Corey said, reaching into his back pocket for his wallet. He pulled out an identification badge, and the bewildered woman took a quick look before Corey pocketed it.

Tessa's eyebrows rose at the use of the phony name and badge, but she was confident that he knew what he was doing. Dressed in dark slacks, a white long-sleeved dress shirt with skinny navy stripes and a tie loosened at the neck, Corey looked the part of a health-department employee. Of course, Tessa wasn't exactly sure what such a person was supposed to look like.

"Are you Robyn Peterson?" Corey asked, sounding authoritative.

"Yes, but I don't understand."

"We're here to investigate an outbreak of head lice at your daughter Katherine's preschool. The people who run the place called and asked if we would visit some of the children personally, because they don't want this thing to spread."

"Lice?" Robyn Peterson's mouth twisted. "Do you mean that Katy could have lice?"

"Don't jump to any conclusions, Mrs. Peterson. This is just a precautionary measure. If you'll let us take a few moments of your time, we'll examine the child and be on our way. There's no reason to panic until we know exactly what we're up against. Even then, head lice is highly treatable. May we come in?"

"Oh, yes, of course." Mrs. Peterson moved out of the doorway to allow them access to her home, and Tessa marveled at how easily Corey had talked his way into her confidence. "Follow me this way to the living room. I'll be just a minute while I round up Katy."

The Peterson home was a charming mix of expensive furnishings and clutter. Discarded toys, coloring books and puzzles sat atop every available surface, giving the house a lived-in appearance. It looked like a swell place to grow up. Tessa pressed her hands together and noticed for the first time that they were clammy.

Before Tessa's anxiety had a chance to build, Robyn Peterson walked back into the room with two blond, blue-eyed girls who could have been mistaken for twins if not for the slight disparity in their heights. Tessa knew instantly that she couldn't have given birth to a child who looked like Katherine Peterson.

"These are my daughters, Katy and Elaine," Robyn Peterson said, and she sounded distressed. The girls each muttered a greeting. "I'd appreciate it if you'd check them both. They're only eleven months apart and do everything together. If Katy has lice, Elaine does too."

"You have a beautiful family, Mrs. Peterson," Corey said, trying to gauge both women's reactions. Robyn Peterson seemed horrified at the thought that her daughters could have lice. Tessa had visibly relaxed since the girls came into the room, and Corey wasn't sure whether it was because she had found some answers or because the answers weren't in this house. "Your husband must be very proud."

"That's an understatement," Robyn Peterson said. "You've never met a man who wanted to have children more than Bill. We got married five years ago, and I got pregnant on our honeymoon."

You're wasting your time, Corey, Tessa wanted to tell him. He was skillfully trying to discover whether her fictitious brother could have fathered Katherine, but Tessa didn't need to hear any more. Chris's eyes and hair had been darker than hers, and the two of them couldn't have produced a child as fair as Katherine.

Even if it were genetically possible, and Tessa supposed that remote chance existed, the fact that Katherine was a ringer for her sister ruled her out. Corey started to ask another question, but Tessa interrupted.

"Grant, I'm sure Mrs. Peterson is anxious to discover if her children have head lice," Tessa said and smiled reassuringly at Robyn Peterson. "He'll just take a quick look, and then we'll be on our way."

Katy Peterson wasn't the right child.

The message came across to Corey as clear as the polished glass in Mrs. Peterson's china cabinet, and he nodded at Tessa to show that he understood. Less clear was how Tessa had concluded after a single look that Katy Peterson wasn't their girl.

"Yes, let's get on with it." Corey addressed Mrs. Peterson. "I need to look through their hair. It'll just take a minute."

Mrs. Peterson instructed her daughters to stand still, and Katy and Elaine stood rigidly at their mother's side as Corey approached and gently ran his fingers through their hair. He made a show of inspecting their scalps.

"Negative," he said after a minute. "I'm sorry we bothered you, Mrs. Peterson."

"It was no bother at all. You can run off and play now, Katy and Elaine," she said, clearly relieved. The two silent children vanished from the room in short order. "I'm just glad you took the time to check on them."

She followed Corey and Tessa to the door, still carrying her youngest child. He babbled happily, calling to Tessa's mind the delightful baby sounds Abby had made in her infancy. Tessa waved goodbye, and he mimicked her with his stubby hands. Everyone laughed, and a moment later Tessa and Corey walked out the door. Robyn Peterson stopped them with a question.

"Isn't it a little odd for the health department to look into something like this? Don't get me wrong, I appreciate it, but it seems like your agency would have more pressing concerns."

"We're always concerned about the welfare of children," Corey said without hesitation. "After all, it's our job to serve you. Taxpayers like you pay our salaries."

Robyn Peterson digested the explanation and smiled, evidently liking the sound of it. She thanked them again before she closed the door.

"Spoken like a true bureaucrat," Tessa said as they made their way back to his car. "Did you ever think of applying at the health department? You were very convincing back there."

"I told you I was good at what I do," Corey said, and his pause was measured. "I also told you not to speak unless spoken to."

"I was just trying to save us from wasting any more time. That little girl isn't related to me."

They reached the car, and Corey pulled open the unlocked door and waited for Tessa to get inside. She did so gratefully, glad for the pause in their conversation. She was beginning to understand how Corey's mind worked, and that meant his next question wouldn't be quite so easy to answer. Corey didn't speak until he was settled in the driver's seat, and then he got directly to the point.

"Why are you so sure that Katherine Peterson isn't the girl we're looking for?"

"Didn't you take a good look at her?" Tessa had decided that the truth might serve her better than another lie. "There's no way that child could be related to me."

"Why not? Maybe Bunny was a blonde."

He had a good point, one which Tessa hadn't stopped to consider. If only she didn't have to lie! But she couldn't tell the truth. Not with Abby's future depending upon his reaction.

"Even so, Robyn Peterson couldn't be Bunny. You heard her say she'd been married for five years. And her oldest daughter was practically a carbon copy of Katherine. I'm completely satisfied that she's not the right girl."

Corey studied her face as she talked, noticing that she seemed earnest. His head started to pound at the effort of figuring out what Tessa was keeping from him. Even more perplexing was the reason she would lie.

The logical conclusion was that she was searching for a child she had given up for adoption, but Abby was the same age as the missing child. Was it possible that Abby had a twin sister and that Tessa had somehow opted to separate them at birth? That, too, sounded preposterous. •

"If you're satisfied, then I'm satisfied. After all, you're the client."

"I'm not completely satisfied. Yet. You said there were three children born in Oak Haven Hospital that October that we needed to investigate. You've checked out two of them. That must mean number three is the right one."

"It certainly seems that way."

"I want to come with you when you go to see her," Tessa said, although she was terrified at the prospect. The odds were good that the little girl would be in perfect health and Tessa could leave Oak Haven with Abby and a clear conscience. But what if her birth child showed signs of developing Cooley's anemia? What then?

"I told you before that it's not necessary for you to accompany me. Hasn't today proved it to you?"

"Quite the contrary. I knew immediately that Katherine Peterson wasn't the right child. I'm not saying you wouldn't have figured it out, but having me along certainly helped."

Yawning silence greeted her pronouncement, and his reluctance to let Tessa accompany him during future investigations couldn't have been more clear. Corey didn't even want her along on this trip.

"When I make the arrangements to see her, I'll call you," he said finally. "We'll talk about it then."

"I'm not going to change my mind," Tessa said firmly, although she considered it a victory of sorts that he hadn't refused her then and there.

"And I'm not going to talk about it right now. We need to get out of here before Mrs. Peterson thinks to call the health department to check up on us." He turned the key in the ignition and felt his stomach grumble with hunger. It served him right for not taking the time to do more than down a glass of orange juice that morning. "I thought we'd stop at a fast-food joint for lunch. I have a lot of things to do in Oak Haven, and I'm in a hurry to get back."

"Fine with me," Tessa said while her visions of white tablecloths and an intimate lunch vanished. She might as well face the fact that something she had done between now and last night had cooled his interest.

It shouldn't have mattered, but Tessa couldn't swallow her disappointment. She was looking for a lost child, but in the process she had found something else. Corey's expression was grim when he started the car, and Tessa was quite certain that she couldn't have what she wanted. That was because she wanted Corey.

The house was so silent when Corey unlocked the front door later that afternoon that he knew immediately that there was no one at home. Two three-year-olds couldn't possibly be this quiet, especially after hearing the door open. Maggie usually bounded into the living room and flew into his arms.

"I don't think anybody's here," Tessa said, stating the obvious. "They probably didn't expect us back so early."

Corey would have gotten them back even sooner, but the tragic automobile accidents he'd witnessed while on the police force had trained him to drive the speed limit. When he'd agreed to take Tessa along on the trip he had envisioned an idyllic day, but it had turned into an ordeal.

He knew inwardly that Tessa wasn't what she seemed, but his body wouldn't make the distinction. He'd spent the past few hours fighting the urge to pull over and take her into his arms. He'd resisted by telling himself he'd be free of temptation as soon as he got home. He'd made it home, but the temptation hadn't gone away.

"Mrs. Miller usually leaves a note in the kitchen when she takes Maggie anywhere," Corey said, striding away from her. Tessa followed, as anxious to be free of his company as he was to get away from her.

When Tessa got to the kitchen, Corey was taking down a note that had been stuck with a magnet to the gleaming white refrigerator. His mouth twisted wryly as he read. Then he glanced at his watch and crumpled the piece of paper.

"We missed them by about five minutes. Mrs. Miller took the girls for a walk and won't be back until four. It's just past two-thirty now."

"Then perhaps I should come back at four," Tessa said, taking a few steps backward.

"Don't be ridiculous," Corey said, without pausing to think about the consequences of what he was about to say. "Of course you can stay here until they get back."

"I know you have things to do. I wouldn't dream of keeping you from your work."

"My work can wait. I never intended to be back from Fox Chapel so soon. You won't get in my way if you stay."

"I'd be even less in your way if I got in my car right now and looked for Abby. They probably went to the park." Tessa backed up a few steps to show that she was prepared to do as she'd said.

"But then she'd be disappointed that she didn't get to play."

I'm not making any sense, Corey thought numbly. *I'm trying to find reasons to keep her in my home when I desperately need her to leave.*

Tessa bit her lip, and her brows drew together so that she looked as confused as he felt. "I don't understand," she said, shaking her head. "You've barely said anything to me all day, and you rushed lunch so you could get back here. I was under the impression you couldn't wait to get rid of me."

"You were right," Corey said, bewilderment seeping into his tone.

"I was right?" Tessa was stung, and it hurt more than any insect bite. "Then why are you trying to persuade me to stay?"

Her question deserved an answer. Corey suspected the honest reply was buried somewhere inside him, but it was somewhere so remote that he couldn't begin to fathom what it was. Tessa had stopped backing away, and her dark eyes were huge in her pale face. Corey didn't even notice that he was moving forward until she was close enough to touch. He shrugged with a nonchalance he was far from feeling and gave her the most honest response he could.

"Damned if I know," he said, and it was almost a whisper. "All I know right now is that I want to kiss you."

"I thought we weren't going to mix business with pleasure," Tessa said, even as his hands covered the flesh on her arms just below her short-sleeved shirt. If it had occurred to her to pull away, she still wouldn't have been able to make herself move. "I thought we had a pact."

"Then let's make another pact where we agree to break the last one," Corey said, and his head moved lower.

"That doesn't make any sense," Tessa said as she tilted her head.

"This doesn't make any sense."

Tessa closed her eyes the moment before their lips touched, and her capitulation rendered Corey powerless to stop what was about to begin. He was past caring about logic, anyway. This might be idiocy, but nothing about this moment seemed wrong.

The sun streamed through the kitchen blinds, illuminating the room and their embrace. Neither of them would ever be able to claim that this wasn't exactly what they wanted.

Tessa's arms snaked around Corey's waist, and she was almost frantic to have him close to her. She heard a soft female moan when he ran his tongue over her lips, and concluded that it must have come from her. His hand cupped the nape of her neck so that he could explore her throat with kisses, and sensations danced through her like ballerinas on a stage.

"Aren't you going to stop me?" he asked, and his breathing was already heavy. His free hand lightly stroked the curve of her breast, and she could barely form a reply. She had on only a wisp of a bra, but she wished she hadn't worn one at all.

"Do you want me to stop you?"

Corey expelled a short breath that sounded like a wry laugh, and his hand covered her breast, kneading and teasing and causing a liquid heat well south of where he touched.

"No, I don't want you to stop me. I don't want you to tell me to answer the telephone, either."

In answer, Tessa covered his lips with hers and plunged her tongue inside his mouth in a pantomime of the way she wanted his body to fill hers. He kissed her back, one of his hands still at her breast while the other left her nape to travel the length of her back and cup her buttocks. He pressed her lower body against his, and she reflexively rubbed her softness against the hard evidence that he wanted her.

Corey dragged his mouth from hers, and another thrill passed through him at the way she cried out in protest. "I want to take you to my bedroom. But if you come, we're not going to stop."

"I don't want to stop," Tessa said clearly.

Chapter 9

Corey lifted Tessa and carried her up the stairs as though she were no heavier than one of his daughter's dolls. Once in the bedroom, he laid her in the center of his king-size bed and began stripping off his clothes.

Tessa merely watched, drinking in the sight of him like a cat lapping up cream. His tie was the first to go, and then he quickly unbuttoned his dress shirt to reveal a chest lightly dusted with dark golden hair. His socks and belt buckle came next, and then he stepped out of his slacks and underwear with brief, fluid motions. Tessa barely had time to admire broad shoulders that tapered to narrow hips and the proof that he wanted her before he was beside her on the bed.

"You're still dressed," he accused, and she smiled contentedly.

"I wanted to watch the show."

"My turn."

He returned her smile and lifted her oversize shirt over her head. He ran his hands slowly, reverently, down her body, pausing significantly at her breasts and then continuing until he reached the apex of her legs. She writhed as his fingers rubbed her there and would have begged him to take off the rest of her clothes if at that moment he hadn't started to slide her panties and leggings off her hips. As he edged them down, his lips kissed the sensitive skin of her stomach and then her hips. His mouth trailed kisses down one of her legs until her pants were off and she was wearing only a bra.

Tessa sat up and undid the front clasp of her bra with trembling fingers, letting her breasts spill free. This time, it was Corey's turn to stare. Even though Tessa had always wanted to be thinner, her self-consciousness vanished in the worshipful look in his eyes. She couldn't savor it for long, because it was only a moment before he was pulling her to him.

Their mouths met hungrily, and Tessa let her hands roam at will, luxuriating in the feel of his chest hairs and powerful muscles, which were pliant to her touch. She responded to his touches with moans and sighs as though she'd been waiting for him, but she couldn't even remember having a sexual thought in the last three years.

When Corey's mouth found her breast, she threw her head back and closed her eyes, loving the way his tongue tasted and teased. But Tessa couldn't just take from him, and her fingers began their quest.

Corey's entire body was an erogenous zone; she had only to touch him to create ripples of feeling. When her hand found his hard shaft, he gasped against her mouth. When she stroked him, tentatively at first and then more boldly, he thought he would lose control before he could join with her.

"I can't wait any longer," he rasped against her mouth.

"I don't want to wait," she answered, and his fingers found her slick and ready for him. And then, for the briefest of moments, she experienced a terrible sense of loss. But Corey was only reaching inside his bedside table for the foil package she should have insisted upon. With a swiftness born out of a sweet desperation, he covered himself and then covered her mouth with his.

She opened her legs so that he could enter her, but cried out at the momentary discomfort when he did. Corey froze, because it had been a long time for her, but in seconds Tessa started to move beneath him.

Had it ever been this way for him before? Corey thought it must have been, but he couldn't remember when. Every movement brought him to the brink of release, and he had to slow his progress to prolong their pleasure. He wasn't thinking clearly, but he knew instinctively that he wanted her as inflamed as he was. But he couldn't have stopped himself from responding even if he lay immobile: Tessa's essence surrounded him like a cloak.

He gave in to the inevitable when he couldn't resist it any longer, and her rhythm was perfectly matched to his. They moved in tandem, giving and receiving and responding until reaching an incredible crescendo of wave after wave of tumultuous release.

Then it was over, but for Tessa it had just begun.

Neither of them moved for long minutes, and Tessa didn't even want to shift her position. Although he topped her weight by at least sixty or seventy pounds, she welcomed the feel of him atop her. It reaffirmed everything they had just shared, and she was afraid they might not be able to hold on to that feeling once they let each other go.

"I must be crushing you," he finally said in a voice slurred by spent passion and rolled away from her before she could protest. Tessa lay still, and the cooled air from an air-conditioning vent blew over her.

They didn't touch, and Tessa prayed that he wouldn't apologize. She had never felt this way with anyone before, not even with Chris, and she couldn't imagine that any other man could ever make her feel this way again. She hadn't imagined that she could be so uninhibited, so unashamed of what a man and a woman could give each other.

She turned her head on the pillow to look at him, and her black hair spilled over one eye. His hand moved as though to brush it back, then stopped. Tessa smoothed it back by herself, trying to believe it wasn't regret that clouded his handsome features.

"Don't say you're sorry," she said, and it was almost a plea.

His eyes met hers, and they were so grave that Tessa thought looking into them was like peering through a window into his very soul. He was waging some kind of battle with himself over her, and he was losing.

"I'm not sorry," Corey said, and refrained from adding a qualifier. He'd taken his pleasure and his body was sated, his passion spent. But there were no guarantees of what the next hour, let alone the next day, would bring. His eyes were wide open this time, and they saw a woman he wanted but could never trust. If he held on to that thought, he could enjoy an intimate relationship without the intimacy.

The resonant chime of a doorbell echoed through the house, and Tessa jumped out of bed so abruptly that her world went temporarily black as spots danced in front of her eyes. The blackness went away, but the sound of the doorbell didn't. It rang again and again, and Corey got to his feet and started yanking on his discarded clothing.

"That's Maggie's calling card," he explained, and they both heard a key turn in the lock. "I figure we have about a minute and a half before she and Abby search the downstairs and figure out we're up here."

"It can't be four-thirty," Tessa protested even as she scrambled out of bed and located her underwear.

"It's not," Corey said, glancing at his bedside alarm clock. "It's four-forty. We should just be thankful Maggie likes to announce her arrival when she sees my car in the driveway."

"Mommy!"

"Daddy!"

The sound of their children calling them spurred Corey and Tessa to dress in record time. She finger combed her hair as they walked out of the bedroom, even though any child old enough to know about sex could figure out what they'd been up to. Fortunately, Maggie and Abby didn't fit into that category. Still, Tessa blushed furiously when Abby spotted them when they were halfway down the staircase.

"Where were you, Mommy?" Abby asked, sounding like an exasperated adult. "Were Mommy and Corey playing hide-seek? We couldn't see you anywhere."

Corey recovered first and descended the last step just as Maggie came around the corner. "Why would your mommy and I want to hide from you?" he asked, putting out his arms to Maggie. Both children went into them.

Mrs. Miller appeared behind the embracing trio and her eyes swept Tessa, who was still standing on the stairs. She nodded her head in acknowledgment, but not before Tessa glimpsed the perception in her eyes. Mrs. Miller guessed what she and Corey had been doing upstairs, but Tessa could swear she saw approval instead of condemnation.

"Hey," Tessa said, lightly stepping down the steps until she was inches away from the man and two girls. "Don't I get a turn?"

Abby reached her first, and her hug was short and intense. Maggie was much slower to break away from her father.

"Can I hug you too, Tessa?" she asked, voice soft and eyes downcast.

Tessa didn't say a word, but swept the little girl into her arms. Maggie's embrace was so sweet it seemed to be drenched in syrup. An irrational wave of anger assailed Tessa, and she wanted to rail at the woman who had so casually abandoned Maggie and crushed her self-esteem. If Maggie had been hers, she would never be able to let her go.

"C'mon, Maggie," Abby said, grabbing her friend's hand and pulling her away from Tessa all too soon. Abby had another hand free, and she latched on to Corey. "We show your daddy our pictures we colored."

Tessa watched her daughter, chattering all the while, lead the two McCashes down the hallway to Maggie's playroom.

"We sure are a pair, Abby," she whispered aloud. "It's not enough that we both love Maggie. We had to go and fall for her father, too."

Tessa had never been one to wait by the phone, her hand poised to grab the receiver, but for two days she had listened for its ring. Worse, she had expected it to ring. But all that came from it was silence.

"Oh, please, Mommy, please." Abby's pleading young voice disrupted the quiet. "I wanna go to the park."

Abby had made her request so many times that Tessa was beginning to think that yielding to her daughter's wish would be easier than listening to her whine. Besides, it wasn't an unreasonable appeal. The sun was shining, the sky was the kind of glorious blue that accompanies a cloudless day, and Tessa was a fool to waste another minute waiting for Corey to phone. If he could act as though their lovemaking didn't mean a thing, she could play the same game.

"Okay, you talked me into it," Tessa told her daughter. "Go get your shoes."

Abby scrambled away at top speed, hunting for a pair of favorite canvas loafers that she was able to slip on herself. She looked as though she was afraid Tessa would change her mind and sentence them to additional housebound hours.

Have I been that bad? Tessa wondered as she bent to retrieve her own shoes. After three years of marriage and as many years of widowhood, she was out of practice with modern dating techniques. Not that she and Corey were dating. Somehow she doubted the modern single woman waited by the phone. She never had before.

During high school, males had been more eager to contact her than she was to hear from them. Chris had been her only serious boyfriend during her college years, and he was so irresponsible that she had never counted on him for anything, not even something as simple as a phone call. After graduation, she'd been married and widowed in the space of a few years.

No man had mattered since. Until Corey. He'd even helped her release the anger she'd built up since Chris's death, allowing her to finally work through the grieving process. She couldn't remember when she hadn't loved Chris, but he'd been a rotten husband. Tessa couldn't let him go after he died, because she would have left him had he lived.

His death had saved her the trouble, and Tessa's guilt had been tremendous. But now, along with the anger, the guilt was gone. Logic took their place. Tessa had realized Chris was flawed long before his death, and that hadn't stopped her from loving him. Having a half-formed plan to ask him for a divorce wasn't tantamount to wishing him dead.

"I'm ready, Mom," Abby sang out, and Tessa reached for her daughter's hand. Even as she locked the door to their rooms she was still thinking about Corey, still listening for the phone.

She should be waiting for him to outline his strategy in approaching the final child on the list, the one who should have been hers. Instead, Tessa was waiting simply to hear from him. She had found something wonderful in their lovemaking, something elusive that she'd never experienced before. It hurt to the quick to think that Corey hadn't found it, too.

Tessa still hadn't shaken her melancholy when she and Abby reached the park. She kept thinking back to the day, not even a week ago, when Abby had broken free of her and run into friendship. Today was much warmer and much earlier in the day, but Tessa half expected to see Corey pushing Maggie on the swing suspended from the wooden play center.

"Look," Abby shrieked, "it's Maggie."

As she had a week ago, Abby set off for her friend in a run. Even from this distance, Tessa could tell that the short, squat figure with Maggie was Mrs. Miller. When she got nearer, Tessa saw that something was wrong. Mrs. Miller was sitting on a swing meant for a child, her face pale and her breathing shallow.

"Tessa!" Maggie yelled in greeting and hugged her around the legs, this time not bothering to ask for permission.

Tessa ruffled Maggie's hair, which she absently noted needed a fresh cut, but her eyes were fastened on Mrs. Miller. Before she could phrase a question, the two girls dashed off to play in the sandbox. They acted as though they hadn't seen each other for a month instead of a few days.

"What's wrong?" she asked Mrs. Miller the instant they were alone.

"Nothing that time won't cure," the older woman said, and even her voice sounded weak. "My sister Betty has the flu, and I think I'm coming down with it."

"You should go home and get some rest."

Mrs. Miller shook her head, and she looked miserable. "I can't. I need to watch Maggie. I tried to phone Mr. McCash, but his answering machine is on. I thought the fresh air would make me feel better, but it hasn't."

"I'll look after Maggie," Tessa said as though it were the most logical solution in the world. "You just worry about yourself."

Relief passed over Mrs. Miller's face, but she quickly masked it. "Are you sure? I wouldn't dream of putting you to any trouble."

"It's no trouble. Abby adores Maggie. I adore Maggie. Don't waste another minute thinking you're inconveniencing me."

This time Mrs. Miller's relief was so tangible it would have been impossible to hide. She fished in the pocket of her housedress and handed Tessa a set of keys.

"Take these keys. Mr. McCash is due home at six. If Maggie's not there, he'll worry." She rose to her feet slowly, wiping at her brow once she was standing. She looked old and vulnerable, not at all like the strong, no-nonsense figure she usually presented.

"Let us walk you home."

Mrs. Miller gave one vigorous shake of her head. "I know I can make it that far, but thank you for asking. You're a good woman, good for Maggie, good for Mr. McCash."

She paused, and the effort of talking seemed to be robbing her of energy. However, Mrs. Miller was determined to finish what she had to say before she took her leave.

"Be patient with him, Tessa. He hasn't had much luck with women, and he's as stubborn as they come. He hasn't realized yet that sometimes it's hardest to see what's directly in front of your face."

A couple of hours later, Tessa snuggled deeper into the leather sofa in Corey's family room and thought about Mrs. Miller's parting comment. She was subtly saying that she approved of the match Tessa made with her employer, while acknowledging that there hadn't yet been one.

Considering the way things had progressed since Tessa left Corey's bedroom, it seemed there wouldn't be a match. Still, Tessa's mind kept wandering back to the previous time she'd been in this house. Her senses came alive with remembered pleasure, and Tessa couldn't accept that he hadn't felt the same sensations.

Sometimes it's hardest to see what's directly in front of your face.

What would Corey see when he arrived home later that evening? The woman to whom he had tenderly made love? Or a nuisance he wanted out of his house?

Tessa knew that she shouldn't fret about which it would be, but she didn't have anything to distract her from her thoughts. Maggie and Abby were napping, having worn themselves out at the park. Corey's essence was everywhere, from his choice of rich masculine furniture to the wood paneling on the walls to the news and sports magazines strewn throughout the room.

Tessa had only to be in this house to yearn to be in his arms again, but forty-eight hours had passed since they'd made love and Corey hadn't attempted to contact her. He had welcomed her into his bed, but Tessa couldn't predict how he'd react when he found her in his house.

She'd had the uneasy feeling in the moments after they made love that he had done so because he couldn't help himself. Tessa sighed, and a solitary tear squeezed from her eye and fell down her cheek.

"Tessa," a soft, troubled voice whispered from somewhere behind her, and Tessa hastily wiped away her tear. She turned and Maggie stood there, her dark hair rumpled and her face wet with her own tears. Tessa was at her side in seconds. She stooped down and gathered the slim child in her arms, sensing what she needed. Maggie snuggled against her.

"What's wrong, baby?" Tessa asked after a few moments, and gently drew back so that she could see Maggie's tear-streaked face. The child's arms remained around her, keeping her close.

"I woke up. Nobody there. All alone," Maggie said on a sob, and Tessa patted her comfortingly on the back.

"No, no, honey. You weren't alone. Abby's asleep in the upstairs bunk bed, and I was down here the whole time you were sleeping."

"You. Not here. Always." Maggie's words were fragmented, but Tessa heard her fear.

"Your daddy's always here."

"Why not a mommy, too? Abby has a mommy."

"Oh, Maggie," Tessa said and smoothed the little girl's hair. Maggie had stopped crying, but tears were still pooled in the dark eyes, which looked up trustingly at Tessa as though she had all the answers. "Not all children have two parents. Abby doesn't have a daddy, but she has me. And you have a daddy who loves you very much. So that makes you very lucky."

Maggie bit her lip, and Tessa couldn't tell how much of what she said had penetrated her three-year-old sensibilities. "Why don't you be my mommy?" she asked finally.

"Me?" Tessa felt as though Maggie had reached out and touched her soul, but the request was as absurd as it was sweet. "It doesn't work that way, honey. You can't just ask somebody to be your mommy. But I'll tell you what. I'll be your special friend."

"Forever?" Maggie asked, her eyes trusting.

Instead of answering, Tessa drew the little girl closer and hugged her. She was everything nice, just like the nursery song about sugar and spice, and Tessa wouldn't lie to her.

Corey's daughter was filling a void in her heart she hadn't even known existed, but Tessa couldn't promise her tomorrow. Once she found her birth child and assured herself that the girl didn't have Cooley's anemia, Tessa and Abby had to leave town fast. Tessa was just starting to realize that she would be leaving something precious behind.

The sun was low in the sky, a hazy red ball, as Corey climbed the steps to his front porch. He moved slowly, showing the effects of a long, tiring day. Yesterday, he had worked even more hours.

Corey supposed he could delude himself into believing that he needed to work extra hard to build up his practice, but that wasn't true. He'd always had plenty of cases, even during his first week back in Oak Haven. The reason he was working too hard was because he didn't want time to think about Tessa Daniel and what was happening between them.

Corey paused before he unlocked the door, mentally preparing an apology for Mrs. Miller. She had expected him home at six, which was a little more than an hour ago, and he hadn't called to say he'd be late. He'd been so engrossed in advising the brain trust of a new company about their security needs that he hadn't noticed the time passing.

Girlish laughter filled the house as he walked inside, and he heard the inevitable shriek that precipitated his nightly greeting. He cocked an ear, immediately sensing a difference. The sounds were coming from two girls instead of one. They were running, but this time he held back his reprimand about running in the hall.

"Daddy!"

Maggie was the first around the corner, and she hurled herself into her father's arms. Corey quickly shifted Maggie to one side of his body and hugged her with one arm, preparing for another assault. Abby came at him even more recklessly, hurling her small body with complete confidence that he'd welcome her. He swung both girls off the ground.

"Hey, wait a minute," he said, laughing along with the giggling girls. "I thought I only had one little girl."

"Big girls," Abby shouted. "Three-year-olds are big girls. Two-year-olds are little girls."

"You're telling me. Did you ever try to pick up two big girls at once? You two must have eaten a ton for dinner," Corey said, pretending to groan, although he wasn't nearly as weary as he'd been a few minutes ago.

"No, Daddy," Maggie said. "We didn't eat ton. We ate pizza."

Corey chuckled. He looked in the direction from which the girls had come, expecting to share his amusement with

Mrs. Miller. Instead of his middle-aged baby-sitter, however, he saw the woman who had been haunting his thoughts. The laugh died on his lips, and he was glad he was holding two children so he wouldn't make a fool of himself by sweeping her into his arms.

Tessa's hair was pulled back from her face, and she was wearing an unglamorous ensemble of blue-jean shorts, a T-shirt and tennis shoes. But Corey saw skin that glowed, shapely legs and the tantalizing outline of breasts.

"I hope you don't mind that we didn't wait for you to come home to have dinner," Tessa said, acting as though there was nothing out of the ordinary about his coming home and discovering her there. "It was getting late, the kids were hungry and all I could find in the freezer was a frozen pizza."

Even though the explanation made perfect sense, it made no sense.

"Of course I don't mind," Corey said, gently putting down the still laughing girls. What on earth was she doing here, especially when he'd gone to such pains to avoid her? When he straightened, he regarded her through narrowed eyes. "But I don't understand. Where's Mrs. Miller?"

Tessa pursed her lips, fighting back disappointment. She hadn't expected a hearty welcome, but she'd hoped for more than this. For a brief moment, she longed to be a three-year-old who merited unconditional affection, instead of a grown woman who hadn't gotten even a smile.

"She has the flu," Tessa said, her voice revealing none of the violent emotion in her heart. She wanted to ask why he hadn't called. She wanted to know if he regretted making love to her. "Abby and I ran into Mrs. Miller and Maggie at the park, and Mrs. Miller was sick enough to be in bed. She said she couldn't reach you, so I volunteered to watch Maggie. She gave me the keys to the house so we could be here when you got home. Mrs. Miller didn't want you to worry."

Corey immediately felt like a heel. Tessa had done him a huge favor, and he had repaid her with suspicion. By hiring him to work on her case and lying to him, she deserved to be treated suspiciously. But he still felt like a heel.

"Tessa let us watch *Cinderemma,*" Maggie supplied.

"*Sisterella,*" Abby corrected.

"And we ate popcorn."

"And crackers."

"I'm sorry if I put you to any trouble," Corey said, realizing that he had. "I appreciate—"

"It was no trouble. I had a good time." Tessa cut him off before he could thank her; gratitude wasn't what she wanted from him. "Mrs. Miller called a little while ago and said she felt better already. She said it was a twenty-four-hour bug that would be gone by morning. And now, Abby and I have to be going. It's getting late."

Abby groaned dramatically in protest, but Tessa walked purposefully across the room and took her firmly by the hand.

"But, Mommy," she said on a wail. "Maggie said I could borrow her Raggedy Ann."

Tessa let out a sigh and released her daughter's hand. "Then go get it and come right back. And don't forget and start playing. We really do need to go."

The girls hurried out of the living room, and Tessa wanted to call them back. Corey was only the second man she'd ever been intimate with, and she needed time and space to deal with his rejection. Unfortunately, she didn't have either.

"Thank you for looking after Maggie," Corey said, determined to convey his gratitude. "And don't say it was nothing. You must have had something else planned to do today."

"You're forgetting that the only reason I'm in Oak Haven is to find my niece," Tessa said, stumbling slightly over the last word. She'd almost said "baby," although the missing child hadn't been a baby in a long time. "I've been waiting to hear from you these past few days. I wanted to know when we could visit the last child.''

That wasn't the only reason she'd been waiting to hear from him, Corey thought and was deluged by guilt. He'd made love to a fair number of women in his life, and he'd never left any of them wondering where they stood with him. Until Tessa.

He believed in complete honesty, even if it meant telling a willing woman that he wasn't interested in a long-term relationship and dooming his short-term chances. But how honest could he be with a woman he knew was a liar? Especially when he wasn't sure what the honest response was?

''I should have called,'' Corey said, but it wasn't clear whether he referred to their business relationship or their personal one. Tessa waited for him to continue.

''The last child, Suzanna Smith, lives in Oak Haven. The reason I didn't check her out before now is that she's been vacationing with her parents. I plan to stop by their house tomorrow after her mother gets home from work.''

And you weren't going to call and let me know, Tessa finished silently. *You didn't want to call me at all.* An ache, throbbing and persistent, began somewhere deep in her chest.

''I want to come along,'' Tessa said firmly.

Corey didn't have a good reason to refuse, because she'd already proven that she wasn't a hindrance to his investigation. After all, she was the one who was paying him. ''Be at my office after dinner. Say about seven o'clock.''

This time, Tessa was the one who hesitated before she spoke. She didn't want Corey to think that she was pursuing him, especially when he had avoided discussing anything personal, but she had to risk it for the sake of his child.

''Why don't we have dinner together?'' she said and then rushed on before he could refuse. ''There's a deli by my place that's open late. I could meet you there at six. I need to talk to you about Maggie, and we can't very well do that with the children underfoot."

"Is it something serious?" Corey's eyebrows rose, and his expression immediately altered from competent business-man to worried father.

"It's nothing that can't wait until tomorrow," Tessa answered, being deliberately evasive because she could hear the children approaching. She turned in their direction, putting her hands on her hips.

"It sure took a long time to get Raggedy Ann," Tessa said. She wasn't angry at Abby, but her frustrating conversation with Corey caused her to sound testy.

"She was lost," Abby said earnestly, her blue eyes large in her small face.

"We had to find her," Maggie added.

That's what I need to remember, Tessa told herself sternly before she ushered Abby and herself away from the father and daughter who already meant far too much to them. *I gave birth to a child and lost her. And now I can't think about losing my heart, because my most important consideration is to find her.*

The Deli, stuck with the most unimaginative name in Oak Haven, was the busiest place in the city when dinner hour rolled around. Businessmen in suits, career women in tailored dresses and friends winding down from a day of shopping or playing all melded together to create a noisy, bustling atmosphere.

Corey and Tessa sat across from each other in a corner of the restaurant, barely speaking. Corey bit into his roast beef sandwich but barely tasted it. He could have insisted they talk in his office, but that would have been even worse. He could deal with uncomfortable silences better than his impulses to reach for her whenever they were alone.

She wore a soft jersey dress of pale purple that hugged her waist and swirled around her hips, and it almost hurt to look at her. Tessa had an innate style that dressed up almost anything she wore, but she looked even better without clothes. Corey watched her pick at her chef's salad, and decided he'd been patient long enough. She had said she wanted to talk about Maggie, and she hadn't even broached the subject.

"If you want to talk about Maggie, I'm ready to listen."

Tessa looked across the table at him, appearing almost startled that he'd said anything at all.

"I did want to talk about her," she said and shrugged her shoulders apologetically. "I'm just not sure that this is the right place."

Immediately he understood that she was concerned that someone dining at the next table might overhear them. He shifted his place setting so that it was adjacent to hers, and moved over a seat. Then he leaned closer and breathed in a floral scent so delicate he couldn't be positive she was wearing perfume.

"Nobody will hear what you say except me."

"Maybe that's what I'm afraid of."

"Come again."

Tessa sighed, wishing he hadn't moved closer but grateful that he had. Thinking clearly with him so close was difficult, but he'd guessed correctly that she didn't want to be overheard.

"I don't want you to think that I'm meddling in your affairs. I wouldn't even mention this, but you seemed so concerned about Maggie the last time we had dinner. I thought that maybe you should know."

"Mention what? Know what?"

"That Maggie asked me about her mother yesterday." Tessa watched Corey process the information and could tell it disturbed him by the set of his mouth.

"Tell me about it."

"I thought she and Abby were napping, but Maggie came out to the den crying. She woke up and thought she was alone. While I was comforting her, she started quizzing me about why Abby had a mommy and she didn't.''

"And what did you say?" Corey's words were clipped, not because he was angry at Tessa but because Maggie's questions were starting sooner than he'd hoped.

"That not every child has two parents and that she was very lucky to have a father who loved her," Tessa said, glossing over the way Maggie had requested that Tessa be her mother.

"Thank you," Corey said sincerely. "It was the best answer you could have given her. You certainly couldn't explain that she has a mother who doesn't care whether she's alive."

Corey lapsed into silence. Maggie would eventually demand to know more about her mother, and he worried about how she would handle the knowledge that Alise hadn't wanted her. But he hoped that confrontation was years away.

He studied Tessa, who seemed even more beautiful now that she had made his problems her own. Her presence in his life presented a problem that was even more pressing than Maggie's questions about Alise.

Maggie was happier than Corey had ever seen her, and that was entirely due to Abby and Tessa. That meant Maggie's happiness was finite, because Tessa had an apartment and a career in another state. How would Maggie handle the pain when they, too, deserted her? How would he?

"It's hard to believe that anyone wouldn't want her," Tessa muttered.

"Oh, Alise doesn't," Corey said, and his laugh wasn't humorous. "If I had any doubts about that, they were cleared up for me yesterday."

Corey paused. He needed to talk about the newest development concerning Alise, and despite everything, he wanted to tell Tessa. Tessa couldn't be trusted, but he didn't doubt that she cared deeply about his daughter. He kept talking.

"I got a letter from Alise saying that she'd met a wealthy man and was moving to Switzerland," Corey said, skimming over the information that his ex-wife had dumped his ex-friend. "It was full of chatty news about herself. She didn't even mention Maggie."

Tessa didn't understand. That was evident in her frown and furrowed brow. Corey didn't completely comprehend it either, but he had learned through painful experience how Alise operated.

"Alise is the type of woman who sets her sights on what she wants and devises a way to get it." Corey paused, again wondering why he was telling her this. "She wanted me a few years back. I'm not sure why, because I didn't have much money. I think it was because I liked to have fun. Back then I rarely stayed home for an evening. I ate dinner out just about every night and then spent the rest of the night drinking, dancing, having fun."

"And after you met Alise, you changed?"

Corey laughed again, a short, harsh sound. "Oh, no. I was never serious about Alise, and she knew it. If she hadn't gotten pregnant, I probably wouldn't even have remembered her name. Even after she got pregnant, I didn't want to have much to do with her. I promised to support her and the child, but I wasn't going to marry her."

"You're not the kind of man who could walk away from that kind of responsibility," Tessa said. It wasn't a question, but a statement.

"I couldn't walk away from my child, so I proposed to Alise," he said, leaving out the fact that he'd done so after Maggie was born. It rankled a little now that the term "illegitimate" could ever have been pinned on Maggie. "Only Alise didn't like the man I'd become. Barely a month after the birth, she wanted to go out dining and dancing and drinking. I wanted to stay home with Maggie."

"What happened?"

"She went out, and I stayed home. And then one day she said she wasn't coming back, and I didn't even care." Corey paused and ran a hand through his thick brown hair. "As long as I had custody of Maggie, what Alise did didn't matter. When we split up, she said Maggie would be better off with me. I've never doubted that was true."

Tessa had stopped eating her salad long ago, and now she pushed the plate away. The thought of eating was as distasteful as Corey's tale about his ex-wife. Maggie would have to know the whole truth eventually, but a three-year-old couldn't possibly understand that kind of rejection. Maybe no child, whatever the age, could.

"There's one thing I don't understand," Tessa said into the silence, knowing she shouldn't ask but not being able to stop herself. "If Alise was so unimportant, why didn't you make sure she didn't get pregnant?"

This time Corey did smile, but his eyes were cooler than the blood that ran through his ex-wife's veins.

"I didn't think I had to, not after she assured me she was taking birth-control pills."

"Wasn't she?"

"Alise never even had a prescription for them. All she was taking was me for a fool." Corey paused significantly. "That's why I can't abide liars."

Chapter 10

Silence reigned during the drive to Suzanna Smith's house, although Tessa would have liked to set things straight. She'd spent her entire adult life living by an unwritten code that had honesty at its base, but she'd been forced to lie to a man who mattered. If it weren't so tragic, it would almost be funny.

Tessa never even told her co-workers that she liked their fresh haircuts or new outfits unless it was the truth. If asked her opinion about something she didn't like, she'd smile and say something innocuous, such as, "It's nice to try something different every once in a while." When Abby was old enough to quiz her about the existence of Santa Claus, Tessa intended to talk about the spirit of Christmas and the wonderful myth of the jolly fat man in the red suit.

But Corey suspected that she was a liar. He hadn't directly said so, but the implication had been clear when he told her about Alise. Tessa wasn't sure what had aroused his suspicions, but she knew they were real. And threatening.

According to the hospital records, only three girls had been born at Oak Haven Hospital during the same period as Abby. By process of elimination, that meant Suzanna Smith was her birth child.

Tessa's heart thudded against her chest, a sensation so shocking that she placed her hand over it until her heartbeat returned to normal. The next hour could be the most significant of her life. She must remain calm enough to keep up the facade about her missing niece. She needed to be the liar Corey suspected she was. If Tessa let anything slip, she risked losing the most important thing in her life.

"Are you going to pose as somebody from the health department this time, too?" Tessa's nerves were stretched so taut it was difficult to form the question, but she forced herself to ask. She needed to know so she wouldn't do or say anything that would jeopardize the investigation.

Corey shook his head, looking at the road instead of at Tessa. "That won't work this time. Oak Haven's not so big of a town that you aren't occasionally asked to investigate people you know."

"You know Suzanna's parents?"

"I've never met her father, but I'm acquainted with her mother. We say hello when we see each other on the street, and she knows I'm a private investigator."

Tessa was dumbstruck. "Then how are we going to pull this off? We can't just tell them the truth."

Especially since I don't know what it is, Corey thought, but refrained from saying the words aloud. He didn't have long to wait for Tessa's lie to blow up in her face. Somehow Suzanna Smith was the key to the mystery of why Tessa was in Oak Haven spinning an outrageous yarn about the child of a dead brother who had never existed.

"Tessa, what you told me was in confidence. Give me a little credit for being discreet."

Tessa sat back in her seat, properly chastised, and didn't speak for a few moments. "What are we going to tell them then?"

"Lynette Smith and her husband both work, so they send Suzanna to a day-care center. I phoned Lynette and told her I was interested in sending Maggie to the same center and wanted to hear her impressions of it. She said I could stop by after she got off work."

"How are we going to explain my presence?"

"You have a daughter, too. It's not much of a stretch for you to say that you're also thinking of sending Abby to the center."

"If she knows you, won't she know you're lying? I mean, doesn't she know about Mrs. Miller?"

"I won't be lying," Corey said, and it struck him again that for a liar she seemed preoccupied with the truth. He pulled the car over to a curb in front of a brick ranch house that looked exactly like a thousand others in western Pennsylvania. "The truth is I am thinking of putting Maggie in day-care."

Truth. There was that word again. "What about Mrs. Miller?"

"I hope she'll still be able to look after Maggie when I need help on evenings and weekends, but I won't need her full-time. Watching Maggie with Abby has convinced me that she needs to be around other kids her age. I don't think a few hours a week at preschool is enough."

"She does cherish her time with Abby," Tessa said reflectively.

"Too much so. When you and Abby leave town, she's going to be devastated. I think that sending her to a day-care center would be the best way to get her to develop other friendships."

No emotion showed behind Corey's words, no hint of what he was thinking. He talked as though their leaving town was an inescapable reality, as though there was no chance they'd decide to stay. And there wasn't, Tessa admitted sadly.

A few days ago, she had found bliss in Corey's arms and fancifully dreamed of a future that included the man and his daughter. But that wasn't possible. Not when every minute she spent in Oak Haven increased the danger to her custody of Abby. Not when Corey acted as though they'd never made love at all. The sooner they left town, the better it would be for everybody.

"Let's get this over with," Tessa said. Her heartbeat had returned to normal, and she was ready to deal with whatever was behind the doors of the innocuous-looking ranch home. Even if it was a child stricken with Cooley's anemia.

The woman who answered the doorbell moments later could have won the Ms. Congeniality award at a beauty pageant. A perky brunette with close-cropped hair, Lynette Smith had an open smile that was all-encompassing. *Great*, Tessa thought as Corey introduced them. *Why do I have to like her? It's just another reason to feel guilty about lying.*

Lynette led them to a family room filled with child's clutter that looked comfortingly familiar. Tessa recognized many of the videos, coloring books and toys as ones that Abby possessed. Missing from the room, however, was any trace of a child.

"Suzanna's class went on a field trip today, and she was so exhausted after dinner that she fell asleep. Bob, my husband, is working late," Lynette supplied, before either of her guests could ask where the rest of the family was. "I'm sure Suzanna will wake up soon, but this is the perfect time to talk. Corey, I've already told you I just adore Suzanna's day-care center. Just ask away."

Swift disappointment coursed through Tessa, and she yearned to break away so that she could look at the sleeping child. Tessa doubted she would glean anything from talking with Lynette. She needed to see Suzanna and study her physical traits. Most of all, she had to look for the

sometimes insidious signs that characterized Cooley's anemia.

"Thanks for agreeing to talk about it," Corey said, addressing Lynette but surreptitiously watching Tessa. Lynette had a gift for welcoming visitors and setting them at
ease, but something was bothering Tessa. Her posture was
rigid, and her palms were pressed tightly together. "I've
heard good things about the Tot Lot all over town, but I've
never had a reason to look into it until now."

Lynette gave Corey a sympathetic look. "Isn't Mrs. Miller
working out?"

"On the contrary, she's fine. It's just that Maggie's kind
of shy, and I think she might benefit from spending her days
with other children instead of an older woman."

Lynette leaned forward in her chair, addressing both of
them, although Corey was the one who had expressed his
concern.

"I know exactly what you mean. A year ago, before I
went back to work full-time, Suzanna was about the most
withdrawn child you'd ever care to meet. I agonized over the
decision to put her in day-care, because I'd heard all sorts
of stories about the home being the best place for a child.
But it was the best thing for her. Suzanna still isn't the most
outgoing of children, but she is happy and well adjusted.
And she has lots of friends."

Lynette smiled at Tessa. "Is your little girl shy, too?"

"Not at all," Tessa said, thinking that Abby was a miniature Lynette when it came to social skills. "But she does
crave the company of other children."

"Don't they all," Lynette said and quickly got to her feet.
"Excuse me for a minute. I think I just heard Suzanna."

"I didn't hear anything," Tessa said as Lynette left the
room.

"I didn't either," Corey said. "But you would have heard
something if it were Abby. You know what they say about
parents being automatically in tune with their own chil-

dren? I've even heard that a mother can pick out her own baby's cry from a dozen others."

Tessa fell silent. If that was true, then this was another dead end. But how could she feel affinity for another child, even a child to whom she'd given birth, when she had Abby? She'd never needed anybody but Abby.

A soft whir invaded Tessa's thoughts, and she couldn't figure out what was making the noise. It sounded like a wheelchair moving across a flat surface. She looked down at the floor and saw that it consisted entirely of tile, without a throw rug in sight. She looked up to see Lynette walking around a corner and pausing, looking expectantly in the direction from which the sound was coming.

A small dark-haired girl in a miniature wheelchair filled the frame of the doorway, and Tessa's hand went to her throat. Tessa had feared that her birth child had a devastating disability, but Suzanna had the wrong impairment.

Cooley's anemia could be a killer, but it didn't put its victims in wheelchairs. It didn't render a child's legs limp and useless.

"Suzanna, this is Mr. McCash and Ms. Daniel," Lynette said brightly, as though nothing out of the ordinary had just happened. "They're here to talk about your school."

Suzanna smiled, and her smile had the same cheery qualities as the woman's next to her. The Smith family might not be blessed with good health, but its members were happy.

"I like school," she said, and then turned to her mom. "Can I color? Please, Mommy."

"Of course you may, Suzanna. Why don't you get your things and color in the kitchen?"

"Okay," Suzanna said and bit her lip as she concentrated on maneuvering her wheelchair. The process was slow and unwieldy, and the wheelchair bumped into the wall a number of times before Suzanna was able to turn it around and head out of the room. Lynette smiled with pride when the child was gone.

"She's had the wheelchair for only a few months, not even long enough for us to get ramps installed. But she's doing better than we'd dared hope. That brings up another point about her day-care center. They don't discriminate. They're just as able to deal with disabled children like Suzanna as they are with able-bodied ones like Maggie."

"What kind of disability does Suzanna have?" Tessa asked. It had never occurred to her that her birth child, if Suzanna were that child, could be stricken with anything other than a blood disease.

"Spina bifida. It's a birth defect in which the spine doesn't fully close," Lynette answered. She sat in a chair opposite Corey and Tessa and smiled her gracious smile once more. "We're luckier than a lot of families, because some children with spina bifida have multiple birth defects."

"I imagine it still must be difficult to live with," Tessa said.

"Actually, it's not. I know that a lot of people are shocked to see a child so small in a wheelchair, and I can understand that. But I've had so long to adjust to Suzanna's disability that I truly don't think of her as disabled anymore. We knew that she was going to have spina bifida when I was only four months along."

"Do you mean when Suzanna was four months old?" asked Tessa.

"Oh, no." Lynette shook her head. "I knew when I was four months pregnant. Tessa, do you remember the Alpha-fetoprotein blood test that you get during pregnancy? Mine came back positive, and subsequent tests showed that Suzanna had spina bifida."

Tessa had been slow to grasp the meaning behind what Lynette Smith was saying, but now she heard the message clearly. Tessa's own AFP test had been normal, which meant that Suzanna Smith couldn't possibly be the child she'd carried in her womb. It meant that Tessa's quest wasn't over.

"It's possible to know that early?" The question came from Corey, who couldn't take his eyes off Tessa. A rainbow of emotions had flickered across her face as she listened to Lynette, but Corey's keen skills of observation hadn't been enough to identify any of them. All he knew for certain was that seeing the disabled little girl had affected Tessa deeply.

"Oh, yes. It was better that way, too," Lynette said. "Because when Suzanna was born, we were fully prepared. Both of you must know that every child is a precious gift. The only true tragedy is losing one."

The sun dipped below the horizon as Tessa and Corey drove away from Lynette's house. Corey thought it was ironic that he now knew all about the day-care center Suzanna attended but was even more in the dark about Tessa's case.

He'd expected something revealing to happen at the Smiths, but Tessa had barely said a word since she'd seen Suzanna. After the child made her appearance and left the room, Corey asked questions about day-care and Lynette answered. He couldn't be sure that Tessa had even listened to anything they'd said.

"We need to talk about the case," Corey said, expecting Tessa to protest. Instead, she nodded and her dark, silky hair rustled about her face.

"I thought we could drop by my office so we can have some privacy," he said, calculating that the need to figure out what was going on was greater than the risk of being alone with her. Tessa nodded again, obviously deeply in thought.

The strip shopping center that contained Corey's office was deserted, a predictable occurrence at this time of night. Although Corey's hours were erratic, none of the other businesses stayed open past five o'clock.

One of the streetlights that illuminated the parking lot had blown out, casting the front of his office in darkness. Corey had drawn the verticals before meeting Tessa for dinner, and the room was black when he opened the door.

He immediately switched on a light, bathing his office in artificial color. He waited for Tessa to precede him and then indicated a leather sofa that was the predecessor of the one in his den.

"Have a seat," he said, trying not to notice how her skirt swirled around her long legs as she walked toward the sofa. She sat down, and in the artificial light her pallor was unnaturally white against the black sofa.

"Are you all right?" Corey asked.

"I'm fine," she said, but she didn't appear fine. Her lips and cheeks, which were usually rosy, looked ashen. Suddenly, at odds with all his principles, Corey was more concerned with what was bothering Tessa than with why she had lied to him.

"Is Suzanna the girl you're looking for? Is that it?"

Corey walked toward her as he asked the question, forgetting his earlier resolve to keep his distance. A coffee table was positioned next to the sofa, and he sat down on it and leaned forward attentively. No more than a dozen inches separated them.

"She can't be the one," Tessa said, shaking her head to emphasize the point. "The child I'm looking for didn't have a birth defect."

"How can you be sure?"

Because I gave birth to a child who didn't have spina bifida, Tessa thought. The question seemed ludicrous until she reminded herself that Corey thought she was searching for somebody else's child. The child she had lost might have been afflicted with a disease even more devastating than Suzanna's problem, but it was an insidious threat, creeping up on the victim in ugly silence.

"I just know," Tessa said, although she realized her explanation was inadequate.

Corey sighed and took her hands in his. They felt cool to the touch, and he rubbed them gently to warm them.

"Help me out here, Tessa. Isn't it possible that the little girl had a birth defect you didn't know about?"

"No," Tessa said, remembering the way the doctor had beamed at her as he pronounced the baby healthy. "She's perfect in every way," he had said.

"Then what's wrong?"

His voice was so gentle that Tessa wanted to cry and let the truth spill forth. But for Abby's sake she couldn't. So how could she explain that seeing wheelchair-bound Suzanna had made her think about children who weren't as lucky as Maggie and Abby? How could she tell him that she feared passing on a disease to an innocent child she never had the chance to protect? She couldn't tell him those things, but she could offer a partial explanation.

"Seeing a child so young sitting in a wheelchair was hard," she said, her voice so low it sounded like a whisper. "I kept thinking how awful it would be if Abby had been born with a problem. Or Maggie."

"But they weren't, and Suzanna's actually quite fortunate," Corey said. "I've seen her before, and she's always seemed like a happy child. A lot of children are in much worse shape than she is."

The child I gave birth to could be one of them, Tessa thought. Even as they spoke, that child could be somewhere suffering. And worse, her doctors might not know exactly what was wrong.

"Why haven't you found her, Corey?" Tessa asked, and he knew at once that she was no longer talking about Suzanna. Tessa closed her eyes, and a tear squeezed out from between her lashes. Corey's heart flipped over violently. "Why wasn't she one of the three girls you investigated?"

"I don't know, Tessa. Perhaps you can tell me." Whenever Corey had envisioned confronting Tessa with her lie, he had boiled with anger. But his voice was soft, even kind.

"I don't know what you're talking about."

"I think you do," Corey said, and he still held her hands. He looked deeply into her wide brown eyes, surprised that he was more interested in knowing the truth so that he could help her than in knowing why she'd lied. "The game's over, Tessa. I know that you never had a brother."

Corey could have sworn that panic glinted in her eyes, but then it vanished as if it had never been. She slipped her hands from his and put them on her lap.

"What game? And how do you know that I don't have a brother?"

"It doesn't matter how I know. What matters is the truth."

"I already told you that," Tessa said, her stomach lurching violently at her initial lie and the ones she would have to tell to cover it. The additional lies that sprang easily to her lips sickened her. "It's true that I don't have a brother by blood, but Steve always felt like one of the family. He lived next door and spent almost all his time at our house. Even my mother thought of him as her own."

Again, some instinct told Corey that Tessa wasn't telling the truth, but he didn't want to heed it. Since he had made love to her, he had thought of little more than that he wanted to do it again. But it was more than that.

Somehow Corey knew that Tessa was beautiful on the inside as well as the outside. He'd seen her interact with her daughter and with his, and telling himself she was a sinner when she acted like a saint was awfully difficult. Corey reached for Tessa's hands again, and she didn't pull them away this time.

"I want to believe you," he whispered.

"Then believe me," Tessa said, hating herself. "Just find that little girl."

"Haven't you figured out yet that I'd do anything for you?"

Tessa closed her eyes again to shut out the honesty in his, and a puddle of tears escaped from her lashes and streamed down her face. Corey brought her hands to his lips and kissed them adoringly while he moved from the coffee table to the sofa. He let go of her hands and gathered her closely as she cried.

"It's true," he said, putting her slightly away from him and gently wiping the still-streaming tears from her face. "I'm either crazy about you or just plain crazy, because I think about you all the time. I can't sleep at night. I can't concentrate during the day. Maggie has to repeat things so often she's starting to think I've lost my mind."

Tessa smiled tremulously, so filled with wonder that she was able to temporarily shove aside the lies she'd told. "Then I've lost my mind, too."

In the instant before he kissed her, Corey smiled so radiantly that Tessa finally knew the truth of how she felt about him. Her life had contained a yawning empty space even before Chris had died, and Tessa finally knew what had been lacking: love.

Not the warm, fuzzy love she felt for her child, but the white-hot passion that flared between a man and a woman who were meant for each other. Even though she'd loved Chris, Tessa had never experienced that. With Corey, there could be no mistake.

Tessa tilted her head to make it easier for his kiss, not caring that they were under fluorescent lights in an office meant for conducting business. She had to seize whatever happiness she could, because it couldn't last. She and Abby would leave Oak Haven soon, and that meant Tessa's time in Corey's arms would be all too brief. She wound her fingers through his thick hair, not wanting to let him go.

Their kiss was fierce, almost desperate. His breath was her breath, and their lips clung as though caught in the force of a magnet. Corey lifted her onto his lap, and she immediately turned her body toward the heat generating from his.

Corey wore a long-sleeved shirt, and Tessa slipped her hand between two of the buttons until one of them popped and gave her access to the hair-roughened plane of his chest. He groaned and impatiently pushed up the material of her dress with one hand so that he could take the same liberties. Her skin was bare under the dress except for slips of material that passed for panties and a bra.

He explored, running his hand over her hips and flat stomach before moving it upward to unfasten her bra. Where she found hair and sinew, he discovered a ripe softness that yielded to his touch. She moaned, and he smiled against her mouth.

"Do you like that?"

"Oh, yes."

"And this?" His other hand slipped inside the waistband of her panties and gently rubbed over her most private part. Hot liquid pooled in Tessa's lower body, and she moaned again.

"Yes," she said, and her breathing was hard. "Oh, yes."

His hands and lips were everywhere, and Tessa squirmed in his lap to allow him better access. Part of her dress was bunched around her throat, and she took her hands from his chest to try to get it out of their way. He helped pull it over her head, and quite suddenly she was gloriously naked in his lap. The blood pounded in his shaft, and his heart pounded for her.

"Touch me, Tessa," he rasped, but she had shifted so that her hand was already working at the zipper on his pants and reaching inside. When she found him, he nearly lost control of himself in her hands. But he wanted this to last, wanted her to experience the same pleasure she gave him.

"You're wearing too many clothes," she said, and Corey laughed delightedly at the frustration in her voice. He knew that she wasn't a woman who said much during lovemaking, so his attempts to pleasure her must be working.

He eased her off his lap, depositing her softly on the couch as he stood and quickly peeled off his clothes. Again, Tessa stared at the magnificence of his body. She hadn't considered the male anatomy beautiful before, but she'd never seen a specimen like Corey in the nude—broad shouldered, lean hipped, long legged and pulsing just for her.

Instead of joining her on the sofa, Corey put out a hand and she took it as trustingly as a child. He pulled her to her feet, and she couldn't resist running her fingers through the sparse hair on his chest. Before Tessa could wonder at what he was doing, he stretched out on the sofa and pulled her on top of him so that every inch of their bodies touched.

"Is this better?" he drawled, cupping her buttocks and moving her lower body against his. Tessa could only nod before hungrily meeting his waiting mouth. She wanted to go on kissing him, tasting the passion between them, but he broke off the kiss and slid her up his body until her breast was at his mouth.

His tongue circled her aureola, teasing and tasting, until her nipples grew hard and she made sensual, throaty sounds that said nothing but told everything. Corey slid her back down his body and reached for his pants, quickly extracting his wallet and one of the packets that were becoming so familiar.

Tessa almost protested that she wanted nothing, not even a sheer sheath of latex, to come between them, but kept silent. She moved to the side so that he could slip on the protection, understanding why he did so and trying not to think of how wonderful it would be to have his seed growing inside her.

She had only seconds to regret what could have been before he maneuvered her atop him so that their pelvises were even. Heat once again saturated her so that nothing mattered except making love with the man she loved.

"Do you want me?" Corey asked, needing to hear the words.

"I want you," Tessa said and lent credence to her proclamation by raising her hips and reaching for him. She guided him inside her on a slippery, white-hot path and started to rock against him.

Further inflamed by her boldness, Corey met her every movement, thrusting deep inside her and wanting to go even deeper. He wanted to lose himself in her, half admitting that he already had.

Tessa answered Corey's every motion, not pausing to reconsider her forwardness because she had acted the only way she could have. Her body's responses to his were pure, natural and entirely uncontrollable.

Billow after billow of sensation built in her until a powerful surge that was almost too much to bear swept through her. Corey cried out at the same time, and he seemed to be swelling inside her.

They shuddered against each other again and again, powerless to stop what was happening to them. When the volcano of feeling had finally subsided, neither of them moved. Corey's arms came around her, holding her there, and she didn't have the strength to tell him that she didn't want to go anywhere. Seconds passed, then minutes, before either of them tried to speak. Then they did so together.

"I shouldn't have acted—"

"I don't want you to think—"

They both stopped in the midst of speaking their thoughts, and Corey smiled against her hair. Even though their lovemaking had come to its inevitable end and he was no longer hard, he still enjoyed being inside her.

"You first," he said.

"I don't want you to think I always act this way," Tessa said, suddenly concerned. She wasn't ashamed of what had ust happened, but she couldn't bear it if he got the wrong mpression. Aside from Chris, Corey was the only man with vhom she had ever made love.

"I didn't think that. Not even for a minute."

"Actually, I've never acted this way before."

"I know that, too."

She kissed his chest, drawing little circles on it with her ongue. He ran his hands down her back, lingering at the :urve of her hips and caressing her buttocks. Tessa would aave sworn that her reservoir of sexual feeling was de-pleted, but sensation danced on her skin.

"Your turn," she said. "To talk."

"I shouldn't have acted as though the last time we made ove didn't matter," Corey said, and his hands didn't halt in their exploration. In answer, she moved her fingers up and down the sides of his body and down his legs. "It mat-ered. So much that all I could think about was doing it again."

She moved her pelvis in little pumping motions against his until she felt him growing hard inside her.

"Is that what you're thinking about right now?"

"Witch," he said, but his voice was anything but dis-pleased. "How can I want you again so soon?"

"Don't ask. Just love me."

Their second climax, although not as shattering as the first, was like a drug-induced haze. Each of them felt as though they had overdosed, yet couldn't wait until they re-covered enough to do it again. They might have, had Corey's eyes, when he was strong enough to open them, not caught a glimpse of Maggie's picture on his desk.

"Uh-oh," he said, and Tessa finally moved so that he slipped from the warm cocoon where he already wanted to be again. She scooted away from him and sat up. He fol-lowed suit.

"What's wrong?" she asked.

Corey grabbed her hand, not wanting to break contact altogether. "I promised Maggie I'd be home in time to tuck her in tonight, and now it looks as though I might not make it."

Tessa glanced at her watch and saw that it wasn't yet nine thirty. "Maybe you can still make it if we hurry."

"You wouldn't mind?"

"Do you think it's comfortable sitting naked on this leather sofa?" she teased. "Of course I won't mind. I already missed Abby's bedtime, or I might rush home to do the same thing."

"Thanks." He smiled and gathered his discarded clothing. Tessa did the same. "I'm already in the dog house with Maggie, and this would shove me in even deeper."

"Why is she upset with you?" Tessa asked as she wriggled into her panties. Corey squashed a powerful urge to reach for her and caress the satiny skin that was still exposed.

His smile was self-deprecating. "The circus is in a neighboring town, and her preschool class is going. Parents are invited, but I can't go because I have an important meeting with the head of the largest and most prestigious corporation in Oak Haven to discuss revamping his security. Maggie can't understand why a meeting I've tried to set up for two months is more important than the circus."

"So she's going without you?"

"There's the rub," Corey said as he fastened the last of the buttons on his shirt. "She can be pretty stubborn sometimes. She says that if I won't go, she won't go, either."

"Ouch." Tessa was fully dressed, and she ran a hand through her hair to try to restore order. When the idea struck her, it seemed so ideal that she put a hand on Corey's arm. "What if Abby and I go with her? If she has us, then she won't feel left out. And we'd love to do it. That is, if you don't mind."

A part of Corey did mind, but it was the selfish little portion that didn't want his daughter to become too attached to another adult. But who was he to keep Maggie away from Tessa when he couldn't stay away from her himself?

"The circus isn't until two o'clock. I'll call her preschool teacher in the morning and make sure she doesn't mind if you go."

Tessa smiled up at him, and he didn't try to ignore the impulse to kiss her. Their lips clung, and he touched her mouth when they drew apart. She puckered her lips so that they kissed his fingers, and her eyes grew solemn.

She had been wonderfully sidetracked and didn't regret the last hour, but the reason she was in Oak Haven with this man still remained. She couldn't leave his office without touching on the subject one more time.

"Do you think you can find her, Corey? Will you try?"

"I already told you that I'd do anything for you," he said, and even though she returned his smile Corey had the strangest sensation that they were treacherously close to a precipice and one of them was going to fall. But then he'd already fallen hard. For her.

Chapter 11

The smells of sugar and freshly made dough assaulted Tessa's nostrils as Mary Moriarty let her in the front door of her home. Little touches like this, Tessa thought, were the kinds of things that made a house a home. Already the rooms she shared with Abby felt like home. Her apartment in Virginia, which she'd never regarded as much more than a temporary stopping point, seemed very far away.

"Let's see if I can guess what you made this time," Tessa said, smiling at her landlady. "Doughnuts?"

Mrs. Moriarty chuckled. "You have a wonderful sense of smell. Would you like to try one?"

"Do you mean that Abby hasn't finished them off yet?"

"Good heavens, no." Mrs. Moriarty feigned insult. "I have more sense than to let a child gorge on treats before bed time. I think she only had two. Or maybe three."

Tessa laughed again, because nothing was going to spoil her mood. She didn't approve of Abby eating so many sweets, but Mrs. Moriarty was like an indulgent grand-mother whose feelings would be hurt if she was repri-

manded. Besides, Abby needed a grandmother figure more
than restrictions on what she could eat.

"Is she asleep?" Tessa asked as she followed Mrs.
Moriarty to the bright, clean kitchen. Tessa had come
through the front door and avoided using her private entrance so that she wouldn't awaken Abby.

Mrs. Moriarty nodded. "She wanted to wait up for you,
but I promised her an extra bedtime story if she'd go to
sleep. I put her down about forty-five minutes ago."

"Did she behave?"

"Of course she did." Mrs. Moriarty's tone was matter-of-
fact, but Tessa suspected that her landlady wouldn't tell her
even if Abby had acted up. "And don't start thanking me
again for watching her. You know there are few things I'd
rather do."

"I know we're lucky to have you around." Tessa sat down
on one of the kitchen chairs as the older woman got out a
doughnut and poured a glass of milk. Tessa wouldn't have
chosen to drink milk with the doughnut, but the flavors
melded perfectly. Caring for Abby and watching over a
roomful of preadolescents was standard fare for Tessa, and
having someone cater to her felt heavenly.

Tessa bit into the treat, leaving traces of powdered sugar
around her mouth. "This is delicious."

Mrs. Moriarty, a doughnut in hand, nodded her thanks
and sat down next to Tessa. The lines in her face grew more
pronounced as she regarded her tenant.

"Did you have a good time tonight?"

"A wonderful time," Tessa answered, smiling. The
question brought to mind Corey's touch, and the tenderness on her face was palpable. For the first time in a long
while she was happy, and she didn't care who knew it.

"Did you know that I baby-sat him when he was a boy?"

"He told me," Tessa said, nodding. She hadn't revealed
that she'd been with Corey, but somehow Mrs. Moriarty
had known. Tessa supposed that Oak Haven was like any

smallish town in that news traveled fast among people who had known each other for a long time. She wondered if one of Mrs. Moriarty's friends had seen her with Corey or if Abby had mentioned his name.

"I used to dread going to his house," Mrs. Moriarty said, raising her eyes in mock horror. "I even raised my baby-sitting fee a few times, hoping that his mother would refuse to pay it. But she always did. I've never wondered why she had only one child."

"He was that bad?"

"Not bad. Mischievous." Mrs. Moriarty tried to put her memories into words. "He liked to have fun, that one. He'd do things like jump into a mud puddle, run into the house and plop himself down on the sofa to watch TV. Or throw a baseball through a neighbor's window. He was always getting into trouble."

"He's changed," Tessa said, wondering what Mrs. Moriarty was getting at. She had difficulty believing that her landlady had brought up Corey's name solely to rehash his childish escapades. "You couldn't find a better man."

"Maybe you should start looking for one."

"Excuse me?" Tessa wasn't sure she had heard Mrs. Moriarty correctly.

The older woman ignored Tessa's question in favor of one of her own. "Do you know that Mrs. Miller and I are friends? She just telephoned a few hours ago."

"To talk about me?" Tessa was aghast.

"Not exactly, but your name did come up." Mrs. Moriarty paused, as though she was thinking about what words to use. "She's worried that you're becoming too attached to Corey and Maggie. At first she thought you were the right woman for him. She still does, but she's afraid he's going to hurt you."

"That's none of her concern," Tessa said, her ire rising at the thought of the two older women meddling into her affairs. She should have stopped the conversation immedi-

ately when she saw the direction it was taking. "It's none of
yours, either."

Mrs. Moriarty held up a hand in apology, but she didn't
stop talking. "I'm sorry, Tessa. But believe me, I have a
good reason for bringing this up."

"Which is?" Tessa's words were clipped.

"Abby. She talked an awful lot about Corey and Maggie
today. I'm afraid that she's gotten quite attached to them."

"She's attached to you, too."

"In a different way."

"Why are you telling me this, Mrs. Moriarty?" Her
landlady was a kind woman, who Tessa suspected normally
shied away from idle gossip.

"Do you know about Alise?"

Tessa nodded, feeling vaguely guilty for discussing
Corey's personal business behind his back. Although her
landlady probably couldn't reveal anything she didn't already know, Tessa couldn't seem to move from her seat.

"Then you know that he married her because she got
pregnant. Did you also know that Alise had an affair with
Corey's best friend?" She paused, waiting for the shock to
register on Tessa's face. "No? I didn't think so."

"What's the point of this, Mrs. Moriarty?" Tessa repeated when she had regained her composure. The new
morsel of information was disturbing. Compounded with
the fact that Alise had lied to him at every turn, no wonder
Corey had such a hard time trusting anyone.

"I just don't want you or Abby to get hurt, dear. Mrs.
Miller said that Corey has repeated over and over that he'll
never get seriously involved with a woman again. I just
wanted you to know the score."

Deep down, Tessa knew that Corey's inability to make a
commitment didn't affect her. As soon as she found her
birth child, she and Abby would head back to Virginia. But
it hurt to hear someone else tell her she didn't stand a chance
with the man she loved.

"I already know the score, Mrs. Moriarty," Tessa said. She had finished her treat, and she stood up. "Now if you'll excuse me, I'm going to turn in for the night. Thank you for the milk and doughnut."

Minutes later, Tessa opened the adjoining door to the bedroom she shared with Abby and shut it softly. Her conversation with Mrs. Moriarty had been troubling. Tessa already knew that leaving the McCashes would create an irreparable hole in her heart, but had she allowed her daughter to become similarly attached to the pair?

"Mommy?" A small voice sounded in the darkness.

"Abby. I thought you'd be asleep by now," Tessa said, crossing the room and sitting on the edge of her daughter's bed. A bed sheet decorated with Minnie Mouse and pink polka dots was tucked around Abby's chin.

"Not tired," Abby said sleepily. "Were you with Corey?"

"Yes, I was."

"Did you kiss him?"

Did I kiss him? Tessa puzzled over how to answer the question, but she couldn't get past the fact that her daughter had asked it. It seemed far too early in Abby's childhood to discuss anything remotely dealing with sex.

"Why do you ask?"

Abby yawned. "Because mommies and daddies kiss."

"That's when they're married to each other, honey. Corey and I aren't married. I'm your mommy, and Corey is Maggie's daddy."

"Can't a mommy and daddy who aren't married kiss?"

"Well, yes. If they're not married to anyone else."

Abby fell silent for a moment, and Tessa had the odd sensation that the child had proven her point. But could a three-year-old be that sophisticated? Abby's next question took her mind off the dilemma.

"Where's my daddy?"

Tessa expelled a long breath. She wondered if Abby and Maggie had been discussing their parentage. A few days ago,

Maggie had asked about her mother. Now Abby was asking about her father.

"We've talked about this before, sweetheart. Your daddy had to go away. He didn't want to, because he loved you very much. But he had to."

"I'd like to have a daddy again." The yearning in her voice was palpable.

"I know, honey."

"Do you think Corey would be my daddy?" Abby sat up in bed, as though the thought was too much to take lying down.

The conversation with Mrs. Moriarty suddenly took on a new light and Tessa wondered if she had been negligent. Instead of protecting Abby from the heartaches of life, Tessa had set her up for a major disappointment that would hit hard when they left Oak Haven.

"He couldn't be your daddy unless I married him."

"Then marry him," Abby said sleepily, wrapping her arms around Tessa's neck and planting a soft kiss on her cheek. As always, a surge of love swept through Tessa. She gently laid Abby back on the bed, and the little girl rubbed her eyes. The night-light gave the room a faint glow. "Maggie said we'd be sisters if you married Corey. She's my bestest friend in the whole world."

Abby's eyes fluttered and then closed, but she kept talking even though she was on the verge of sleep. "I love them, you know."

Out of the mouths of babes, Tessa thought as she watched Abby drift off to sleep. Love acted in funny ways, creeping up on you when you least expected it and gripping so hard you couldn't let it go. Tessa knew about that kind of love, and now Abby knew too. She planted a kiss on her fingertips and gently deposited it upon Abby's cheek.

The circus had ended more than an hour ago, but it still lived in the minds of the children in Mrs. Arnold's preschool. They chattered nonstop about the clowns, elephants and acrobats during the hour's bus drive back from Crest Ridge.

The trip reminded Tessa that she'd spent far too little time on having fun. Not that she'd relaxed much at the circus. While the children delighted in the antics of the performers, Tessa carefully examined each little girl on the chance that one was her missing child. She'd even briefly considered asking the girls their birth dates. If she hadn't known Maggie was born in Philadelphia, she probably would have deemed Maggie a candidate, too.

The large yellow school bus pulled into the parking lot adjacent to the Oak Haven preschool, and Maggie tugged on Tessa's sleeve.

"Wanna see my preschool?" she asked so timidly it was as though she expected the answer to be negative. "My pictures are on the wall."

Tessa couldn't have dashed the hope on Maggie's small face even if she had been in a hurry to get someplace. "Sure, honey. We'd love to see them. Wouldn't we, Abby?"

Abby, who had been staring out the bus window, smiled and nodded. Tessa was quite sure she had no idea what they were talking about.

Minutes later, the three of them stood next to a wall of "artwork" in the building that housed Maggie's preschool.

"I didn't know you could draw so well," Tessa exclaimed enthusiastically over a self-portrait that was missing a mouth, torso and legs.

"Wait'll you see this one," Maggie said, tugging at Tessa's hand to propel her in another direction. This time she indicated a rough coloring of a purple pig. At least Tessa thought it was a pig.

"That's great, Maggie," Tessa said, mussing her hair affectionately. "This sure must be a fun place to come to school."

"Uh-huh," Maggie said, and dropped Tessa's hand in favor of Abby's. "Wanna see the gerbils, Abby?"

The girls shot off in the direction of a pair of caged rodents before Tessa could say it was time to leave. But she didn't truly mind lingering, because Maggie was taking such joy in sharing her school.

"I'm so glad you could come," said a voice directly behind her, and Tessa turned to see Mrs. Arnold walking toward her. A small, thin woman in her twenties, Mrs. Arnold had nondescript features enhanced by a pair of luminous green eyes. The teacher had been too busy up to this point to speak more than a few words to Tessa.

"I am, too. I was just thinking how well Maggie seems to be doing. She's certainly taking great pride in the things she's accomplished here. You must be a very good teacher."

"Thank you for the compliment," Mrs. Arnold said, but then her expression grew troubled. "But to be honest, this is the first time I've gotten any inkling that Maggie enjoys preschool."

"Maggie's a bit of an introvert," Tessa said, touched by the woman's concern. Maggie wasn't her daughter or her responsibility, but somehow it felt right to be discussing her as though she was. Was that because Tessa was in love with Maggie's father?

"Don't we know it, but I was encouraged by her behavior today. Her friend is quite an outgoing child, and because of that I noticed Maggie interacting with many more children than she usually does."

"Yes, Abby's quite the extrovert. To state the obvious, she really enjoyed the circus. I should thank you again for letting us tag along."

"Don't be silly." Mrs. Arnold dismissed her thanks with a wave of the hand. "An extra child doesn't make much difference when you already have a dozen, and you're welcome anytime. I can't tell you how glad I am that you've finally come home."

"Excuse me?"

Mrs. Arnold continued talking as though she hadn't heard Tessa's question. "If ever I saw a girl who needs her mother, it's Maggie. Corey worries so much about her social skills and her moods, but I'm sure those problems will disappear now that you're home. There's nothing like a mother to make a child feel secure."

"But I'm not Maggie's mother," Tessa said, shocked that the teacher had jumped to that conclusion.

"Excuse me?" Now it was Mrs. Arnold's turn to look confused. "Aren't you Alise?"

"No." Tessa shook her head emphatically. "I'm Tessa Daniel, a friend of the family. Didn't Corey tell you that over the phone?"

"Well, no, I don't think he did." Mrs. Arnold's face was the shade of her pink lipstick and getting more pink by the minute. "He said that Maggie would be going to the circus after all and that I should count on another mother and a child. When I saw you, I just assumed . . ."

"You assumed incorrectly."

"I know that now. I'm so sorry."

"I'm sorry, too," Tessa said, turning at the sound of footsteps rushing toward them. The feet belonged to Maggie and Abby. "Believe me, I'd be thrilled if both of these girls were mine, but I have only one daughter."

"Tessa," Maggie yelled, coming to such an abrupt stop she almost toppled over. Tessa put out a hand to steady her. "We got an idea."

Tessa smiled. Maggie was forever announcing that she had an idea, and she knew the correct response from watching her with Corey.

"What's your idea about?" Tessa asked obligingly.

"It's about finding Daddy and eating pizza," Maggie announced, and Abby nodded vigorously. "Don't you 'member? When we had pizza, you said we could have a rain hat."

"Rain check," Tessa said, laughing. She turned to Mrs. Arnold, who was looking at them curiously. "I said we'd take a rain check."

"Please, Mommy, let's take the rain hat," Abby said, and Tessa didn't bother correcting her. The thought of taking a rain hat with Corey held a delicious charm. Even after last night's conversation with Mrs. Moriarty.

Tessa couldn't worry that the bonds she and Abby had formed with the McCashes were too strong. Chris's death had taught Tessa to enjoy her time on earth, because it could end at any time. While in Oak Haven, they would enjoy the time they spent with Corey and Maggie. When the time came to leave, they'd cherish the memories.

Tessa looked at her watch, saw that it was almost six o'clock and grabbed each little girl by the hand. "Tell you what. Let's go to Maggie's house. If Corey's there, we'll ask him about the rain hat."

A chorus of hurrays greeted her pronouncement. Mrs. Arnold looked on approvingly, her mouth creased in a smile, her green eyes shining.

"'Bye, Mrs. Arnold," Maggie called.

"'Bye," Abby added.

Tessa smiled at the teacher over the children's heads, and paused when Mrs. Arnold spoke.

"It doesn't really matter who you are, Tessa, because you're exactly what Maggie needs," she said. "And I imagine the same goes for her father."

Maggie giggled wildly at something Abby whispered in her ear, and Abby joined her laughter until they sounded like candidates for the laugh track of a television sitcom. Corey exchanged a puzzled look with Tessa and shrugged; he didn't have any more insight into what they were talking about than she did.

"I'm starting to forget I ever thought Maggie was shy," Corey said, and the undercurrent of worry Tessa had detected whenever he talked about his daughter was gone.

They sat in a booth at the only pizza parlor in Oak Haven that boasted genuine Italian owners. The town had the usual chain outlets, but Corey preferred authenticity to fast food. The parlor was crowded, the lights were dim and Tessa was just inches away on the same bench seat he occupied. Her nearness brought to the surface erotic memories he struggled to eradicate, because their daughters were with them. The girls, who had insisted on sitting next to each other, let out another peal of laughter.

"That's because she isn't shy anymore," Tessa said, not worrying about whether the girls heard her. They were in their own little world, and for the moment it didn't include adults.

"At least not around you and Abby."

"She wasn't shy around the preschool kids at the circus today, either. Mrs. Arnold even remarked upon it. She said it was the first time she got the impression that Maggie enjoyed preschool."

Corey studied Maggie from across the table. The sight of her was familiar, yet he could pinpoint distinct differences. Her dark hair and small features were the same, but her face was stamped with a radiance that hadn't been there a month before.

Why had he ever thought a relationship with Tessa and her daughter would harm Maggie? Why had he imagined that the closer Maggie got to Tessa, the farther she would stray from him? The Daniels had been good for Maggie— they had been good for him.

"That's good news." He slanted a look at Maggie to make sure she wasn't listening, but her dark head was huddled close to Abby's lighter one. "Sometimes I question whether I'm doing the right thing by taking her to preschool when she says she doesn't want to go. I hope she acts the same way around the other children when you and Abby aren't around."

"You know, I think she will," Tessa said, voicing what had been only an abstract thought until that moment. "Now that she's out of her shell, I don't think she'll ever want to go all the way back in. Granted, Abby was the one who started talking to the other kids today. But Maggie didn't hesitate to join in."

"Then that's one less thing to worry about."

Tessa immediately sensed that something wasn't quite right and guessed it had to do with his appointment that afternoon. "Does that mean you didn't get the security contract?"

"Actually, I did get it," Corey said, glad to have someone who would listen to him. Maggie was great company, but she couldn't discuss anything more complicated than what Big Bird had said on Sesame Street that morning. "It's just that they want me to take a hands-on approach to implementing the new security system. They even want me to stick around for a few months after it's in place. If I agree, I'd be developing a reputation as a corporate-security specialist."

Tessa remembered other corporate-security jobs he'd discussed, and she tilted her head as she considered him. "Haven't you been moving in that direction anyway? I got the impression that you wanted to keep your evening hours free for Maggie."

Corey gave her a half grin. She was even more perceptive than beautiful, and he couldn't think of a thing wrong with the way she looked. He even liked the dip her nose took and the way the few extra pounds she didn't want rounded her figure.

"You're right, but I didn't think it would happen quite this quickly. Corporate security is lucrative, but there's more excitement during a slow day at Maggie's preschool. I'm not sure I want to give up the investigative part of the business.''

''Then don't,'' Tessa said firmly. ''Make corporate security your bread-and-butter, but keep your options open so you can take an occasional case. That way, you can work only on cases that really interest you.''

''Like yours?''

''Yes, like mine.'' At the mention of her case, Tessa's voice lowered and the worry that was never far from the surface showed in the faint lines around her mouth. Again, Corey was left with the impression that finding the missing girl was of vital importance. Again, he suspected that Tessa hadn't told him the whole story.

''You give excellent advice,'' Corey said, ignoring his hunches and keeping to their discussion of corporate security, ''and I'm going to follow it. As soon as I solve your case. I told my new clients that I wouldn't be available until I finished what I was working on.''

''Thank you,'' Tessa said and squeezed one of his hands in appreciation. He turned his over so that their palms touched, and Tessa felt as though their hearts were also connected when she looked into the blue eyes that had become so familiar.

''Hurray, pizza!'' Abby's shrill pronouncement and the arrival of a waiter broke the tender mood. Small hands claimed individual pieces, and Corey laughingly poured soda from a pitcher into four glasses.

A half hour later, full of pizza and soda, Tessa and Corey sat in their booth and watched their daughters with amusement. The girls pumped quarters into a video machine, valiantly trying to play a game designed for children years older.

''They'll never figure it out,'' Corey observed. He draped his arm over the back of the booth, and his fingers idly played with her shoulder.

''You didn't have to give them the quarters.''

"What?" he asked in mock horror. "And miss this show? Look how they're giggling. I bet nobody who ever played that game had more fun than those two."

"Chris and I used to go out for pizza and play video games all the time before Abby was born," Tessa said, and she was barely aware that she had voiced the thought until he commented upon it.

"Do you still miss him?"

He asked the question as though he really didn't want to hear the answer, as though he was afraid of what it might be. But Tessa was no longer afraid to confront the past. She wiggled her ring finger, drawing Corey's attention to the faint white line that told of a bond he feared hadn't yet been broken.

"I finally took off my wedding ring."

"I noticed," Corey said, neglecting to add that he'd been watching her finger for days and could pinpoint the night she'd removed the ring. "But that doesn't mean you don't miss him."

"I think I'll always miss him, but not in the way you mean," Tessa said, her voice contemplative. Discussing Chris with the man she loved was odd, because she'd also loved Chris. Only now it felt as though a girl had loved Chris, while a woman loved Corey. "I was finally able to admit to myself that I never should have married him, but I'll always be glad that I did because he gave me a child."

"Did you love him very much?" The surge of jealousy was so strong Corey experienced a physical jolt. He gave himself a mental one, because it was foolish to be jealous of a dead man.

Tessa was silent for a moment. She'd come to terms with the truth, but she hadn't shared it with anyone else. She'd thought she never would, but she felt compelled to explain how she felt to Corey, if only to wipe the concern off his face.

"I was too young to know the difference when I married Chris, but I loved him like you love a friend. Not the way you should love a husband," Tessa said. *Not the way I love you,* she added silently, and the words were in her eyes even though they didn't touch her lips.

"Mommy!"

"Daddy!"

The shrill summons from their children snapped the invisible connection that held Corey and Tessa together, and they looked toward their daughters. Maggie and Abby, their supply of quarters apparently exhausted, hurried back to the booth. Tessa stifled an urge to scold them for running in the restaurant. She didn't want anything to spoil this moment, especially since she didn't know how many more she and Abby had left to spend with Corey and Maggie.

"I won," Abby said, beaming.

"We both won," Maggie corrected.

Corey was sitting toward the outside of the booth, and both girls crawled into his lap. Laughing, he balanced them so that neither would slide to the floor. He resembled a boy himself, with his brown-gold hair tousled and his blue eyes sparkling from the wide smile that creased his face.

"Don't you think you girls are a little heavy?" he asked, feigning a protest.

"No," they shouted in chorus, and Corey's deep, rich laughter mingled with their high-pitched giggles.

Tessa watched them, her smile tinged with sadness. For the first time since Chris had died, Tessa felt as though she and Abby belonged somewhere. Corey and Maggie were the missing links in their lives, and anyone looking at the four of them would think they were one big happy family. But it could all end as soon as tomorrow.

Corey was a top-notch investigator, and solving her case wouldn't take him much longer. Tessa memorized the sight of Corey and the girls laughing sheerly from the pleasure of being together and tucked it away. She'd need her memories for the empty years ahead of her. As soon as Corey found her birth daughter, Oak Haven would no longer be a safe haven.

Chapter 12

Something doesn't add up, Corey thought as he tossed a pile of records onto the stack in front of him. Weak sunlight filtered through the verticals of his office windows, telling him it had been hours since he started searching for clues in the birth records.

Each of the three girls he had investigated had a separate cache of paperwork. It included newborn identification sheets, pediatricians' notes, laboratory results, nursery observation records and much, much more. Not a line of it gave Corey any indication that he was on the right track.

He stood abruptly and stretched his long arms overhead. For the first time, he wished he hadn't taken Tessa's case. Something precious had started between them, and it was strong enough to stamp out the burning anger that had lived in him since Alise had left. But he feared it wouldn't be strong enough to survive the truth behind Tessa's secrets.

Corey rubbed his brow; the puzzle only made sense if Tessa was holding back a vital morsel of information. Otherwise, Corey would have solved the case days ago. The irony was that Corey no longer cared about the mystery surrounding Tessa—he cared about her.

He would have liked to turn the case over to another private investigator, but Tessa had looked at him with pleading eyes and trembling lips and asked him to find the child. Corey never backed down on a promise, especially not to someone like Tessa.

The phone rang, and Corey's large hand pounced on the receiver. He'd welcome a respite, however short, from thinking about the convoluted case of the missing child.

"McCash here."

"Corey." His name on her lips sounded like a caress, and he imagined her fingers running over his skin. "It's Tessa."

"Tessa." Her name came out on a sigh of frustration, and Corey wasn't sure if that was because of her case or her absence. "I was just thinking about you."

"Normally I'd consider that a compliment, but you don't sound pleased. What kind of things were you thinking?"

Corey laughed, and the sound was rich and warm. "I should have said I was just thinking about your case. If I had been thinking about you and me, I definitely would have sounded happy. Either that, or frustrated because you're not within touching distance."

She returned his laughter, and the sense of foreboding Corey had been experiencing lifted slightly but didn't dissipate. "You'll have plenty of opportunities to touch me."

"I'll take that as a promise."

He could almost see her blushing at the other end of the line, and the thought pleased him. Tessa Daniel had been married and had borne a child, but she wasn't a woman who entered a relationship with a man lightly. That she had singled him out made him feel special.

"Isn't the case going well?"

"No," Corey said, aware that she had deliberately changed the subject when the conversation became intimate. He didn't bother to hide the truth or his frustration.

"I can't figure out why I haven't solved it yet. One of those three girls should have been the one you're looking for."

"But none of them was. I'm positive of that, Corey."

Corey sighed. They were back to square one, and he wasn't sure which direction to take next.

"Are you sure you've told me everything?" He asked the question as gently as possible and hoped that this time the answer would be different. He waited for the pause he had come to expect, but Tessa didn't hesitate before she answered.

"I'm sure," she said. "Maybe the records you have aren't complete."

"I've already thought of that, but my contact at the hospital swears he gave me everything."

"Then he must be wrong," Tessa said, and there was conviction in her voice. "There has to be another child, Corey. There just has to."

"You may be right," Corey said, although he wasn't sure what he believed anymore in relation to her case. He wasn't getting anywhere, either in her case or in this conversation. He decided to change the subject. "I hope you didn't call just to talk about your case."

"Actually, I didn't." He heard the smile in her voice, but her explanation wasn't what he expected to hear. "I called about Maggie. The movie theater is having a matinee showing of *Bambi* that starts in about an hour. If it's okay with you, Abby and I would like to take her along."

"Sure. Just give Mrs. Miller a call and tell her I said it would be all right," Corey said without hesitation. He glanced at his watch, angling for a way to work himself into her plans. "I'll be ready to call it a day at about the time the movie ends, so why don't I meet you at my house?"

"That sounds great. I'll be looking forward to it."

"Not as much as I will."

After replacing the receiver, Corey sank back into his chair. The conversation had given him something to look forward to, but it hadn't lightened his spirits or lifted his dilemma. He was a respected investigator who was stumped by a case that should have taken him a few days to solve.

He had a sudden flash of the way Tessa, gloriously naked and flushed from their lovemaking, had looked on his leather sofa just the other night, and he knew why the case had stymied him. He had violated an unwritten rule of every investigator in the land: Don't get involved with your client. Only he had shattered the rule into a million pieces by falling in love.

Love. The word frightened him more than the two former football linemen who had come up on him from behind one night while he was a policeman on patrol. He had escaped and eventually arrested them, but he couldn't escape this.

The feeling was overwhelming, possibly because Corey hadn't experienced it before. Oh, he'd had the usual infatuations when he'd been a teenager and then a college student. And he'd been attracted to a fair number of women in the years since, but Corey had reached the age of thirty-two with his heart relatively unscathed.

Love had a funny way of creeping up on him. It had happened almost the same way with Maggie when he'd seen her in the hospital nursery. He hadn't particularly wanted a daughter then, just as he didn't want a relationship now. But wham. When the feeling hit, it hit hard.

Love hadn't struck when he'd met Alise, even though at one time he'd certainly desired her. What he felt for Tessa was different, unique. It was as though he was standing under a waterfall and his emotions were cascading over him.

The sensation wasn't comforting, especially since it had blinded his judgment. He'd known from the first that the way to solve Tessa's case was by locating the mother, not the child. When Tessa had revised her story and told him that "Steve" was a close friend instead of a relative, he should have asked his surname. With that information, he could have gotten Mike Turner to run another background check and possibly come up with a marriage license containing Bunny's real name.

But Corey hadn't asked Steve's surname, because he already knew what Mike would turn up: nothing. Corey didn't want to believe it, but he was quite certain that Steve didn't exist. Bunny probably didn't, either. So he was stuck with a pile of birth records and the nagging feeling that he was missing something obvious.

The private investigator in him knew that Tessa was holding something vital back. He knew it, but he didn't want to accept it. Just days ago Corey had spoken of trust and truth, and she had reiterated the story about the "brother" she'd loved, lost and wanted to find again in his child. Just moments ago over the telephone, she had insisted that she'd told him the entire truth.

An idea crystallized in Corey's mind, one that had nudged him before. This time, however, he wasn't able to dismiss it before it infiltrated his consciousness. If Tessa was lying, there was a way to find out. Corey determinedly flipped through some papers sitting atop his desk until he came to a sheet listing a name and address that Mike Turner had provided. Corey picked up the telephone and dialed before he could reconsider his actions.

"What city, please?" The impersonal voice of the operator came over the line.

"Richmond. I'd like the number of a Mrs. Teresa Hutton. She lives at 513 Willow Lane."

A moment later, Corey stared down at the scribbled telephone number that would link him to Tessa's mother. Until he solved Tessa's case, he was stuck in a limbo from which there was no escape—unable to start another job, unable to plan for a future with a woman who could be playing him for a fool. He picked up the phone and dialed before he could have second thoughts.

By the fifth ring, Corey was tempted to replace the receiver. Maybe fate had intervened, decreeing that he leave well enough alone. He could take another route to solve Tessa's case, bypassing the family members who could tell him if a "brother" named Steve had ever existed. The phone rang for a sixth time, but a familiar voice answered before Corey could hang up.

"Hello." It was a lilting sound, at once reminiscent of Tessa. Corey was momentarily speechless, and the woman repeated the greeting. "Hello?"

"Could I please speak to Mrs. Hutton?"

"She can't come to the phone right now. This is her daughter. Can I help you?"

"Susan?" Corey remembered the name of Tessa's sister from the information Mike Turner had dug up on her family. He wondered if she had the same delightful combination of dark hair and pale skin as Tessa.

"Yes, this is Susan." She sounded surprised. "Do I know you?"

"Actually, we've never met." Corey debated briefly over how much information he should reveal. He decided upon the minimum. "I was a friend of your brother."

"My brother? Are you sure you're talking to the right Susan? I don't have a brother."

"My mistake," Corey said, fishing for more information. "I guess Steve wasn't officially your brother."

"Steve?" Now she sounded really confused. "Who's Steve?"

The question sliced through Corey like a knife. *Who's Steve?* She asked it as though she didn't have the vaguest idea what he was talking about. Corey forced himself not to jump to the obvious conclusion, not yet, not until he had given her every chance to confirm Tessa's story. He held out a vague hope that Susan had forgotten the boy next door, the one who had been like a brother.

"Didn't you have a next-door neighbor around your age named Steve?"

She laughed. "Hardly. The only Steve I know is seventy-five and crotchety. Are you sure you have the right telephone number?"

Corey was silent for a moment as the implication behind Susan's denial registered on his resisting brain. He couldn't fool himself about Tessa any longer, when the truth had resounded like a bell over the telephone line. Not only didn't Tessa have a brother named Steve, but she didn't even have a neighbor by that name. The depth of her lie shook him so that his fingers gripping the telephone trembled.

"I'm starting to think that I've been wrong about everything."

"Excuse me?"

"Can I ask you just one more question, Susan?"

"Well, I guess it wouldn't hurt."

"Do you have any nieces or nephews?"

The question was an odd one coming from a stranger, and it wouldn't have mattered had Susan refused to answer it. Corey knew what the answer would be even before she phrased her response.

"Just one niece named Abby. She's my sister's child." Susan paused, and Corey heard the suspicion in her voice when she continued speaking. "But what does my niece have to do with anything? This is a wrong number, right?"

"Right," Corey answered slowly as pain pierced him like needles entering a pincushion. "Sorry to bother you. I must be looking for some other Susan."

After he rang off, Corey stared unseeingly at the papers on his desk for a full fifteen minutes. How could he have been so wrong about Tessa? The fiasco with Alise hadn't taught him a damn thing, least of all how to spot a liar.

It wasn't as though Tessa hadn't given him plenty of chances to tear apart her story. First she'd lied about having a brother, and then she'd lied about having a friend who was like a brother. She'd probably gone to bed with him to keep him from asking questions she didn't want to answer.

It had worked, too. Not only had Corey gone about the investigation the way Tessa suggested, he'd neglected to follow leads that could have revealed her as a fraud. It hadn't taken Sherlock Holmes to figure out that a simple telephone call to Tessa's family could verify her story.

Oh, he was a fool, all right. He still was. Despite Tessa's treachery, Corey couldn't quite believe that she'd made love to him solely to keep him from discovering too much about her case. Not when he thought of the way she had wrapped her legs around his waist and moaned softly, as though she wanted to lose herself in him.

"Fool," Corey said aloud, pounding the desk with his hand to crush the image. Not more than an hour ago, he had thought that the mystery enshrouding Tessa was no longer important. Now he wanted desperately to know what had driven her to lie to him. He closed his eyes and silently counted to ten in an effort to control his temper. He needed a clear head to unravel the mystery that had brought deceitful Tessa Daniel to Oak Haven.

Whatever way Corey looked at it, her lies didn't make sense. Tessa was searching for a child, which was hardly a crime in itself, but the search had been fruitless. None of the three children he'd investigated had been the right girl. Why?

"There has to be another child, Corey. There just has to."

The words Tessa had spoken on the phone just minutes ago echoed in his ears, and Corey yanked open the desk drawer containing the rest of the birth records.

The documents atop the stack weren't a surprise, because Corey had recognized the coincidence as soon as Tessa mentioned her niece's birth date. He stared at the name, regretting that he had let Alise choose it. Margaret Alise McCash. The name was much too stuffy for a baby girl, but Alise had insisted upon naming their daughter after her late mother. When Alise referred to Maggie at all in the six months after her birth, she'd called her Margaret. But to Corey, his daughter had always been Maggie. His Maggie.

Corey looked at the date on the sheet of paper. October ninth. He wasn't sure why he hadn't told Tessa that Maggie had been born on October ninth in Oak Haven Hospital nearly four years ago. He supposed it was because his sweet memories of newborn Maggie were laced with bitter ones of Alise.

He shrugged off the memories, focusing once again on his task. Excluding Maggie, three girls had been born in Oak Haven Hospital during that October. Tessa was completely satisfied that the girl she sought wasn't Lisa Jones, Katherine Peterson or Suzanna Smith.

There has to be another child.

Corey remembered that he had been in a hurry to get home to Maggie when he had sorted the records, and he supposed it was possible that he had misfiled a female child with the stack of males. It was a long shot, but Corey was running out of shots.

The rest of the pile was thick, but Joe Schwinn had helpfully paper-clipped each child's documents together. Corey started to sort through them, this time checking the line on the in-patient medical record sheet that specified the sex of the child. Corey went through five males before he came across a female.

"Eureka," Corey said, picking up the sheet to study it further.

His smile faded and the blood ebbed from his face when he read the name in the upper left-hand corner of the document: Abby Teresa Daniel. He knew what it would say, but he still searched the page for the name of the traitor listed under "relative information." Teresa Anne Daniel. He didn't realize he was clutching his heart, as though the pain was too much to bear.

* * *

"Well, girls, what did you think of the movie?" Tessa asked cheerfully, as she pulled her car into the driveway of Corey's home. She'd avoided asking the question until now because of the traumatic scene that occurred halfway through *Bambi*. The cute little deer with the big eyes lost his mother to hunters' guns, leaving him to walk alone. The scene had bothered Tessa as a child, but it was even more poignant now that she was an adult. Her birth child, too, had lost a mother.

"Wunnerwul," Abby sang out.

"Can we see it again tomorrow?" Maggie asked, and Tessa's fears were unfounded. The scene had gone straight over their small heads.

"Not tomorrow, darling," she said, laughing. "But I'm sure you'll see it again someday."

Tessa cheerfully went about the task of unbuckling their twin car seats while listening to chatter about what the four of them should do once Corey got home. *I could get used to this,* Tessa thought. She loved her teaching job, but there was nothing more fulfilling than spending the day with your children and the night with the man you loved. *Careful, Tessa,* an unwelcome little voice warned. *Maggie isn't yours, and neither is Corey. At best, they're on loan until you and Abby return to Virginia and real life.*

"Your father should be home at any minute," she said to the girls, determinedly ignoring the little voice and living out her fantasy. "Why don't we sit on the porch and wait for him?"

"Let's play cars," Abby yelled, referring to a favorite game in which each player chose a color and counted how many vehicles of that color passed by. "I get red."

"I get blue," Maggie chimed in, although she'd never played the game and couldn't have any notion what Abby was talking about.

The girls sprinted for the porch. Tessa followed more leisurely, still smiling.

"How could I have been so stupid?" Corey asked himself aloud as he got into his car for the drive home. "I knew all along that she was lying, but I wouldn't believe it. I acted like a teenager with overactive hormones. I acted like a fool."

He'd thought that the debacle of his marriage to Alise had taught him the importance of concepts such as trust and honesty, but he'd disregarded everything when he'd looked into Tessa's big brown eyes. It was as though she had him under some sort of spell. He could have forgiven her anything, but not this.

A lie was the knife that slashed apart relationships; once they were torn, they weren't worth putting back together. At least Corey hadn't been stupid enough to tell her he loved her. That kind of humiliation would have been unbearable. This way, even though his heart was in shreds, he could walk away from her with his pride intact.

And he would walk away, Corey told himself firmly, just as soon as he got some answers. He knew he wasn't thinking clearly, but the entire episode still didn't make sense. Questions swirled in his brain like ants swarming over an anthill.

Why had Tessa made up a farfetched tale about a nonexistent adopted brother and his missing wife? Why didn't she want him to know that she had given birth to Abby in Oak Haven Hospital? Why was she looking for another child?

The last question was the most puzzling. Thanks to Joe Schwinn, the records Corey had were extensive. He'd spent the last hour going over all the information in the hope that it would provide a clue, but he was no closer to uncovering the mystery behind this case than he'd ever been. He'd initially thought that Abby had been a twin who had somehow been separated at birth, but records clearly indicated that hers had been a single birth.

He'd considered the possibility that Tessa had met one of the other mothers while in the hospital and needed to find her again. But why? And if that was the case, wouldn't she have asked him to search for the mother? And wouldn't they have found her by now?

Corey pressed his foot down harder on the accelerator, because his ruminations were driving him nowhere except crazy. The only person who could provide him with answers was waiting at his home, and he refused to wait any longer than necessary to get them.

The windows of Corey's car were rolled down, and he heard the squealing even before he realized that Maggie and Abby were on the porch with Tessa awaiting his arrival. She must have told them not to rush his car until he turned off the ignition, because they waited until the engine started to die before running to him.

"Daddy, Daddy, can we get pizza again?"

"Corey, do you want to play cars? You can have orange."

The girls spoke at once and then fired question after question until he wasn't sure who was who or what was what. They didn't notice his lack of enthusiasm, or the fact that he hadn't said a word, and went tearing back toward the house and Tessa.

Corey was almost to the porch when he finally looked at her. The sun hadn't yet set, and it bathed Tessa in a soft glow that highlighted her delicate features. Then Maggie tugged at her sleeve, and Tessa bent to listen to what his daughter had to say.

The curve of their cheeks, the slight dips in their noses, even the hues of their complexions were nearly identical. In profile, they were mirror images. The questions died on Corey's lips, and his heart began a slow, painful thud.

He no longer needed to ask Tessa why she was searching. Preposterous as it seemed, he knew without a sliver of a doubt that Maggie was the missing piece of the puzzle. Tessa was looking for her daughter, and Maggie was that child.

Chapter 13

Tessa laughed at Maggie's nonsensical babble about pizza, video games and carnival rides, and kissed the child's brow. Oblivious to the turmoil swirling inside Corey, she turned to him with a smile. He wondered how she would react if she knew she had just kissed her own daughter, and the answer terrified him. To know Maggie was to love her. Alise's behavior had been unthinkable; he couldn't believe another mother could willfully abandon her own flesh and blood.

"These children have pizza on the brain. I've told them over and over that Mrs. Miller left a casserole for dinner, but they just won't hear me. Maggie suggests that you freeze it, and find a carnival to take them to after you buy them pizza."

The last part of Tessa's sentence trailed off until it was barely a murmur, and her smile faded. Corey hadn't said anything since he'd gotten out of the car; his body was rigid and he was visibly pale. She'd once considered becoming a physician and had taken a few college courses in physiology, and he appeared to be in a state of shock.

"C'mon, girls, into the house," Tessa said overly brightly, taking Maggie and Abby by the hand and steering them toward the door. "I want you two to play in Maggie's room, and I don't want either of you to come out until we call. Now go."

Even before the door thudded behind her, Tessa was descending the steps. Corey still hadn't moved, and he stared at her in that same blank way. A light seemed to have gone out deep inside him, somewhere vital and virtually impossible for her to reach.

"Corey, what's wrong?" Tessa put a hand on his arm, and he vehemently recoiled from the contact as though her touch were anathema. Stunned and hurt, she had a flashback to the day they'd met and the suspicion in his eyes. But this was much worse. This time his blue eyes were filled with anger and what looked to be hatred.

"What's wrong?" she repeated, and this time her question was heavy with fear. She had hidden too much and had too much to lose, including the man himself, if Corey should uncover the truth.

"We can't talk about this out here," Corey bit out, and a muscle throbbed in his temple. He might have been in shock moments ago, but right now he was trying to hold on to the remnants of his temper.

He brushed by her and walked briskly up the stairs and into the house, letting the door thud to a close behind him. Tessa stood unmoving, watching his progress. Something was frightfully wrong, and it would be a miracle if it didn't concern Abby. *Be strong,* she implored herself, praying that he hadn't discovered the truth. She drew her lungs full of air, bracing herself for what he'd uncovered, and slowly followed him into the house.

Corey reached his study a full minute before she did and tried to reason with himself through the anger and shock. His trump card was that he knew Maggie's true identity and Tessa didn't. He had to handle this confrontation in a way that dismissed Tessa and the threat she carried from their lives without revealing what he knew.

He thought of the day he had returned home from work to find Alise gone and six-month-old Maggie in a neighbor's care. Maggie had been sobbing copiously, instinctively knowing that something was wrong but not understanding what. Corey had cradled Maggie against himself, trying to soothe her with his love and the whispers assuring her he'd never leave her. He never had, and he never would.

"Are you going to tell me what this is all about?" Tessa, framed by the French doors, stood at the opening to the room. Her shoulders were slightly slumped and her voice quivered, as though she was the injured party. Corey's first instinct was to gather her into his arms to comfort her; his second instinct was to be furious. This was a woman who had wriggled her way into his life, making him care for her even while her mouth spouted lies. This was a woman who, if she knew the truth, would try to take his daughter away.

"Don't play the innocent with me, Tessa," Corey said, disgusted with her and himself. "We both know that the innocent don't lie."

"I don't know what you're talking about."

"You just can't stop lying, can you?" Her eyes glistened with unshed tears, and again he wanted to comfort her. Raw, red hurt pulsed in Corey as he reminded himself that she had played him for a fool. His voice was harsh when he spoke again. "You know exactly what I mean. The game's up, Tessa. I know about Abby."

The words hit Tessa like a punch struck to the chest, directly over her heart. She closed her eyes briefly, not wanting to face the inevitable. She'd been so careful to safeguard the knowledge, but she'd never truly believed she had the hospital's only record of Abby's birth. This moment had been inescapable since she'd hired Corey, but that didn't make it any less frightening.

"What do you know?" she asked softly, fearfully.

They stood about a dozen feet apart, and Corey moved forward purposefully as he talked, closing off the hope that Tessa could get out of Oak Haven both with her child and her heart.

"I know that all you've told are lies," he said, his voice like a growl deep in his throat. "I know that you never had a real brother or an adopted brother or any kind of brother. I know that Bunny and your poor, lost niece don't exist.

"And I know that Abby was born in Oak Haven Hospital on October ninth almost four years ago."

"How do you know that?" she asked when he stopped talking. Just inches separated them, and he was so close that she could hear the uneven way in which he was breathing. He didn't resemble the man who had looked at her so tenderly just days ago, the man who seemed to be falling just as hard for her as she already had for him.

"I have the hospital's birth records, remember? Abby's documents were there all along, but I misfiled them. Did you really think I wouldn't find out?"

"What else do you know?" Tessa asked, ignoring his question. Anything she could have answered would only make the situation worse.

"Why don't you fill in the blanks?" Corey rasped.

Tessa met his eyes bravely, and saw that her fight was already lost. She could make a stab at another lie, but he'd almost certainly see through it. Her only hope was to try to make him understand, not for her sake but for Abby's. She'd already lost her chance at making him love her, but she hadn't lost her daughter.

"All right. I did lie to you, but only because I had to. Abby's all I have. I couldn't let anyone know about her."

"Know what?" His voice hadn't lost any of its harshness.

Tessa's shoulders slumped in defeat, and she squeezed the answer through lips that were suddenly parched. "I couldn't let anybody know that she wasn't really mine, that she and another child had gotten switched at the hospital."

Corey's breaths came in quick, hard gasps, because her testimony had just made the surreal real. Before Tessa had admitted that Abby wasn't her daughter, the possibility remained that he had imagined the resemblance between Tessa and Maggie. But he hadn't. Maggie was Tessa's daughter, not his.

The truth almost made him laugh in irony. The entire time Alise was pregnant, he had wondered whether he was truly the baby's father. After Maggie was born, he'd fallen in love with her so swiftly that it hadn't mattered if he wasn't really her father. But never once, in all these years, had he wondered about the identity of Maggie's mother. At least he didn't have to adjust his thinking in one regard: he'd always known Maggie's mother was a scheming liar.

"Why did you switch your baby with someone else's, Tessa?" Corey still didn't touch her, but his words were like blows. "Wasn't she perfect enough? Did she weigh five pounds instead of eight? Did she have brown eyes when you wanted a baby with blue eyes?"

"I would never give up my baby. Never!" Tessa's cry was impassioned and injured. He believed the worst of her, and that hurt even more than it had to reveal the information about Abby. "It was the hospital's mistake, not mine. Can't you see that? How could you think such a thing of me?"

Corey grabbed the collar of her shirt roughly, and his eyes bored into hers. "Why would I think anything more of a woman who lies as easily as another woman smiles? Tell me, Tessa. Did you come to Oak Haven because you couldn't live with the guilt of giving up your child any longer?"

"I don't have anything to feel guilty about," Tessa managed on a sob. He didn't release her, didn't seem to notice or care that she was on the verge of tears. "I've racked my brain trying to figure out how it could have happened, and

I still can't come up with a way. I just know that it happened.''

He ignored her protestations, even though it was ludicrous to think that Tessa had replaced her daughter with a child she had snatched from its hospital bassinet.

"You hired me because you want your child back, isn't that right?" Corey asked. "That's why you were waiting outside the preschool that day. If you had known which child was yours, you would have taken her. Isn't that right?"

"Of course it's n—"

"Come off it, Tessa. Why should I believe a thing you say? You never even told me what city you're from, or anything about yourself except that you're a teacher. But I'm a step ahead. I have a friend in Richmond, and he's told me everything there is to know about you."

"You had me investigated?" Tessa asked, appalled.

"To think I actually felt a little guilty about it," Corey said, shrugging away the unwelcome memory of how he'd waited fruitlessly for Tessa to tell him what he already knew. "This way, even if you do find your child, you won't be able to take her and disappear without a trace."

"No," Tessa sobbed. "No. I wasn't planning to do anything like that. You've got it all twisted."

Corey released her collar so abruptly that Tessa stumbled and almost fell, but he made no move to help her. There was no trace of softness in the slash of his lips, no compromise in the set of his shoulders. He had acted as self-appointed judge and jury and found her guilty. "No. I was twisted to fall for you, but I'm finally straightening things out."

"You're a cruel man," Tessa said, wiping impatiently at the tears streaming down her face as anger filled her. Tessa's only sin had been loving Abby so much that she would do anything within her power to keep the little girl at her side. She didn't expect Corey to forgive her lies, but she thought a man with a treasured daughter of his own would at least try to understand. "I should have stuck to my first impressions of you. You're rude, insufferable and vile."

"Do you really think I care what kind of names a liar like you calls me?" Corey asked, even angrier than before because her barbs had stung.

"I'd rather be a liar than a cold-blooded snake who doesn't have a heart," she hurled back, vaguely aware that she and Corey had moved from an argument about her lies to a skirmish about their relationship. "I can't imagine what I ever saw in someone like you."

"Can't you?" Corey covered the distance between them in one long stride and hauled her into his arms. She pushed at his chest, but he held her tight with her arms pinned between their bodies. He hardly knew what he was doing and was propelled by a mesh of anger and hurt that threatened to choke him. "Why don't I show you then?"

"Let me go," Tessa shouted before her further protests were silenced by the cruel press of his mouth on hers. She tried to close her lips, but his tongue penetrated the ineffective barrier and plundered deep into the recesses of her mouth. One of his hands roughly caressed her buttocks, and her lower body was pressed tight against his. To Tessa's horror, her own desire stirred deep within her when she encountered the evidence of his desire. Self-loathing gave her enough strength to push him away.

"I hate you," she spat out, breathing hard with shame because her body's reactions didn't back up her words. She took a wild swipe at her hair, which was partially covering her face. "I never want to see you again."

"That's just fine with me," Corey bit back, "because I can't be held accountable for what I'll do if I ever see you around me or my child again."

They fell silent while they glared at each other, and the air was thick with unspent passion and soft sobs. Corey and Tessa turned simultaneously, searching for the source of the crying and saw their daughters huddled together in the doorway. Strands of golden-brown hair mingled with strands that were almost black as Abby and Maggie held onto each other tightly. Their faces were wet with tears and misery.

Before Tessa and Corey could make a move toward them, the girls turned and ran. Without a backward glance, Tessa followed. Corey, however, sat down heavily on the edge of his desk. In the instant before she had fled, he had gazed into Abby's militant, miserable face and seen something he hadn't picked up on before: himself.

In the past few hours as he'd puzzled over Tessa's lies and Maggie's parentage, somehow he had missed an irrefutable truth. If Maggie was Tessa's natural daughter, then sweet, precocious Abby was his. Had Corey still been standing, the knowledge would have knocked him over as easily as a bowling ball that strikes a pin. As it was, it drained the blood from his face. He bent over and put his head between his knees, trying to regain some semblance of normalcy. But his world had just gone topsy-turvy, and he couldn't set it right.

"Girls," Tessa called as she entered Maggie's room, desperately wanting to find them and fix the hurt but knowing it was beyond her scope. She and Corey had said some dreadful things to each other, things two three-year-old children should never have heard. But they had, and nothing was going to change that or the fact that the conversation had signaled a death knell for their friendship. How could she explain to two small girls that they couldn't be friends any longer because their parents were enemies?

I shouldn't have allowed them to become so close, Tessa chided herself. She'd driven into Oak Haven not more than a month ago to make sure her birth child wasn't afflicted with a blood disease, and now the town and two of its people were in her blood. She'd vowed not to become close to anyone in Oak Haven, but she'd fallen in love with a man she hated and allowed his daughter to wrap herself around two hearts.

"Abby. Maggie," Tessa called again, her concern for the children overriding her heartache. A hiccuping sob that came from the direction of the closet gave away their hiding place. She slowly pulled open the closet door to reveal the two crying children sitting on the floor. Tessa hunched down so that she was at their level.

"I'm sorry you had to hear that, girls," she said softly. "So sorry."

Abby just stared at the carpet in the closet, but Maggie raised her tear-streaked face. "I thought you liked us."

"Oh, I do," Tessa said, stopping short of telling the little girl that she loved her. Adults found it difficult to understand why people who loved each other sometimes had to part; to a child, it would be incomprehensible.

"Then why did you tell my daddy you hate him?"

"Oh, Maggie," she said on a sigh. "Sometimes adults say things when they're angry that they don't really mean."

"Then you don't hate him?"

"When I said it, I hated him," Tessa said, trying without success to sort out her emotions. The only thing she was sure of was that she was through with lying. "Sometimes when you care a lot about someone, everything you feel is magnified a hundred percent. The love is richer, and the hate stronger."

The look on Maggie's face was of utter incomprehension, and Tessa reminded herself that she was speaking to a three-year-old. But how could she explain to anyone, let alone a child, what she herself didn't understand?

Abby looked at her then, her eyes glistening with tears and her lower lip thrust forward. "Do we have to go home?"

Tessa nodded, biting her lip to keep it from quivering. They not only had to go home, they couldn't come back. She didn't know how much the girls had witnessed, but it was far too much. They were so young that they couldn't yet grasp the concept of permanency, but they seemed to know that their days as a foursome were over.

"But I don't wanna," Abby wailed, and her outburst caused Maggie to surrender to fresh tears. Tessa gathered them both closer, thinking abstractly that her heart was as full as her arms.

After a few minutes, the girls quieted and Tessa extracted herself from their clinging arms and determinedly stood up. Corey had ordered her out of his house fifteen minutes ago, and it was past time she left. The longer she delayed their leave, the harder it would become. She put out a hand to each girl and hoisted them to their feet. When they turned, Corey stood in the doorway, bringing back a memory flash of the day he had looked at her with undisguised need.

His expression now was inscrutable, a vague improvement over the glare that had chilled her in his study. Tessa let go of Maggie's hand, bent down and kissed her soft little-girl cheek.

"Go to Daddy, honey," Tessa whispered in her ear. *And always know that I love you,* she added silently.

Maggie went, and Tessa scooped Abby into her arms. Tessa lifted her chin and willed her expression to be as stony as possible as Corey lifted his daughter.

"We'll be going now," Tessa said and started to brush past him. Abby's words stalled her.

"'Bye, Maggie. 'Bye, Corey," she said, directing a watery smile at the latter. "Maybe you can bring Maggie over to play tomorrow."

"'Bye, Abby." Corey's voice was thick with an emotion Tessa couldn't identify.

In light of all that had happened and all that he'd said, Corey's next move stunned Tessa. He reached across the chasm separating them and bestowed the softest of kisses on her daughter's cheek. Abby smiled, certain that everything was all right again, and seconds passed before Tessa swept by father and daughter and out of their lives.

The illuminated dial on the bedside clock showed that it was well past midnight when Tessa slipped into bed, but she knew it would be hours before she slept. Her eyelids were heavy and her body lethargic, but her mind was running a race that would do a stock-car driver proud.

Abby had gone to bed at her regular time, naively thinking that her smile and Corey's kiss had made everything right with the world. Tessa punched her pillow, because everything had gone wrong since they'd arrived in Oak Haven.

She'd gotten past being heartsick, and the emotion that remained was anger. She was still steaming at Corey for refusing to listen to her explanation about why she'd lied to him. He'd jumped to so many farfetched conclusions that she hadn't even had a chance to tell him about the blood test that proved she was a carrier of Cooley's anemia. He'd been so closeminded to her plight, the knowledge probably wouldn't have made a difference anyway.

But why had he been so angry?

The question was like a thorn imbedded in Tessa's brain. Upon reflection, it seemed that his rage had been way out of proportion to her lie. She knew about Alise and the way she had tricked Corey into marriage and fatherhood, but all Tessa had done was fib to protect her child. They were hardly equal crimes, but Corey had acted as though she was Alise reincarnated.

She supposed it was possible that, since his experience with Alise, Corey abhorred liars of any kind. Especially if the liar was a woman he was beginning to love. Before the theory could inflate Tessa's hopes, she had a deflating thought. Any embryonic love Corey felt for her had surely died in his study that afternoon. Tessa could justify blaming Corey for a lot of things, but not that.

Budding love could be as fragile as the seed that forms a beautiful flower, and she'd trampled on it when it started to bloom. She had a moment's remorse that her love for him wasn't equally frail. Once it had taken root, nothing—not even anger and ugly words—could kill it.

She supposed the death of his love could explain his re-action to her lies, but she couldn't shake the nagging feel-ing that something more was feeding his ire.

Had he discovered the identity of her birth child? Tessa turned the possibility over in her mind and rejected it. She'd never before hired a private investigator, but she assumed they were obligated to reveal any information they uncov-ered in the course of an investigation.

Tessa sighed and turned over so that she faced Abby's bed. She couldn't make out any of her features in the dark-ness, but Tessa knew well how the little girl looked as she slept. Even in her darkest moments, Tessa had been able to derive strength from just looking at Abby. She needed that energy now more than she ever had.

She had to figure out where they went from here. Tessa was no closer to finding her birth child than she'd been be-fore hiring Corey. She stared up at the ceiling, searching for answers where there was only darkness. Should she aban-don her hunt and return to Virginia? Now that Corey knew the truth about Abby, she couldn't be sure that they were safe in Oak Haven.

But her reasons for looking for her birth child weren't any less urgent than they'd been yesterday. How could she in good conscience abandon a quest that could improve the quality of life for an innocent child who should have been hers to love? At the same time, how could she jeopardize the happiness of a child she did love?

"I have to make Corey understand," Tessa whispered aloud. "I have to get him to promise that he won't tell any-one about Abby."

The decision made, Tessa fell into a fitful sleep, but not before she felt a rush of guilty pleasure that she hadn't seen the last of Corey McCash.

The phone rang six times before Corey's rich, familiar voice came on the line, and Tessa's legs suddenly felt so weak that she sat down.

"Hello."

"Corey, it's—" Tessa started in a rush before she lost her nerve, but she needn't have bothered saying anything.

"This is McCash," continued the voice on the other end of the line, a voice that had been prerecorded. "You can leave a message at the beep."

Tessa hung up and quickly dialed Corey's office number, which she knew by heart. This time she was prepared for the mechanical voice, because she was beginning to get the impression that Corey McCash would go to any lengths to avoid her. Short of showing up at his door and getting it slammed in her face, she was going to have a devil of a time getting him to listen to her story.

"Who you callin', Mommy?"

Tessa quickly hung up the receiver when she spotted Abby in the doorway, looking hopeful.

"Nobody important," she said, determined not to mention either of the McCashes by name. Abby's refrain that morning had been about visiting Maggie, and Tessa didn't want to give her another chance to recite it. She swiftly changed the subject. "What are you doing here? I thought you were helping Mrs. Moriarty bake a cake."

Abby threw up her hands in a gesture of annoyance, just like a miniature adult.

"I am, but we ran out of sugar. Do you have some?"

"I think I can find some," Tessa said, thankful that the interruption was only temporary. She couldn't seem to think clearly with Abby around and had thanked providence when

Mrs. Moriarty invited the child to participate in yet another baking project.

In minutes, Abby disappeared through the connecting doors with an unopened bag of sugar in her hands intent on joining their benevolent landlady. *Mrs. Moriarty is such a dear woman,* Tessa thought. *If I asked, she would probably do anything for me.*

I bet she'd even deliver a letter to a man who wouldn't take it from me.

Tessa didn't stop to examine the wisdom behind her thought, and in moments had found some stationery and a pen. A half hour later, she had a letter. She read it over carefully, making sure she hadn't incriminated herself or Abby in the text.

Dear Corey,
Please give me a chance to explain before you toss this letter away. I admit I lied, and I know how you feel about liars. Just let me tell you why.

About a month ago, I found out I was a carrier for a genetic blood disease called Cooley's anemia. At the same time, I discovered the truth about Abby. I didn't want to come to Oak Haven, but I couldn't do nothing. Although the disease usually strikes children under age two, a milder form can show up in slightly older children. Both forms are often troublesome to diagnose.

So, you see, I had to come. Not because I planned anything wicked. All I planned to do was find her, make sure she was okay and leave. I never planned on anyone finding out about Abby. I never planned on falling in love with you.

I'm not asking you to love me back. I'm not even asking you to forgive me. All I ask is that you don't tell anyone about Abby, because I can't leave town. Not yet. Not until I've done what I came to do. Please understand. And know that I would never deliberately hurt you.

Tessa stared at the letter for long minutes, debating whether to tear it up and write another in which she didn't admit her love. But she did love Corey, and she'd told him so many lies that he deserved the truth. Tessa scribbled her name, folded the letter in thirds and shoved it into an envelope. She walked briskly to the other part of the house in search of Mrs. Moriarty before she could change her mind about sending it.

Tessa glanced at the digital clock in the sitting room and saw that it had clicked off only six minutes since she had last looked at it. Where was Mrs. Moriarty?

She'd agreed to the errand readily enough. Although Tessa was quite sure Mary Moriarty wasn't often asked to take the place of the post office, the landlady hadn't asked questions. She'd simply nodded, told Tessa she had known Corey since he was a boy and was on her way. That was shortly after noon. Mrs. Moriarty had been gone for nearly three hours.

Tessa once again picked up the novel in her lap and tried to read. She favored romance, possibly because she'd always been an optimist who believed in the power of love and happily ever after. But she couldn't enjoy this book, because Corey McCash had shaken her beliefs. She'd never before been involved with a man whose passions, much like a faucet, ran white-hot and bone-chillingly cold.

Tessa hadn't known Corey long, but it was long enough to know that she'd always love him. It was long enough to suspect that, when he wasn't hating her, he loved her too. Her nerves frayed when she thought of the passage in the letter in which she revealed her feelings. Had that been a mistake?

"Mommy, I'm tired of coloring." Abby, who was stretched out on the floor, sat up. Tessa hadn't bothered to tie back her hair, and it was badly in need of brushing. "Please can we go to the park? Please, please."

"Not now, Abby," Tessa said, feeling slightly guilty for keeping Abby housebound on a beautiful summer day. "I told you that I was waiting for Mrs. Moriarty to come back."

"But I said please."

For the first time that day, Tessa smiled. Her efforts to turn Abby into a polite young woman were working, maybe too well.

"I know you did, honey. But remember what I said about please? Saying please doesn't mean you get what you want, but not saying it is a sure way to not get what you want."

"What?" Abby screwed up her forehead comically, and Tessa started to rephrase her statement when there was a knock on the door.

"I'll get it," Abby sang out and rushed the few steps to the door. Tessa, no less anxious but able to camouflage it better, was directly behind her. Tessa didn't even bother to warn Abby not to open the door to a stranger. She knew it wouldn't be anybody other than Mary Moriarty.

"Aunt Mary," Abby sang out, "we've been waiting for you for hours and hours and hours."

"I was afraid of that. I should have told you I was going to have my hair done," Mrs. Moriarty said, and Tessa noticed that her salt-and-pepper hair was immaculately styled. "Can I come in?"

"Certainly," Tessa said, stepping back and silently chiding herself for her lapse in manners, considering her lectures to Abby about the subject. Even so, she wondered how much longer she could be polite without demanding to know what Corey had done with the letter. As it turned out, Tessa couldn't wait any longer than it took her chattering daughter to pause for breath.

"Hush for a minute, Abby. Would you please go play with your dolls while Mrs. Moriarty and I talk? Please." Abby looked about to protest, but in the end she shrugged and skipped away. Tessa waited until Abby was in the bedroom with her toys before she spoke again. "Mrs. Moriarty, did he read the letter?"

"He took the letter," she said, clearly uncomfortable discussing the subject. "I can't say for sure if he was going to read it."

"Why not?"

"Do you really want the truth?"

"I really want it."

Mrs. Moriarty squared her shoulders, as though getting ready to deliver bad news. "He asked me to come into the house before he knew why I was there. When I told him the letter was from you, he threw it into a wastebasket without looking at it."

Tessa's spirits sank. The man she loved not only didn't love her, but didn't want anything to do with her. Not only that, he had the power to throw her life into turmoil with a single telephone call. She was sure that the local newspaper, among others, would be interested in a sensational case involving a baby switch.

"I'm sorry," Mrs. Moriarty said, accurately reading Tessa's reaction. "I hadn't realized you two had a spat."

"It was more than a spat, Mrs. Moriarty. It was a break. Only for me, it wasn't a clean one."

The older woman shook her head sadly, and not a strand in her newly styled hair moved. "That's such a shame, not only for you but for him. That man deserves some happiness after what happened with that Alise Tyner he married. He seemed so different when he came back from Philadelphia, not at all like the man who left beaming with that baby daughter in his arms. I hoped he would finally get that happiness back with you."

Tessa didn't hear Mrs. Moriarty's last sentence, because the previous one still reverberated in her ears. "What did you just say?"

"That I hoped he might be happy with you."

"No, before that." Tessa's tone was urgent.

"Just that Corey seemed so happy after Maggie was born."

"Maggie was born in Oak Haven?"

"Well, yes. Corey and Alise moved to Philadelphia when she was just a few weeks old."

Tessa's world spun, and she put a hand to her head in an attempt to steady it. She had to make sure that she wasn't jumping to conclusions, that she wasn't twisting what she was hearing.

"Do you remember what month they moved?"

Mrs. Moriarty looked as though she thought Tessa had taken leave of her senses, but she tried to remember anyhow. Her eyes narrowed as she thought. "I remember that the weather was turning, and I was surprised the cold had set in so early."

"Anything else?"

"There were leaves on the trees, I think," Mrs. Moriarty said, clearly taxing her memory. "Wait a minute. My sister was visiting, because I remember talking with her about what a shame it was that Corey was leaving town. Rose visits at the same time every year, so it must have been late in October."

That meant that Maggie had been born in Oak Haven Hospital in October during the same year as Abby. Scenes from the past month came randomly to Tessa. The instant affinity she had experienced when she first saw petite dark-haired Maggie. The lady on the Good Ship *Lollipop* at Story Book Forest who had thought Abby belonged to Corey and Maggie to her. The preschool teacher who had assumed that Tessa was Maggie's mother.

That's because I am her mother.

The realization stole Tessa's breath, and she took a number of short gasps to try to get it back. How could she have missed the obvious all these weeks? Maggie was practically a miniature version of herself, and all she'd needed to do to make Tessa love her was exist. Mrs. Moriarty was instantly at Tessa's side, holding on to her arm.

"My dear, is something wrong? Can I help?"

"Yes, something's wrong," Tessa said when she had partially regained her composure. If she was Maggie's natural mother, then Corey was Abby's biological father. Furthermore, he must have already figured out the relationships. That explained why Corey had been so upset when he shouted at Tessa in his study, and it explained the way he had tenderly kissed Abby afterward. "But you can't help. It's something Corey and I have to work out on our own."

Chapter 14

Tessa's hands were steady on the steering wheel, but her lips trembled as she covered the familiar route from Mary Moriarty's home to Corey's. Her landlady hadn't asked any more questions after Tessa's declaration that she and Corey needed to work things out, but had graciously offered to look after Abby. Now Tessa wondered if she and Corey would be able to come to a solution.

She'd been incredibly naive to think she could drop into Maggie's life, assure herself that the girl was disease free and disappear for the rest of it. Her love didn't work that way. From outward appearances, Maggie was as healthy as she had dared hope.

But Maggie was also her daughter, and that was never going to change. The love she felt for Maggie was as strong and as binding as the love she had for Abby.

The seed for that love must have sprouted in the first stunned moments she'd spent in Dr. Morgan's office, even before she'd come to know Maggie. That's why Tessa had never allowed herself to think of the missing child as her daughter. As long as Tessa mentally referred to her unknown baby as her birth child, she had been able to keep her emotions detached.

But her blood ran through Maggie's, and her features were imprinted on hers. She could no more walk away from Maggie than she could from Abby. Could Corey?

"Oh, Corey," Tessa said aloud, drawing a shaky breath. Merely uttering his name brought tears to her eyes, because of what could have been. She loved Corey as much as she loved either of her daughters, but she couldn't permit herself to fantasize about the four of them becoming a family. Her lies had seen to that. "What are we going to do?"

Tessa still didn't have an answer minutes later as she knocked on Corey's front door. She prepared herself to brace her body against the door while she pleaded her case, so Corey wouldn't have the opportunity to slam it in her face. Corey had refused to read her letter. She didn't expect him to welcome her into a home from which he had warned her to stay away.

Tessa knocked on Corey's door once again, more insistently this time. She was willing to create a scene before she'd be turned away. Maggie was her daughter, and Corey had to face that. Tessa was so surprised when the door opened a crack that she forgot to stick her foot in the opening to prevent it from closing. Mrs. Miller peered out from the opening, but her expression wasn't any more welcoming than Tessa had imagined Corey's would be.

"I need to see Corey, Mrs. Miller."

"You're not supposed to be here," the older woman said, and she sounded uneasy. Tessa frowned. Mrs. Miller might not consider her a friend, but she thought they had formed an alliance with a goal of what was best for Maggie. Knowing that she had a mother who loved and wanted her was best for Maggie.

"I know I'm not supposed to be here, but everything's changed. This is very important."

"He told me not to let you in the house if you came," Mrs. Miller said, and her voice contained none of its usual authority. "Please understand, Tessa, I'm just doing my job. I'm not saying I agree with him."

"I know that, Mrs. Miller, and I don't want to make trouble between you and Corey," Tessa said, desperate to make her see reason. "You don't have to let me in the house. All I ask is that you tell Corey I'm here. Tell him that I'm not going away until I talk to him."

"I would," Mrs. Miller said, and Tessa glimpsed a faint ray of hope before it went dark. "But he's not home."

A childish shriek so piercing that it cut to Tessa's soul and filled it with icy fear drowned out her reply. Tessa had never heard a child, or even an animal, scream like that. She would have pushed past Mrs. Miller into the house had the older woman not turned and run in the direction of the anguished cry. The door, which had seemed like an impenetrable barrier just moments ago, was left standing open. Tessa followed Mrs. Miller into the house, running on adrenaline and fear.

The next scream came from Mrs. Miller, who had stopped just short of Corey's study. Tessa rounded the corner in the hallway and pushed past her, thinking only about getting to Maggie. The sight that greeted her made her stomach curdle with fear. Broken shards of glass were scattered around the closed french doors, and Corey's daughter—*her* daughter—stood in the midst of them. She wore a short-sleeved white shirt that was spattered with blood, and one of her bare arms was red. Maggie's face was devoid of color, and Tessa feared the child was going to faint.

"Call 9-1-1!" Tessa screamed to Mrs. Miller as she plowed her way through the glass, thinking only of reaching Maggie. When the woman didn't react, Tessa shouted as loudly as any drill sergeant. "Do it now! Call 9-1-1! Hurry!"

Then Tessa was at Maggie's side, unmindful of the tiny glass pieces that pricked her bare legs or the blood that flowed from her child onto herself. She lifted the hysterical girl and quickly moved her to a carpeted place in the room that was devoid of shattered glass.

Think, Tessa, think, she implored herself, casting her mind back to the first-aid course she had taken before becoming an elementary school teacher. She had signed up for a refresher course sponsored by the Virginia school district a few years back, but had gone into labor with Abby—no, Maggie—the day it was scheduled. Tessa put her mind on autopilot, not daring to think about what could happen to Maggie if her memory were faulty.

"Tessa...heard...you...don't... tell... Daddy... running," Maggie sputtered between sobs, and Tessa made her voice as reassuring as possible. The girl had just had a terrible accident, no doubt because she had been running in the hallway and hadn't been able to stop when she came to the French doors. But the cause didn't matter—all that mattered was seeing that Maggie lived through the aftermath.

"Shh, honey. It doesn't matter. Just lie still, and everything will be all right," Tessa said, willing it to be true. But if her statement was going to come true, Tessa had to act quickly, because she was the only person in a position to help Maggie. Her daughter. Some of the techniques Tessa had learned in the first-aid course came rushing back to her as swiftly as the blood that was flowing from Maggie.

Raise the wound above the level of the heart.

Tessa cradled Maggie's head in her lap and lifted her arm slightly. She pressed her bare hand against the wound, attempting to stem the flow of blood, but the liquid kept streaming. The rich red color signaled danger, because Tessa was almost certain that Maggie had sliced a major artery. She put her bloody hands together, praying that she'd remember what to do when the bleeding doesn't stop.

Squeeze the sides of the wound together gently but firmly.

Tessa squeezed, but it was frighteningly clear after a few moments that her ministrations weren't helping. Maggie was whimpering now. The child's eyes were unfocused, deep dark pools that didn't seem to have pupils, and she had started to sweat even though her skin was cold. That could only mean that her blood pressure was dangerously low. Tessa looked wildly around the room for Mrs. Miller, who appeared in the doorway with a pallor even whiter than Maggie's.

"Help is on the way," the older woman shouted, but Tessa needed help in that very instant. One look at Mrs. Miller's wild-eyed expression told her that the housekeeper would be no help. Time. She needed time, But that was the one thing Maggie didn't have. By the time the paramedics arrived, it would be too late.

Think, Tessa, think. She had brought this child into the world, and only she was in a position to keep her here. Surely there must be some technique just beyond the grasp of her memory that she could try as a last resort. *Think, think, think.*

Press your fingers between the muscles on the underside of the upper arm.

Not daring to doubt her sudden snippet of memory, Tessa squeezed and pressed upward against Maggie's humerus. She vaguely remembered that the action was supposed to compress an important artery and stop the blood from flowing. There was blood everywhere. On Tessa. On Maggie. On the floor. There was so much that at first Tessa thought this attempt too had failed, but then she realized that none of the blood was flowing.

Tessa wasn't even aware of the tears falling down her face in thick streams. The crisis was far from over, because Maggie had lost a tremendous amount of blood already, but they had been granted a temporary reprieve. Now if only she could remember how long she could hold her child's arm this way without damaging it.

"I hear the sirens," Mrs. Miller said and rushed from the room. Tessa bent over Maggie, whose eyes were opening and closing like the wings of a butterfly. She was as fragile and as precious as any creature.

"Hold on, sweetheart, hold on," Tessa whispered, and the plea came from her heart. "I can't lose you now. I won't let you leave me."

Tessa's relief was overwhelming when the emergency medical technicians rushed into the room, intent on saving her daughter's life. Everything was out of Tessa's control as she allowed the professionals to do their job, but she adamantly refused to leave Maggie's side.

She was there when the paramedics wrapped Maggie's arm to stop the dangerous loss of blood, and she was there during an ambulance ride to the hospital, which seemed to take hours when in reality it lasted only minutes. All the while, she held Maggie's hand, whispering reassuring words she desperately wanted to believe.

At Oak Haven Hospital interminable minutes later, a harried emergency-room doctor sounded desperate when he told her that Maggie needed an immediate blood transfusion if she was to survive.

"What are you waiting for? Give her one," Tessa demanded, forgoing politeness. Her daughter was dying, and he had the nerve to stand idly by when he could save her.

"You don't understand." The young doctor, dressed in green scrubs, took her arm as he talked. She would have yanked away from him in anger, but he had kind eyes that cut through her hysteria and showed her that he wanted to help. "There's no time to type her blood, and I just performed a surgery that wiped out our supply of blood that's safe to use in these cases. I'd rather not, but I'm going to have to use an artificial plasma substitute."

"No," Tessa said, recoiling at the words although she wasn't sure of the meaning. She spoke so rapidly that some of her words blended into others, but the doctor understood. "Use my blood. Maggie and I are the same type, *O*-negative. Even if we weren't, I'm a universal donor."

The doctor hesitated. "You're sure?"

"I have the card in my purse to prove it," Tessa said and then realized that she didn't have her handbag with her. It was probably lying in a pool of blood at the McCash house.

"If you're positive, I'm going to trust you. Because time is running out," the doctor said, ushering Tessa into the operating room. "The nurse will hook you up to an IV, but I'm afraid your little girl's going to need more than one pint of blood."

"Take as much as you need," Tessa said, vaguely remembering that the standard contribution was a pint per donor. "Don't worry about me. All that matters is Maggie."

Tessa seemed to be watching the medical procedure—the needles, the IV bags, the instruments monitoring blood pressure and body temperature—from a distance even as the lifesaving liquid streamed from herself to Maggie. The needle was in her arm before she recalled the fainting incident at the blood bank and the way she had recoiled from needles since that day.

"Maggie," Tessa mumbled, turning to stare at the little girl lying on the makeshift bed next to her. Maggie's eyes were closed and she was deathly pale, but Tessa detected a fluttering of the child's eyelids and her hope soared.

The bond she'd formed with Maggie before birth had never been severed, and Tessa would do anything to see that it remained strong. She couldn't give Maggie back the years she had spent without a mother, but she could make her coming years better simply by being a mother who loved and needed her.

Tessa's life in Virginia had been just a shell of an existence since Chris had died, and there was nothing stopping her and Abby from moving to Oak Haven. Tessa was a good teacher, and she felt confident that she could secure a job somewhere in Oak Haven before the school year started. Abby would be thrilled at the news, especially because it meant she wouldn't have to leave Maggie.

As for Corey, he would simply have to accept her presence in Maggie's life. He'd already admitted that Maggie needed a woman's influence, and what better woman was there to influence Maggie than her mother? Tessa had just as much claim to Maggie as Corey did, especially considering that she was entirely blameless in the events that had led to their separation.

Staying in Oak Haven wouldn't be easy, because her heart would ache each time she saw Corey and knew that he couldn't return the love she harbored for him. But leaving her natural daughter—and the man she loved—would be even harder. Having a little piece of Corey, even if it was because of his daughter, was better than nothing at all. It was settled. Tessa was staying in Oak Haven, and no one was going to change her mind.

"Maggie," she said again, this time more groggily. Tessa wanted to keep watching her newfound daughter, as though she could will her to survive just by looking at her, but her own eyelids started to close.

Tessa's thoughts didn't stick together any better than the red cells of two people belonging to incompatible blood groups. She thought about the blood test that had forced her to come to Oak Haven, and her blood dripping into Maggie. She thought about the way her love for Abby flowed through her veins, and the way Corey had wound himself around her heart. She tried to keep her eyes open, but her head swam and the room took on a dark, fuzzy glow.

But the face that floated before her eyes was Corey's, not Maggie's. He gazed at her with the same tender expression that he'd worn after they made love, before circumstances had blown their relationship to bits. He looked wonderful, as though he just might understand why she'd resorted to deception in the hunt for her natural daughter.

"Please understand, Corey. Love her, love you," she whispered desperately, but her words ran together so that the last part was hopelessly garbled. Her energy spent, Tessa surrendered to the weakness invading her and closed her eyes.

Corey shifted his position on the uncomfortable vinyl upholstery that covered the hospital chair and rubbed his eyes. He looked at his watch and calculated that he had been waiting for Tessa to wake up for more than an hour.

The doctor insisted that she hadn't lost consciousness and was merely asleep, but Corey couldn't distinguish much of a difference. A plastic bag suspended by a metal pole dripped intravenous liquid into her veins, and she wore a pale green hospital gown that spoke of sickness. Her dark hair fanned the pillow, and her always pale complexion had taken on a chalky appearance. Even her lips looked pale.

Corey swallowed hard. The doctor had also explained that he'd been forced to take twice the normal donation of blood from Tessa because of the gravity of Maggie's condition. Corey knew on an intellectual level that Tessa was suffering from nothing more serious than the aftereffects of giving too much blood, but he was illogically frightened that she wouldn't wake up.

He'd been so hard on her yesterday in his study, hurling accusations that he couldn't back up. He'd treated her worse than some of the criminals he'd arrested when he was a cop. But damn, he had hurt. One minute he was daydreaming about making love to her, and the next he was faced with the knowledge that his daughter was actually hers. Then there were the lies.

Even if he was able to forgive her for lying to him, how could he ever trust her? Tessa's story about trying to locate her dead brother's child had always seemed preposterous, but it wasn't because of her delivery. Lies dripped from her lips like the sweet juice of an orange. She was even better at camouflaging the truth than Alise had been, and Alise had been a master.

Corey expelled a long breath. He'd spent the past few days and especially the past few hours operating on auto-pilot, and the emotional upheaval was taking its toll. He'd nearly lost the most important person in his life today, and the close call had left him feeling vaguely sick. Maggie had looked so small and vulnerable when he'd arrived at the emergency room, reminding him of how fragile life was. If it hadn't been for Tessa . . . Corey deliberately cut off the thought, not wanting to think about what could have happened to his daughter.

Except Maggie really wasn't his daughter. It was so bizarre, it was difficult to believe even now. Then Corey thought about the way he'd been drawn to sweet-faced Abby from the instant he'd seen her in the backseat of Tessa's car, and the bizarre really wasn't so bizarre at all. Corey's heart ached when he thought of the years he and Abby had missed, and he wondered if it was possible that he already loved both girls. Tessa claimed she did.

Tessa. It always came back to her. Maggie had asked for Tessa and not Corey when she'd finally regained consciousness, and he had rationalized that it was because Tessa had been with her after the accident. He knew now that wasn't completely true. Maggie might not know that she had come from Tessa's womb, but she loved her just the same. And so did he.

"I love Tessa Daniel," Corey whispered aloud, but Tessa wasn't awake to hear him. It was just as well, because he didn't want her to know. The usual sweet sensations that accompany love didn't fill his heart. Instead, he was seized with despair because it was a hopeless sort of love, doomed before it had gotten off to a proper start.

Long before he'd figured out that Tessa was Maggie's biological mother, Corey had stood across the street from a playground and thought she was capable of snatching a child and disappearing into the countryside. He knew too much about Tessa for her to disappear now, but he dreaded the lengths she might undertake to reclaim her child.

The bald truth was that he didn't trust her and probably never could. It didn't matter why Tessa had deceived him or the way she'd kept up the charade even after they'd become intimate. All that mattered was that she had started to lie to him and never stopped.

Corey sighed again, trying to make sense of why he sat at Tessa's bedside. He wanted to thank her, yes. And he supposed his debt was so great that he owed it to her to listen to her side of the story.

In retrospect, he shouldn't have refused to read the letter she'd sent with Mrs. Moriarty. The letter! Corey stood abruptly and almost landed on the floor because his leg had fallen asleep. He shook off the effects of sitting in one place for too long and fished in his pocket until he found her letter. Even before Maggie's accident, he'd had second thoughts about throwing it away. It was slightly crumpled, because he'd retrieved it from the trash can.

The letter was enclosed in a plain white envelope and neatly handwritten on a single sheet of white paper. Corey unfolded it and started to read. Fear, hope and disbelief came and went on his face as the words registered. When Corey finished reading, he took another look at Tessa to assure himself that she was still asleep. Then he hurried out the door and down the hallway.

Chapter 15

Her arm ached.

Tessa, still half asleep, reached across her body with the arm that wasn't so sore and rubbed in the area just above her elbow. She stopped abruptly when she encountered a bandage on one arm and felt the prick of a needle in the other.

Her eyes snapped open, and the unfamiliar surroundings enveloped her in fear. Tessa was lying on a small bed wearing an unfamiliar cotton gown in a room with stark white walls, and she was alone. An IV bag dripped liquid into one of her arms, and the other was bandaged and black-and-blue.

Tessa's momentary confusion gave way to renewed fear when she remembered lying on another bed with a still, silent Maggie across from her. She struggled to sit up, pushing aside the white sheets bunched at her side, but weakness assaulted her and she was forced to lie back against the bed.

Tessa had been in a hospital only once, but she remembered how to operate some of the standard equipment. She felt at the side of the hospital bed for the controls.

When the bed was in a sitting position, Tessa slowly swung her legs over the side. The thought of walking was tiring her before she even took a step, and Tessa briefly wondered what had become of her stamina. Then the need to see her daughter crowded everything else from her brain. She looked up to plot the path she would take, and her eyes slammed into Corey.

He stood about ten feet away with golden brown hair that was mussed, clothes that were wrinkled and a look she could have sworn was panic. His eyes were opened wider than usual and his mouth was slightly agape, as though poised to yell a warning. In a few quick steps, Corey was close enough to the bed to block any progress she could have made.

"What do you think you're doing? You're not supposed to get out of bed."

Tessa wasn't sure if his words were glazed with harshness or concern, but she didn't have the energy to figure which it was. She could ignore the way her heart had fluttered at the sight of him, because at the moment there were more important matters than her aching heart.

"Maggie," Tessa said, not comprehending why he was trying to stop her. Didn't he understand that she needed to get to Maggie? "I have to find her. I have to see her."

She was almost delirious with worry, and her body wobbled when she tried to push herself to the edge of the bed. She stopped for a moment, trying to regain her equilibrium, and her breathing was shallow.

"Maggie," she repeated, and Corey realized that she didn't yet know the little girl's condition.

"Maggie's fine," he said, but his voice wasn't quite steady. She cocked her head, and the concern in her eyes said she didn't entirely believe him. "Well, not fine, but improving. She lost a lot of blood, and she's weak and a little disoriented. She's asleep now and has to stay in the hospital for a few days. But she's going to be fine."

Tessa closed her eyes in relief, but she didn't enjoy a corresponding physical benefit. Lethargy overtook her limbs and Corey's face swam before her in much the same way it had in the emergency room, but this time she didn't black out.

Corey's warm, strong hands half lifted her to a sitting position and manipulated the bed controls so that she was half sitting and half lying. He covered her with the thin white sheet that was bunched at the foot of the bed.

"You were there," she said groggily, trying to focus on the face that had become so dear to her even while she was hating him. "In the emergency room."

He nodded. "I got home soon after the accident, and Mrs. Miller told me what happened. When I got to the hospital, the crisis was almost over."

Corey didn't explain the pulsating fear that had gripped him when he saw the woman he loved and the daughter he cherished lying prone and helpless in the emergency room, and he didn't mention the way Tessa had rambled about love. Clearly she didn't remember a word of what she'd said, and he hadn't been able to make out all of it anyway. But he had a trump card—the letter.

"Maggie's really okay?" The words were fearful, as though Tessa couldn't yet believe he wasn't holding back bad news.

"She's really okay."

"And Abby? Oh, gosh, I have to call Mrs. Moriarty and ask her if she can keep Abby overnight."

"Already done," Corey said, before she could reach for the phone. "Mrs. Moriarty sent her love and said not to worry. She said she needed some help trying out a new recipe, and Abby was the perfect candidate. They might even bring you a sample in a little while. I think they're planning to be here for visiting hours."

"Thank you," Tessa said and tried to smile, but even the thought of Abby "helping" Mrs. Moriarty whip up another culinary concoction couldn't make her mouth curve.

Now that she was lying down, Tessa had regained her composure. With it came a sort of pain from merely looking at Corey. She didn't want to notice that he looked slightly rakish, and immeasurably appealing, with stubble on his chin and unruly hair. Even as a child at Christmas, Tessa had never wanted much from life. But she wanted Corey, and it hurt that she couldn't have him.

The probability that she'd never live in the same home as Maggie compounded the pain. The little girl had almost died earlier that day, but harsh experience had taught Tessa that there was more than one way to lose a child. Circumstances had been beyond her control when she'd unknowingly left newborn Maggie in the hospital years ago. They might be equally out of her control now that she'd found her again.

What did she really know about Corey except that she loved him? Tessa knew that he loved his daughter so fiercely that he wouldn't give up even a part of her without a ferocious fight. Corey might even bring lawyers into the picture, meaning that Tessa could lose any chance of being a mother to Maggie. She might even lose Abby.

"How'd the accident happen, Tessa?" The question penetrated her mental ramblings, and Tessa concentrated on answering it instead of torturing herself with possibilities that might never come true.

She again saw Maggie, her dark eyes paralyzed with fear, holding out a blood-drenched arm. Tessa blinked to exorcise the image and focused on keeping her tone steady while she retold the nightmare.

"I was at the door talking to Mrs. Miller, and I think Maggie heard my voice and came running. I figure she rounded the corner too fast and tried to stop from crashing into the French doors by putting out her arm."

And then came the unearthly shriek of pain, Tessa thought, but she didn't say it. Corey loved Maggie as much as she did, and she could spare him a few details.

"She probably cut herself when she pulled her arm back through the shattered glass," Corey said, shaking his head. His eyes were downcast, revealing only his long lashes, but Tessa knew his eyes were pained. "I've told her again and again not to run in the hall."

"I figured that," Tessa said softly, sympathizing with him. Every loving parent tried to keep his child safe, but it was impossible to deliver anyone from every evil the world harbored. "Even while she was bleeding, she was worried that you were going to be angry at her for not listening to you."

"I can't be angry at her after something like that. How it happened doesn't really matter. All that matters is that she's okay."

Funny, Tessa thought, as she listened to Corey's impassioned denial. *Those were my sentiments almost down to the very word. I should have met him long ago, before I married Chris and before I came to Oak Haven full of lies. But then I never would have had Maggie—or Abby.*

They fell silent, and Tessa stared down at the bed covers. She was in a hospital room with a man who'd known her intimately, and she felt as awkward as a teenager who couldn't get up the nerve to talk to a boy she had a crush on. She wanted to tell him to leave, but was afraid he'd ask why. She decided on a neutral subject.

"How long do I have to stay here?"

"Just the night. They took a lot of blood from you, twice what they should have, and it takes the body a while to replenish itself. The doctor said it was normal for you to feel weak, and he wanted to keep you overnight for observation. I think that he's doing it partly because he's afraid of getting sued."

"Sued? Why would I sue him?"

"Hospitals are supposed to keep a supply of *O*-negative blood for emergencies, because it's relatively safe to use when you don't know a patient's blood type. But this hospital let its supply get dangerously low and then exhausted it when what was supposed to be a routine surgery turned complicated. They were expecting a shipment at about the time Maggie had the accident."

In other words, Maggie had almost died because of the inefficiency of the same hospital that had bungled her birth. The news was stunning, but Tessa couldn't get angry. At the moment, she was too grateful that Maggie was safe. Suing the hospital wasn't an option in either of their minds.

Tessa needed to know the extent of the hospital's incompetence, but she and Corey were dancing around the real issue. She was a mother who was talking to her daughter's father, and that was something they had to discuss. Still, she said nothing.

"The doctor said Maggie would have died if you hadn't been there," Corey said after another stretch of silence. "He said you managed to stop the arterial bleeding until the ambulance arrived and then you insisted on donating as much of your blood as she needed.

"I can't express how grateful I am. I'll never be able to repay you."

Tessa waited until she was sure he was through with his speech, watching his face for any telltale sign that he knew he was talking to Maggie's mother. There was none, and she swallowed the hurt that suddenly swelled in her throat. He knew, but he didn't trust her with the truth.

"You're not indebted to me, Corey," she said, tired of skirting the issue. She paused before she delivered the blow. "I didn't do anything more for Maggie than any mother would have done for her child."

She knew. Corey had suspected it, but he hadn't been sure until that moment. He tried to keep his expression neutral, but doubted that he was succeeding. Now that she knew, everything he had to say would be so much easier. He could feel a smile creeping onto his face, so he bit his lip to stop it from spreading.

"How long have you known?" he asked, stalling.

"Just since this afternoon. It was something Mrs. Moriarty said. Something about how happy you'd seemed with Maggie in your arms when you left for Philadelphia. I'd always assumed you moved to Philadelphia before Maggie was born. It never occurred to me that she could have been born in Oak Haven Hospital."

"Alise was the one who wanted to move to Philadelphia, and I didn't marry her until after Maggie was born."

Tessa nodded, digesting the information. What they'd done in the past wasn't nearly as important as what they were going to do in the future, but they needed to talk about the mistake that had irrevocably changed their lives.

"When did you realize that I was Maggie's mother?"

"Yesterday on the porch steps. I was pretty angry, because I had just found out you had been lying to me. Then you bent down to listen to something Maggie was saying, and the resemblance hit me like a Mack truck. Funny thing, though, it didn't sink in that Abby was my daughter until I saw her in the doorway."

They lapsed into silence, and Tessa remembered the ugly ensuing argument in his study. Tessa had said she never wanted to see him again, and Corey had yelled at her to stay away from Maggie. Then the children who were inexorably tied to both of them had appeared.

This conversation was so much less volatile than their previous confrontation that Tessa couldn't juxtapose them in her mind. Was he being kind because she had just saved a little girl they both loved or because he was afraid of what she would do with her newfound knowledge?

"I see you're awake. Welcome back to the world." The cheerful voice of a nurse carried from the doorway, and they both turned at the sound. A middle-aged woman in a starched white uniform quickly crossed the room to Tessa's bedside, and Corey stepped out of the way.

She thrust a thermometer in Tessa's mouth and fastened a blood-pressure cuff above the bandages on her arm. Tessa was glad that the nurse couldn't measure heartache, because she was sure her reading would be off the chart. After checking the readings, the nurse efficiently removed the intravenous needle.

"You're still a little weak, and you need to drink lots of liquid. But you'll be as good as new in no time," the nurse said in a jovial voice. She slanted a look at Corey, theatrically narrowing her eyes. "You be sure you take good care of her, young man."

Her proclamation made, the nurse hustled from the room. Her entire visit had taken no more than five minutes, not nearly enough time for Tessa to get her emotions under control. She'd need a lifetime for that.

"Oh, Corey," she sighed when the nurse was gone. "What are we going to do?"

"What do you plan to do?"

"I don't know," Tessa said truthfully, studying the bed sheets before she raised her eyes to his. He still stood at the side of her bed, but he didn't seem to fear her answer. He looked as though he was about to start grinning, and that didn't make sense. She felt closer to sobbing than to smiling. "I never thought about what I'd feel when I found her. I thought it would be easy to walk away once I made sure she was healthy."

"Maggie is healthy," Corey said before she could finish her thought. "I just got through talking to the doctor. He's familiar with Cooley's anemia, and he doubts very much that Maggie has it. He says she almost certainly would have shown signs of it by now. But he's running some tests on her blood anyway, and he'll have the results in a few days."

A weight that had been crushing Tessa's heart lifted with his news. She'd been so afraid that her family's awful legacy had been passed down to her child that she should rejoice, but something nagged at her.

"How do you know about the Cooley's anemia?"

"You told me," he answered, grinning. He pulled a sheet of white paper out of his pocket and held it up for inspection. Tessa instantly recognized it as the letter she'd written him, the one she'd thought he hadn't read.

She died a little inside, because that wasn't all she'd told him. Color finally began to return to Tessa's face, but it wasn't the glow of health—it was the telltale red of a blush. Too late, she regretted penning a declaration of love. She might have been able to handle unrequited love as long as Corey didn't know it for what it was. Tessa cast about wildly for some way to take back the words she had written, but there was none.

"I thought you threw that letter away."

"I had second thoughts," Corey said and sat down on the edge of her bed. She self-consciously inched her legs across the bed so that they weren't touching any part of his body. She avoided looking directly at him, but she knew what she would see if she did: a smug, handsome man she'd never be able to stop loving. Maybe she could avoid reaffirming what she'd written if she focused on the other parts of the letter.

"I wrote that before I found out that Maggie was my daughter, but I already loved her."

"I love her too." One of Corey's large hands snaked across the bed and caressed one of her smaller ones. He turned her hand over so that the palm was facing upward and lightly rubbed his thumb back and forth across her smooth skin.

"I can't walk away from her, Corey. I just can't," Tessa said, discovering that she couldn't quite reclaim her hand, either. She craved his touch, no matter how fleeting it was. She talked about how she felt about Maggie, but her body responded to the way she felt about him. Her nipples grew taut under her hospital gown and the tiny hairs on her arm stood at attention, all because he'd offered her a morsel of affection.

"I'm not asking you to walk away from her."

"Then you must have had a change of heart since yesterday," Tessa said, her harsh tone at odds with the sweet softness invading her body. "I distinctly recall you telling me to stay away from Maggie."

"A lot of things have changed since yesterday."

His mysterious statements gave Tessa the strength she needed to snatch her hand from his. She folded both hands primly in her lap and glared at him unhappily. She didn't like being toyed with, especially by a man who held the controls.

"Like what?"

Corey stroked his chin while he considered the anger in her flashing eyes and the petulant set of her lips. Her dark hair was mussed, faint smudges were under her eyes and she wore the most unattractive hospital gown he had ever seen. He imagined stripping it off and making love to her on the hospital bed.

"Yesterday I didn't know that you came to Oak Haven to make sure your missing daughter didn't have a frightening disease."

"I tried to tell you, but you weren't in the mood to listen," Tessa said, wondering where this conversation was headed. Why couldn't he allow her to preserve the vestiges of her dignity by leaving her alone?

"I'm listening now."

"There's not much more to tell except that I've decided to stay in Oak Haven." Tessa couldn't read his reaction to her news. She didn't want to discuss this, not now when she wanted to pull the covers over her head and curl up into a little ball. The reality was that she might not have a better opportunity. "I can't leave Maggie now that I've just found her."

"What about me?"

"What about you?" Tessa asked, fidgeting. He scooted closer to her on the bed, and she tried to back up against the pillow.

"Could you leave me?"

"You changed the subject. We're not talking about you."

"Then let's change the subject."

"Okay, Corey. You win," Tessa said tiredly, because he wasn't going to let her rest until he had thoroughly humiliated her. "You know how I feel about you. I told you in that letter. Do I have to spell it out?"

"Please."

"Please?"

"Yes, please. I'd like to hear you spell it out."

"Okay, then. I love you," Tessa said, and tears flooded her eyes. She tried to close them so he wouldn't see that she was crying, but the tears squeezed out of her lashes and wet her face. "Why did you make me say it?"

Corey took both her hands in his. Defeated, she let them stay there. "Because I was afraid you'd try to tell me you didn't mean it if you didn't say the words aloud."

"I meant it," Tessa said miserably. She opened her eyes, and the tears that were welling there dripped down her face. There were so many of them, she didn't even bother to wipe them away. "Now just go away and leave me alone."

"Why would I want to do that," Corey whispered, closing the gap between them so that he could kiss the salty tears off her face, "when I love you so much?"

More tears squeezed between Tessa's lashes and ran down her cheeks, because she didn't believe him. She had just saved his daughter's life, and he was confusing gratitude with love.

"But I lied to you," she said on a sob.

"For a good reason." Her eyes were closed again, and he pressed a soft kiss against each eyelid. His tenderness made her cry harder.

"I told you I never wanted to see you again." She opened her eyes, and he was still there. The tears had served as a bath, cleaning up her vision and allowing her to see him more clearly than she ever had.

"Only because I was acting like a bastard." He stroked her hair with one hand and applied some comforting pres-

sure to her shoulder with the other, being careful not to
touch the bruised part of her arm.

"You don't love me." Tessa shook her head to emphasize her words. "What you feel for me is gratitude."

"I do love you." Corey softly kissed her brow. "What I
feel for you is love."

The words finally pierced her stubborn doubt, and Oak
Haven Hospital suddenly seemed like the most wonderful
place in the world. If somebody hadn't carelessly mixed up
their daughters in the hospital nursery three years ago, they
would never have met. Tessa gave him a watery smile.

"Then you'd better marry me, because I'm not the kind
of woman who believes in having an affair with her daughter's father."

Corey smiled—a warm, wonderful smile. "I assure you,
my intentions are completely honorable. After all, you are
my daughter's mother."

Tessa wasn't sure who moved forward to eradicate the last
of their doubts, but it no longer mattered. They clung together with their lips, their arms and their hearts. Corey's
tongue encircled hers, and she was seized by a languor so
sweet that she forgot they were in a hospital room. She
pressed herself against him, frustrated that the ugly green
hospital gown was between them.

"Mommy, what are you doing?"

The sound of a small voice drifted through the room,
dimly registering in a recess of Tessa's brain. Abby. That was
Abby's voice. The realization must have struck Corey at the
same time. He was lying half across her body, and he hoisted
himself on one arm and turned. Both Tessa and Corey saw
Abby's small face, not more than a foot away, peering at
them curiously.

"Why, I was, uh, kissing Corey," Tessa stammered. Abby
nodded gravely, as though studying a particularly puzzling
phenomenon under a microscope. Corey chuckled. Behind
Abby, Mrs. Moriarty kept a respectable distance. She too
was smiling.

"Does that mean you're not mad at Mommy anymore, Corey?"

"That's exactly what it means, sport," Corey said, drawing the rest of the way back from Tessa and lifting his daughter. She giggled. "In fact, your mother and I have something to tell you."

He balanced Abby on one hip and held out a hand to Tessa. "Do you feel up to visiting our other little girl?"

"Big girl," Abby corrected as Tessa nodded. "I'm a big girl, Corey."

Moments later Corey, Tessa and Abby crowded around Maggie's bed. The child had been awake only for minutes and she was drowsy from painkillers, but she was grinning. First at Abby, then at Corey and finally at Tessa. Maggie's hand reached out to Tessa, and her mother clasped it in hers.

"We have some wonderful news," Tessa said, glancing from Maggie to Abby. Corey smiled at her with his warm blue eyes, and Tessa couldn't imagine ever being happier than she was at that moment. "We're going to be a family."

"Tessa and I are going to get married," Corey finished for her.

"Does that mean you'll be my mommy?" Maggie asked eagerly, squeezing Tessa's hand hard. She didn't look like a child who had almost lost her life hours before or one who was stricken with a terrible disease. She looked happy. And hopeful.

"And will you be my daddy?" Abby piped in, throwing her arms around Corey.

"We already are, girls," Corey said, his love for all three of them shining on his face. "We already are."

* * * * *

HE'S AN

AMERICAN HERO

January 1994 rings in the New Year—and a new lineup of sensational American Heroes. You can't seem to get enough of these men, and we're proud to feature one each month, created by some of your favorite authors.

January: CUTS BOTH WAYS by Dee Holmes: Erin Kenyon hired old acquaintance Ashe Seager to investigate the crash that claimed her husband's life, only to learn old memories never die.

February: A WANTED MAN by Kathleen Creighton: Mike Lanagan's exposé on corruption earned him accolades...and the threat of death. Running for his life, he found sanctuary in the arms of Lucy Brown—but for how long?

March: COOPER by Linda Turner: Cooper Rawlings wanted nothing to do with the daughter of the man who'd shot his brother. But when someone threatened Susannah Patterson's life, he found himself riding to the rescue....

AMERICAN HEROES: Men who give all they've got for their country, their work—the women they love.

Only from

Take 4 bestselling love stories FREE

Plus get a FREE surprise gift!

ROMANTIC TRADITIONS

Paula Detmer Riggs kicks off
ROMANTIC TRADITIONS this month with
ONCE UPON A WEDDING (IM #524), which
features a fresh spin on the marriage-of-
convenience motif. Jesse Dante married
Hazel O'Connor to help an orphaned baby,
underestimating the powers of passion and
parenthood....

Coming to stores in January will be bestselling
author Marilyn Pappano's **FINALLY A FATHER**
(IM #542), spotlighting the time-honored secret-
baby story line. Quin Ellis had lied about her
daughter's real parentage for over nine years.
But Mac McEwen's return to town signaled an
end to her secret.

In April, expect an innovative look at the
amnesia plot line in Carla Cassidy's
TRY TO REMEMBER.

And **ROMANTIC TRADITIONS** doesn't stop there! In
months to come we'll be bringing you more
classic plot lines told the Intimate Moments way.
So, if you're the romantic type who appreciates
tradition with a twist, come experience
ROMANTIC TRADITIONS—only in

SIMRT2

INTIMATE MOMENTS®
Silhouette®

CONARD COUNTY

continues...

Welcome back to Conard County, Wyoming, Rachel Lee's little patch of Western heaven, where unbridled passions match the wild terrain, and where men and women know the meaning of hard work—and the hard price of love. Join this bestselling author as she weaves her fifth Conard County tale, LOST WARRIORS (IM #535).

Vietnam veteran and American Hero Billy Joe Yuma had worked hard to heal the wounds of war—alone. But beautiful nurse Wendy Tate wouldn't take no for an answer, staking her claim on his heart...and his soul.

Look for their story in December, only from Silhouette Intimate Moments.

And if you missed any of the other Conard County tales, EXILE'S END (IM #449), CHEROKEE THUNDER (IM #463), MISS EMMALINE AND THE ARCHANGEL (IM #482) or IRONHEART (IM #494), you can order them by sending your name, address, zip or postal code, along with a check or money order (do not send cash) for $3.50 for each book ordered, plus 75¢ postage and handling ($1.00 in Canada), payable to Silhouette Books, to:

In the U.S.
Silhouette Books
3010 Walden Avenue
P.O Box 9077
Buffalo, NY 14269-9077

In Canada
Silhouette Books
P.O. Box 636
Fort Erie, Ontario
L2E 7G7

Please specify book title(s) with your order.
Canadian residents add applicable federal and provincial taxes.

SILHOUETTE.... Where Passion Lives

Don't miss these Silhouette favorites by some of our most popular authors!
And now, you can receive a discount by ordering two or more titles!

Silhouette Desire®

#05751	THE MAN WITH THE MIDNIGHT EYES BJ James	$2.89	❑
#05763	THE COWBOY Cait London	$2.89	❑
#05774	TENNESSEE WALTZ Jackie Merritt	$2.89	❑
#05779	THE RANCHER AND THE RUNAWAY BRIDE Joan Johnston	$2.89	❑

Silhouette Intimate Moments®

#07417	WOLF AND THE ANGEL Kathleen Creighton	$3.29	❑
#07480	DIAMOND WILLOW Kathleen Eagle	$3.39	❑
#07486	MEMORIES OF LAURA Marilyn Pappano	$3.39	❑
#07493	QUINN EISLEY'S WAR Patricia Gardner Evans	$3.39	❑

Silhouette Shadows®

#27003	STRANGER IN THE MIST Lee Karr	$3.50	❑
#27007	FLASHBACK Terri Herrington	$3.50	❑
#27009	BREAK THE NIGHT Anne Stuart	$3.50	❑
#27012	DARK ENCHANTMENT Jane Toombs	$3.50	❑

Silhouette Special Edition®

#09754	THERE AND NOW Linda Lael Miller	$3.39	❑
#09770	FATHER: UNKNOWN Andrea Edwards	$3.39	❑
#09791	THE CAT THAT LIVED ON PARK AVENUE Tracy Sinclair	$3.39	❑
#09811	HE'S THE RICH BOY Lisa Jackson	$3.39	❑

Silhouette Romance®

#08893	LETTERS FROM HOME Toni Collins	$2.69	❑
#08915	NEW YEAR'S BABY Stella Bagwell	$2.69	❑
#08927	THE PURSUIT OF HAPPINESS Anne Peters	$2.69	❑
#08952	INSTANT FATHER Lucy Gordon	$2.75	❑

	AMOUNT	$ _____
DEDUCT:	10% DISCOUNT FOR 2+ BOOKS	$ _____
	POSTAGE & HANDLING	$ _____
	($1.00 for one book, 50¢ for each additional)	
	APPLICABLE TAXES*	$ _____
	TOTAL PAYABLE	$ _____
	(check or money order—please do not send cash)	

To order, complete this form and send it, along with a check or money order for the total above, payable to Silhouette Books, to: *In the U.S.*: 3010 Walden Avenue, P.O. Box 9077, Buffalo, NY 14269-9077; *In Canada*: P.O. Box 636, Fort Erie, Ontario, L2A 5X3.

Name: _____

Address: _____ City: _____

State/Prov.: _____ Zip/Postal Code: _____

*New York residents remit applicable sales taxes.
Canadian residents remit applicable GST and provincial taxes.

SBACK-OD

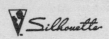